W9-CDI-137

A Deadly Grind

"Has all the right ingredients: small-town setting, kitchen antiques, vintage cookery, and a bowlful of mystery. A perfect recipe for a cozy."

— Susan Wittig Albert, national bestselling author of *The Darling Dahlias and the Texas Star*

"Smartly written and successfully plotted, the debut of this new cozy series . . . exudes authenticity." — *Library Journal*

"The first Vintage Kitchen Mystery is an exciting regional amateur sleuth . . . Fans will enjoy this fun Michigan cozy."
— *Genre Go Round Reviews*

"*A Deadly Grind* is a fun debut in the new Vintage Kitchen Mystery series . . . Fans of Joanne Fluke or of Virginia Lowell's Cookie Cutter Shop Mysteries will feel right at home in Queenstown." — *The Season*

"Hamilton's Jaymie Leighton completely captivated me . . . I'll be awaiting [her] return . . . in the next Vintage Kitchen mystery." — *Lesa's Book Critiques*

"I really loved the hometown feel that Victoria Hamilton brings to this book. This is the start of the Vintage Kitchen Mystery series, and I felt this book was smart, funny, and quirky. I smiled in places, blushed for the embarrassing moments, and fell in love with cooking all over again as I read this book." — *Two Lips Reviews*

Muffin but Murder

VICTORIA HAMILTON

BERKLEY PRIME CRIME, NEW YORK

THE BERKLEY PUBLISHING GROUP
Published by the Penguin Group
Penguin Group (USA) LLC
375 Hudson Street, New York, New York 10014

USA • Canada • UK • Ireland • Australia • New Zealand • India • South Africa • China

penguin.com

A Penguin Random House Company

MUFFIN BUT MURDER

A Berkley Prime Crime Book / published by arrangement with the author

Berkley Prime Crime Books are published by The Berkley Publishing Group.
BERKLEY® PRIME CRIME and the PRIME CRIME logo
are trademarks of Penguin Group (USA) LLC.

For information, address: The Berkley Publishing Group,
a division of Penguin Group (USA) LLC,
375 Hudson Street, New York, New York 10014.

ISBN: 978-0-425-25884-2

PUBLISHING HISTORY
Berkley Prime Crime mass-market edition / July 2014

PRINTED IN THE UNITED STATES OF AMERICA

10 9 8 7 6 5 4 3 2 1

Cover illustration by Ben Perini.
Cover design by Lesley Worrell.
Interior text design by Kristin del Rosario.

For Melanie, who loves Hannah as much as I do.

ACKNOWLEDGMENTS

This book, as a finished product, has been made so much better by the close attention of a wonderful copyeditor. Thank you, Andy Ball, for making my prose more elegant, more sensible, and entirely more grammatical!

Chapter One

RIDLEY RIDGE. HOW had I lived a whole month and a half at Wynter Castle, my inherited digs near Autumn Vale in upstate New York, without visiting Ridley Ridge, the next closest town?

Just lucky, I guess.

And I, Merry Wynter, an almost-forty not-so-merry widow and apparent inheritor of a nineteenth-century mill baron's castlelike home, would not be visiting the town again unless I had to. I looked up and down the windswept road—gray, drab buildings, litter on the streets, one person peeping out at me from between horizontal blinds—and shivered. The winds of October in upstate New York were upon us, and I was in Ridley Ridge because I had it on good authority that they had—wait for it—a party store in town. A party store. In the drabbest, saddest town I had ever seen. Who in their right mind would open a party store in Ridley Ridge?

Did they also own a bikini shop in Anchorage? A liquor store in Salt Lake City?

Standing in a puddle of gum on the dirty sidewalk, I blew a puff of air through my pursed lips, wondering which way to go. I had not been able to confirm beyond a shadow of a doubt the existence of this party store. But Pish Lincoln, my New York friend who was living at the castle for the time being, had insisted that, if I wanted to sell Wynter Castle, I needed to introduce it to potential buyers, also known as his complete little black book of influential city dwellers.

We had a game plan. Halloween was coming up, so I would host a costume party; it would be a fun gala with lots of wine and music and many of his friends, acquaintances, and former business associates from that mythical land, my former home, New York City. Since Pish was a financial advisor—the successful kind, not one of the ones who had crashed and burned in the last decade—he knew people with a *lot* of money. I hoped that one of his clients would be interested in turning an authentic American castle into an inn, an event venue, or a retreat.

We weren't counting on just Pish's friends, though. As a former stylist to the occasional star and many more models, I too knew a fair number of folks, some wealthy and others loaded with connections. I desperately needed to sell Wynter Castle if I was to return to the city with money in my pocket.

The only problem with that bright and bubbly scenario was that I had already made friends in Autumn Vale. Jack McGill, the real estate agent who had been trying to sell the castle while I ignored the problem from New York for nine months, had managed to enchant and woo my quirky gypsy model friend Shilo Dinnegan. They were now a couple, and I would not have been surprised if wedding bells were in the works. I had become fast friends with Gogi Grace, the owner of a local retirement home, and one of her residents, oddball oldster Doc. Most special of all, I had made friends with Hannah, the librarian.

I had *even* made friends with Binny Turner, though her brother, Tom Turner, had been murdered on my property a couple of days after I arrived. At first she'd thought I was involved, but that suspicion didn't last and was completely eradicated when I found Binny's frightened father, then connected Binny with Lizzie, a local teenager I had befriended, who had turned out to be Tom's unacknowledged daughter. If that seems like a busy month or so, it certainly had been. I was just supposed to be at Wynter Castle long enough to fix it up to sell, but with each new friend made, I realized how difficult it would be parting from them all when I had to leave.

I sighed and looked around. None of this musing was helping me a bit now, on the lonely streets of Ridley Ridge. Could I perhaps find a friendly local to guide me, or was that an oxymoron in this place? The blind twitched again and I realized I must look suspicious just standing in the middle of the sidewalk gawking like a lost tourist. The scenario did feel suspiciously like the opening of a suspense movie of the week, the kind where a lone woman goes missing and is in peril for the two hours until she is finally rescued or found dead just before the credits roll. I glanced over at the café; there was a blinking *pen* sign in the window. Being naturally bright, I surmised that the *O* had died, along with any semblance of hope in this town. But coffee shops are always a good source of information.

If only Shilo had come with me, or Pish; but no, they were both too busy. Ever since we had unsuccessfully tried to decode my eccentric late uncle's scavenger hunt, concealed in a code in Becket the cat's tag, they had been whispering and laughing together a lot, and I had a feeling those two were coming up with some gag that would explode over my poor, unsuspecting head at some point in the next week or so.

Ah well, it would be a welcome break from worry. Worry about money. Worry about selling the castle. Worry about Cranston Higgins, and yes, that was the real name of a person, a fellow who had shown up two weeks before. He had rung the sonorous bell on the big oak doors, apologetically claiming to be a rightful co-inheritor of Wynter Castle. It's a long story, and I'll get to that soon.

I opened the door to the café, expecting the fragrant scent of java and donuts to wash over me. Instead, all I smelled was burnt coffee, old grease, and apathy. A chubby waitress looked up from her cell phone, on which she was busy thumbing a text, no doubt saying, *Help me get out of the hell that is Ridley Ridge!* One customer sat in a booth, his head down on the tabletop. Drunk? Asleep?

Dead? The fact that I considered that a real possibility shows you the depth of my loathing of the town so far.

"Hi," I said, crossing the gummy floor, shoes sticking at every step. "I'm looking for the Ridge Gift and Party Stop."

She stared at me for a long moment, smudgy eyes wide. "The Party Stop?"

I bit back my first instinct, which was to check for an echo. "Yes."

She gulped and said, "Well, you go down Ash to Birch, left on Birch to Danver. It's on the corner. You *sure* you want to go to the Party Stop?"

"Yes, I'm sure!" I said, uneasily. "Why?"

"Oh . . . no reason."

"Okay, then. Thank you so much." As she again began madly texting, I pried my gummy foot off the floor and left.

Outside, I found the car—I had handed in the rental that was costing me several limbs a month and was using Shilo's quirky rattletrap she had named Jezebel for some unfathomable reason—and followed the waitress's directions to an unpromising semi-industrial section of town, more weed infested and lonely than I had expected. In fact, the Ridge Gift and Party Stop sign was peeling and pitted with random buckshot, and I wondered if the place was truly open. The parking lot in front was empty, so I pulled in, turning the car around and pointing it toward the road in case I needed a quick getaway. I turned the motor off. It didn't rattle as it died, which in this case was not reassuring. Rattling and groaning were the car's primary signs of life.

I got out and slammed the door. The car sighed and huddled where it sat, with a final murmur of worry. I sympathized; I was not reassured by the store's appearance either. The Party Stop looked like a warehouse, a big, sagging barn of a building constructed of concrete and corrugated steel. Weeds, withered now in the chill embrace of autumn, grew from the foundation. There were no windows on the front, only a fireproof metal door with store hours posted. If the sign was to believed, the store was open for business.

"In for a penny," I murmured, striding up to the steel door and jerking it open. The place was cavernous and looked deserted. Ah, we were still in the first act of our movie of the week, *Losing Merry*, wherein the heroine of the piece walks into trouble, not heeding the ominous *scritch* of a violin bow being drawn harshly over the strings. At least if I disappeared, the waitress at the café would remember where I had been going. I hoped. Maybe she'd text another *Help me* on my behalf.

It was the party shop I had been told about, I supposed, and had the requisite Halloween decorations, which did not make it look any more reassuring. Plastic gravestones and webby ghosts, mummies and spiders plastered around a metal detector entrance do not make for a cheery "come and spend" welcome. Even weirder, though, was the echoed whispering I heard from somewhere. Did I mention the place was cavernous? It had thirty-foot ceilings with dusty light fixtures up in the rafters that some bright fellow had supplied with twenty-five-watt yellow bug bulbs.

We were moving from suspense to horror, I decided. As I advanced, I was reminded of that scene in every slasher movie where the stupid girl keeps going forward, even when the ominous soundtrack is getting louder and more insistent. Everyone in the theater is saying, *Don't do it*, but she keeps just bumbling along, saying, *Hello?*

"Hello?" My voice echoed . . . no, really! It did. *Hello . . . ello . . . ello.*

There was a rustling sound, and movement. Along one of the cramped, dimly lit aisles came a figure, and it turned out to be . . . a completely ordinary looking guy, mid-thirties, slim, glasses, beard, and a smile, an out-of-place hipster dude. "Hi, there," he said as he advanced toward where I stood, near a cluttered customer service counter that was jammed with boxes of bubble gum and playing cards, fake poop and hand buzzers, the kind of jokey junk you find at gag shops. "Les Urquhart at your service." He slipped behind the cash desk where a copy of *Moby-Dick* was over-turned and a half-drunk cup of coffee cooled by the cash register.

With a sigh of relief, I smiled, reassured by his normalcy. "Hey, hi. I was beginning to think it was a ghost shop."

"What do you mean?"

"Oh, you know, I heard whispers when I couldn't see anyone."

He just stared at me. "Uh, there were no whispers. No one else is here."

I thought he was joking for a moment, but he seemed serious. I glanced around the place and said, "It's a little gloomy in here. Is that on purpose?"

"I like to save on electricity. Times ain't exactly blooming," he said with a wry grin. "So what can I do for you?"

"I'm throwing a kind of fallish Halloweenish party at Wynter Castle."

He started. "*The* Wynter Castle?" he blurted out.

"Have you heard of it?"

He paused, scruffing his goatee, then said, "Well, *yeah*! Everybody has. Last fall a bunch of kids from town got together and took a tour out there to see if it was haunted. That was about the time the old man who owned it got killed, right?"

"He actually died a little after that, in November, and it was a car accident," I said, not mentioning that it had been murder and that the person responsible, Dinah Hooper, was now languishing in a federal prison awaiting trial. Too much detail. "That was my Uncle Melvyn."

"Sorry. No offense intended."

"None taken. The castle isn't haunted, by the way, just in case you hear of anyone intending any more midnight rides. I've been living there over a month, and I haven't heard anything. Anyway, I'm looking to decorate on the cheap and I'm hoping you can help me. I need a lot of stuff, but I don't want to make it scary Halloween: no skeletons, no zombies, no mummies. I'm looking to do more Phantom of the Opera retro cool, you know?"

"So, not kiddy Halloween, more Count Dracula's castle from an old movie?"

"Only not *quite* so kitschy. Kind of kitsch lite," I said. I jumped and whirled around when I heard something at the back fall with a huge clatter. "What was that?"

"Nothing important. Happens all the time here, stuff falling over. It's just storage back there." He smiled, and I got the feeling he was enjoying my jumpiness. "Your castle may not be haunted, but this warehouse is. So let's get started," he said, clapping his hands together and rubbing them, perhaps at the anticipation of some actual business.

He led me past a section labeled *Costumes for Rent*, and then past racks and racks of commercial costumes for sale: French maids, saloon girls, zombies, and such. In half an hour he had me back at the checkout with bags of spider webbing, bolts of maroon and gold fabric to drape down the stairway, a little bit of kitschy Halloween junk, and the promise of more to come, if I so wished. Next time maybe I'd send Pish and Shilo. That would keep them busy for a few hours, which would be a blessing. As much as I love my friends, together they have the energy and imagination of a class full of kindergartners.

"Thanks so much, Les," I said, holding out my hand. We shook. "Would you like to come out for the party? I'm planning to have some locals there, as well as a lot of out-of-towners."

"Doesn't sound like my thing," he said.

"There *will* be girls," I said, eying him with raised eyebrows. "In costumes. Some probably skimpy." Why was I trying to lure him to come? I guess I just thought the more variety the better. A party isn't a party without a lot of people to mingle.

"Maybe I will, then!" he said.

There was another crash, and I eyed him with interest. He had blinked, but that was all, but I could tell he wanted to go back there. I wondered if the back of his store was the local pot stop. I knew from my not-too-lengthy experience that there's one in every small town, a place where all the teenagers and stoners know to go to get an ounce for a party or a kilo to sell. I stood for another moment.

"Well, have a good day," he said, fidgeting and yet resolutely not glancing behind him.

I chuckled. "You, too. Hope business gets better." Pot dealing would explain how he was able to survive with such a dusty, dingy shop in a town like Ridley Ridge.

I drove away, out of town, down the highway, and took a detour back through Autumn Vale. As I tootled through town, I waved at Doc English, the old dude who had been a friend of my uncle's from way back. Today the eccentric doctor was dressed in a camouflage jacket and pith helmet—for him that was just another clothing option in an endless line of weird outfits. I did not want to know where he got his array of headwear; in fact, I existed in blissful ignorance. It was one of the mysteries of life in Autumn Vale, a town considerably cheerier than Ridley Ridge, if just as weird in its own way

I was tempted to stop at Janice Grover's store, Crazy Lady Antiques and Collectibles, to see if she had anything new, but there was no guarantee she would be there, since her Main Street shop full of junk was only the beginning of her horde. She rented a vast warehouse on the edge of town, where, among other things, she had garden furniture and statuary, some of which I had already bought for use at Wynter Castle. She also had some wrought iron stuff I was trying to figure out a use for. I had taken photos of it all and would decide in the next couple of days. I already had dibs on an oak casket for the main hall to present the proper Halloween feel. I was only borrowing the coffin and hoped I wouldn't need it anytime soon. Though I didn't want a traditional Halloween feel for the party, it *was* a masquerade ball, so the coffin was my nod to the season.

I drove back out of town, taking the ascending road up out of the valley that gave Autumn Vale its name. A car rocketed toward and then past me, and ahead I saw Virgil Grace just getting back into his police car. Virgil is the sheriff of Autumn Vale. I'm not exactly sure of his age, but I fear he's a little younger than me, and despite my attraction to him—he is a good-looking man—I won't be pursuing that particular relationship for a number of reasons.

I'm a widow of over seven years, but there will never be anyone for me after Miguel. Once you've been loved by a man like that, there is no use trying second best. I only had two years with my husband, who was a fashion photographer, but it was two years of a bond so close I still feel him with me. I went back to my maiden name after his death only because his mother, who never liked me anyway, asked me to. She blamed me for his death, even though I wasn't with him on the day he was killed in a car accident on his way to a shoot.

I pulled up alongside Virgil's car and rolled down my window. "Hey, who was that? Did you have them stopped?"

"Yeah, routine traffic stop. Some weird out-of-towner with frizzy bleached blonde hair and strange clothes. Told her to stop driving so fast on gravel roads if she's not used to them. I was actually just coming from the castle—delivered some papers to Pish. The Feds are still roaming around AVCB and see fit to use me as their messenger."

AVCB is what locals call Autumn Vale Community Bank; after the debacle with Dinah Hooper, Isadore Openshaw, and the mismanagement of Simon Grover, the Feds had swooped in to see if there was *just* negligence or actual malfeasance. Pish, a financier of some repute, was helping them with the aim of keeping the local bank open for the citizens of Autumn Vale. It was complicated and tedious, both things Pish relished.

"Fun for you," I said, with sympathy. "So you stopped the girl for speeding. Weird place to be driving if you don't know the area, don't you think? A backwoods road like this?"

"She's just passing through. I warned her about her speed and a brake light that wasn't working and that was it."

He eyed Shilo's decrepit car, and I ignored his cocked eyebrow . . . it was a game we were both used to by now. It was cheaper to pay the tickets than fix the car and he knew it. Eventually we would come to an impasse where he wouldn't ignore the problems with Shilo's bucket, and when that time came, we'd have to do something.

"So, Virgil, are you coming to the party?" He had waffled a bit about it, but his mom, Gogi Grace, with whom I had become fast friends, was coming.

"Mom wants me to. I probably will. No dead bodies, right?" he said, eyes narrowed. "No Halloween crap like that?"

"It's not that kind of a party," I assured him, crossing my fingers because of the planned presence of the casket and a mannequin inside it. "We won't be going with a graveyard theme or have a haunted house or anything." Mostly, anyway.

"Okay. I'll have to see if I'm busy that night."

He presided over a very small police force of three other full-time and two part-time officers that patrolled a large township, so he wasn't being coy; even in his off hours he was on duty. Still, his caginess was annoying. His radio crackled to life, and he responded, then waved and headed off toward town.

"Don't do me any favors, buddy," I muttered. It was strange; the very first time I'd met him he had outright flirted with me, but ever since he had kept his distance. But I wasn't bothered by that, not one little bit.

Okay, maybe a little.

I drove on, rounding a bend in the road that was closed in on either side by pine forests. I then passed the stake that demarcated the beginning of my property, where it met the road. At first I had needed that indication to know where I was, but now I noticed the subtle change in trees; Wynter Castle had a wonderful forest that was actually a fifty-year-old arboretum planned and planted by my uncle. I turned into the lane that wound through the forest, then came out into the open and caught my first sight of Wynter Castle. It never failed to take my breath away, and with the improvements I had made, in a good way.

It's a real castle, built in the early nineteenth century by my mill-baron ancestor. The stone was quarried locally, a mellow cream, gold-and-gray granite that picked up the sun's rays and looked warm and inviting even on a chilly October day. There were three vehicles already there, and I groaned. It wasn't Jack McGill's Smart car with the Autumn Vale Realty sign on the side, nor the mower tractor that indicated that Zeke and Gordy, two local lads I hired to do exterior maintenance, were working that caused me to groan. It was the rented car parked haphazardly that told me Cranston Higgins was on-site.

Chapter Two

❊ ❊ ❊

CRANSTON HIGGINS. HE was a nice enough guy in his way, well mannered and jovial. Obliging, even. But he was not only trying to horn in on my inheritance, claiming he was the long-lost grandson of my uncle Melvyn, but he was constantly, cheerfully *in my way*. Some people manage to be quietly helpful, but Cranston wouldn't have known *quietly* if it had slapped him across the cheek and called him daddy. He wanted to help, he said, but all I heard when he said that was that he wanted to keep his eye on the prize, to be sure we got top dollar for "our" inheritance. I was doing my best to keep it all in perspective until I figured out what to do about him.

I spotted Cranston directing Zeke and Gordy. Wynter Castle is big enough, but not Highclere or Windsor Castle huge. It's a more manageable American-sized castle, thank goodness, and has an amazing gothic arched window directly above the huge double oak doors that illuminates the great entrance hall. Ivy had grown up over the years and obscured the light, and the window was filthy. I had asked Zeke and Gordy to clear away the ivy while leaving the vines not directly on the window alone; the ivy added character to the castle and possibly hid other problems that might be revealed if the plant matter was torn away. They were then supposed to clean the glass. I hoped the ivy removal and glass cleaning would not only flood the great hall with light, but also illuminate the rose window that's on the opposite wall over the double staircase. The rose window is amazing, a gorgeous rose-and-blue stained glass masterpiece.

Zeke and Gordy, up on matching twenty-foot ladders I had borrowed from Turner Construction, knew what to do . . . I hoped. They had assured me they did. I had even written out the instructions to be absolutely clear: *Tear ivy from window* only, *then clean window!* That was clear, right? I certainly didn't need Cranston giving them conflicting directions. Heaven knows they could make up enough conflicting instructions between them to hopelessly confuse the matter. Cranston was trying to get them to pull *all* of the ivy down; he wanted it "clean and tidy," he yelped up at the pair. Zeke, bless his heart, was arguing that I had been very specific, even while Gordy began to obey.

"No! Leave it alone," I hollered at Gordy as I stormed across the parking area, some of my bagged goodies in my arms. "Cranston, as much as I know you're trying to help, please don't!"

All three men gazed at me with wide, unblinking stares. I am accustomed to that. I am normally a soft-spoken woman, and that lulls people into thinking I'm a pushover. I'm not. Gordy and Zeke went back to the task at hand, which, since they had finished removing the ivy covering the window, was now to wash said window with long-handled squeegees.

Cranston, my round-faced, doughy possible cousin, just stood regarding me much as he might a pretty puppy that had bitten his hand, leaving him with a gash long enough to need stitches.

"Well, okay, Merry," Cranston said with a disappointed frown. He shoved his hands into the pockets of his corduroy sports jacket. "If you think the ivy is okay, then we can leave it in place for now. But I heard that ivy has little roots that get into mortar and could make our castle crumble eventually."

I smiled evenly, trying to ignore his use of *we* and *our* in the context of the castle, and said, "When it falls down around our ears in a couple hundred years, I'll be sure to let you say, 'I told you so' as much as you want."

As we watched the boys work, he began a long story about his past life in Buffalo with his beloved Granny Violet. Whenever Cranston started to drone, I drifted off.

I was of two minds regarding Cranston Higgins's claim to being a Wynter by birth, if not by name. Skepticism comes naturally to me, so my first thought was: *Con artist, grifter, fake!* I was *not* going to be taken, and I was a little tired of being *told* I must not be taken in by the well-meaning folks around me. My theory is, if you are suspicious of someone, it's wise to be kind and lovely to them so they'll be lulled into a false sense of confidence and expose themselves at some point. It also gives you time to do some background checks. From what I had discovered so far, Cranston Higgins had indeed lived in Buffalo for most of his life, attended the schools he said he had attended, and lived where he said he had lived.

Cranston had never once asked me outright for money, just for a portion of the estate if he could prove his claim. I was keeping things polite and pleasant while we sorted it out. Melvyn, my great uncle, had apparently had a sweetheart named Violet round about 1940. He would have been in his late teens, fresh out of high school, when he enlisted in the army in '42, after Pearl Harbor. When he headed off to basic training, there was apparently some kind of rift between them, and though she was pregnant, she never told him. She married some other fellow and moved away, but years later, just before she passed on, she told her grandson about his Wynter heritage and the castle his biological grandfather lived in.

He had a few photos of him with his granny as he grew up and in later years, but the one thing he had that connected him to the Wynter estate was an old gold-colored locket with her picture in it as a young woman. It was engraved *Forever Yours, Mel*.

I wouldn't even be giving him the time of day except that Doc English, one of the few old enough to remember the old days and a great friend of my Uncle Melvyn, agreed that Melvyn had been going with a girl named Violet and that she married a fellow and moved away very soon after he and my uncle left for the war. So the tale *could* be true. If she had been pregnant with Melvyn's baby but they argued and broke it off, she may have felt she had no recourse but to marry a nice 4-F fellow and raise the baby as his, rather than endure the shame of being an unwed mother in 1942.

Andrew Silvio, the estate lawyer, said he had never heard of another descendant. We could just let Cranston take us to court, the lawyer told me, but he warned that if that happened, the fight would be long and I might end up with nothing in the end even if I won, because legal fees could eat up the estate. He urged me to offer the guy a settlement to walk away. But in my gut I believed that if Melvyn had known he had a grandson, he might have handed the whole estate over to his closer male heir. Cranston just wanted half, which he said was only fair.

However, I wasn't going to just hand half the estate over to him. I needed some ironclad proof. I asked Cranston if he was willing to do DNA testing, and he agreed. That took me aback. If he was a grifter, wouldn't he kick up a fuss, knowing the DNA wouldn't match? Silvio didn't want me to do the DNA test. What if it came back positive? Then I would *definitely* be in for a court battle, because despite what he said right now, Cranston *might* sue for the whole estate, and he'd have a case. Melvyn's stated wish—everyone in town knew about it—was to keep the castle in the family. My expressed intent to sell could be used against me, though I would argue the same would go for Cranston.

It was complicated. If Cranston and I were related, we'd be second cousins, or something like that. I didn't have any relatives that I knew of, since I was an only child and both my parents were gone. It would have been kind of cool to have a cousin, but on the other hand, I could go from being owner of the estate to maybe visiting there occasionally. And the trouble with *that* was, I was beginning to like Autumn Vale and its inhabitants.

So we hadn't done the DNA test yet, but I was leaning toward it. If Cranston ended up with the whole shebang, then that was how it was meant to be, and I'd find a way to make a fresh start. Maybe I'd move to California and become a stylist to the stars, I thought, in my more flippant moods. I just didn't know which way I wanted to handle it yet.

It was possible that the decision would be yanked out of my hands, though, because Cranston was starting to insist. That made me lean toward the idea that, true or not, he at least believed he was the grandson of Melvyn Wynter. Silvio *still* thought I should just offer the guy a settlement. If he had any doubts about his granny's story, he might take it, since at least he'd walk away with something. But exactly what could a muffin-baking former stylist and one-time assistant to a diva model who was as broke as a dollar-store watch offer as compensation? I had no real money. My only asset was the castle, which would not be liquid until it was sold.

I came back down to earth with a thud, aware that the bags were starting to get heavy and Cranston showed no sign of stopping. He was talking about the great Buffalo, New York, snowstorm of 1977, when he had been just a little guy. "I bounced out of the house and straight into a drift so high it came up to my eyebrows!"

I sighed, shifting the bags. "In case you hadn't noticed, Cranston, I am loaded down and there's more in the car. You can stand there and talk, or you can give me a hand." I trudged into the castle and attempted to slam the door, but no dice. Heavy doors like the double oak ones that lead into the great hall do not slam; they swing majestically shut. I took a deep breath and sighed, letting it out gradually. The great hall always had a calming effect on me.

Gordy and Zeke's work had already made a difference, because for the first time I could see into the corners of the enormous space, and the rose window opposite the big window over the doors was lit up nicely to show the gold and royal blue panes that offset the crimson and greens of the floral pattern. And now I could actually see the fabulous curved and carved ceiling, with its ornate gold-painted plaster curlicues, the broad border painted with a rosy sunset sky with puffy clouds illuminated by a setting sun. The big, dusty tapestries were more visible, too, with their scenes of stag hunting, fruit sellers in marketplaces, and ladies sitting in gardens being wooed by medieval knights. Gorgeous. I smiled as I set the bags down and moved to the center of the great hall, under the majestic chandelier, letting the peace of the big space fill me, edging out the irritation Cranston had incited.

How had this happened to me? Just ten or so months ago I was doing my best to keep tyrannical model Leatrice Peugot happy. I had been a struggling stylist a couple of years before when she decided I was her savior. She offered me an insane wage, so I grabbed it like a large-mouth bass snapping at a wormy hook and soon found out that being her assistant meant active duty as her flogging girl, scapegoat, gofer, and everything in between, as well as taking over a starring role in the Leatrice Peugot drama *The Reason Everything Goes Wrong in My Life*. I dealt with it all as best I could for a while, muffin baking being my only outlet and link to sanity.

When Leatrice started stealing and scarfing them down in private, she gained a couple of ounces, which threatened her career as professional stick woman. It was my fault she kept filching them, apparently, and she was horribly angry. Angry Leatrice was volatile, like nitroglycerin in a room full of sugar-hyped toddlers. On rocking horses. With pellet guns. I took a lot of abuse before I figured out she was filching my muffins. I could handle her accusations that I was undermining her out of jealousy, but once she accused me of stealing a valuable necklace that had been loaned to her by Tiffany, I knew I had to leave. The police did not arrest me, but they filed a report in which I was named prominently. I don't think *anyone* took it; I think she either lost it or pawned it.

I was in the middle of all of that when Andrew Silvio called me and told me the news; I was heir to the Wynter Estate, castle and all. It seems odd now, looking back, that I put off coming to Autumn Vale for so long, but I was desperate to right things in my life. I thought that meant staying in the city and dealing with my multitude of problems, among them suspicion from the police, Leatrice's backstabbing, having no job, dwindling resources, and an industry poisoned against me by gossip and innuendo. I enlisted the help of Jack McGill, Autumn Vale's only real estate agent, to put the castle on the market.

It didn't sell, and finally I gave up trying to clear my name and deal with the crapstorm that was the web of lies Leatrice had woven. I left New York in the middle of the night with my worldly belongings in a rented sedan, leaving what didn't fit in a storage unit in Manhattan, one that I had since cleared. Now everything I owned was around me in the castle, and it felt good.

Many of my problems had magically vanished the moment I left New York City. Industry gossip and Leatrice's backstabbing became moot points once I was no longer confronted by former friends and allies at every event or club. I held fast to the knowledge that gossip dies and everyone would eventually move on to some new scandal.

"Merry, you home?" came a bright shout.

I smiled. I had *left* NYC alone, but I wasn't on my own for long. In fact, my best friend, a model named Shilo Dinnegan—whose shout now welcomed me back to the castle—had followed, arriving just hours after me. Then, before long, my other best friend, dapper retired financier-to-the-stars Pish Lincoln, had arrived, anxious to see the castle for himself. Both were now staying at the castle with me.

"I'm ho-ome," I sang back.

Cranston, Gordie, and Zeke came in the front door at that moment, loaded down with the rest of the stuff I had bought at the Party Stop, just as Shilo, trailed by a smiling Pish, came down the stairs to greet me. The resulting clash was tumultuous. Shilo threw herself at me with some complaint about something Pish wouldn't let her do—I think it was paint her room fuchsia—and Cranston preened, telling

Zeke and Gordy where to deposit the bags. Becket strolled into the great hall at that moment and began washing his butt; a cat can get away with that in polite society. I smiled happily. I was home.

Cranston futzed around for a while longer, then headed off to wherever he went when he left. For the first few days of our acquaintance he had hinted that he would love to stay at the castle, but I dug my heels in. Until I knew he was Melvyn's grandson, I wasn't going along with that. He was staying at some bed-and-breakfast or boarding house nearby, as far as I knew.

That evening Pish and Shilo told me some of what they had found up in the attic while I was slithering through Ridley Ridge. There was, according to Pish, an embarras de richesses. Shilo said she wasn't embarrassed at all, and in fact thought all the riches were cool. There was no point in explaining what that meant to Shilo, and why would we bother? Not everyone needs to get every snobbish literary or classical reference.

There were oodles of furniture up there, as well as trunks and trunks of random goodies, they told me. While Shilo rhapsodized about the vintage clothing—she was toying with dressing as a flapper girl for the party—Pish was intrigued by what appeared to be boxes of financial records of the family dating back many years. While I couldn't muster any excitement over those, I was interested to learn that there were old photo albums up there, too.

We spent the evening planning the party décor and the placement of the casket, which Zeke and Gordy were bringing to Wynter Castle on a flatbed truck that Gordy would borrow from his uncle, the farmer. The coffin, with a mannequin, was going to sit on a low table in the great hall and be the welcome to the castle; Pish was planning to rig up the sound system he was working on so some maniacal laughter would emanate from the half-open oak casket. That was as far as I wanted the décor to go in that direction, I reminded him. I did not want kiddie Halloween party gruesomeness or a funhouse atmosphere.

The alarm clock woke me the next morning just as a ray of autumn sunshine peeped past the drawn curtains. I rolled out of bed, groaning, "Time to make the muffins!" Mornings dawn early when you've promised four dozen muffins to an old-age home and another dozen to the local café. Muffins, my downfall in New York City, had proved to be my saving grace in Autumn Vale, New York. My temporary business, called The Merry Muffin for obvious reasons, was going great guns now that I had the castle kitchen vetted and licensed as a proper place in which to bake food for the masses.

I showered and snuck downstairs, trying not to awaken my friends, who were still on New York City time, where nothing gets going until ten AM. Or at least not in my circle. I let Becket out the door—he had his own mysterious catty business to take care of, I suppose—donned a hairnet and got to work, baking two dozen spice muffins, two dozen bran, one dozen carrot, and one dozen apple.

Since my stuff had come from storage, I had made myself comfortable in the kitchen, which boasted, thanks to my uncle's ambition, an industrial-size oven and stovetop and stainless steel countertops worthy of any inn kitchen. Whatever holes there were in my equipment supply I had been able to fill from Janice's junk store, so I even had industrial-size baking sheets for cookies and squares, which I had added to my repertoire.

The kitchen was a long room, and now had a cozy nook at one end where the fireplace was topped by a mantel adorned with oil lamps and the more rustic of my teapot collection. I was using what I could of my own stuff to mingle with all that had been left in the castle when I inherited it, which was a lot. The huge Eastlake-style furnishings—including a marble-topped maple sideboard in the dining room that was eight feet tall, which fit the grand size of the room—along with random samples of furniture from every era in American history, made the castle a warm environment, but it was my decorations that were bringing it to life. When I had time, I was going to work on the dining room, where a long oak dining table and a huge Eastlake china buffet were currently cluttered with the remainder of my rather large teapot collection.

I was just taking the last of the muffins out of the oven when Pish, looking spiffy and dressed for town, jogged into the kitchen and grabbed a cup of coffee. He was followed by Shilo, still wearing footie pajamas—charming on her: she's twenty-nine but looks about ten years younger—and carrying Becket.

How had he gotten back in? "No cat in the kitchen," I told her sternly, but she didn't listen to me and set him down in one of the big armchairs near the fireplace.

"I have to go into town today, my *darling* dumpling," Pish said, laying a kiss on my floury cheek. He grabbed an apple cinnamon muffin and perched on a stool by the distressed wood worktable.

I eyed the sport coat and sweater vest he wore and smiled. Pish can be flamboyant, his dialogue sprinkled with exaggerated emphasis and wild hand movements, but he buttons it down when need be, like while talking to the federal agents who were examining Autumn Vale Community Bank. He was working with them to try to uncover and minimize the damage done to the bank by the scheming Dinah Hooper, who now languished in a federal prison awaiting trial for the murders of Tom Turner and Melvyn Wynter. She had not been granted bail, as she was considered a flight risk.

I said she was a flight certainty, but then I had looked down the barrel of her rifle and survived. To say I was happy they were keeping her out of circulation would be a vast understatement. "I'm going in about twenty minutes," I said. "Is that too early for you?"

"Not at *all* my dear. I'm going to see Isadore this morning before the bank."

Isadore Openshaw, a former teller at the bank, had not been arrested—yet—and was cooperating with the federal agents. Pish felt sorry for Isadore, and I think she had become something of a pet project of his, the plan being to keep her out of trouble and reform her life. He told me that she reminded him of an aunt who had floated in and out of his life when he was a kid. That poor woman eventually died alone in a house overrun by cats, and he foresaw a future like that for Isadore if someone didn't intervene. Given how unpleasant she could be, I wasn't sure Pish was ever going to succeed, but his charm and good nature gave him a better chance at it than most.

"Will you invite her to the party?" I asked.

Shilo snorted. I turned to where she sat, curled up in a chair by the fire with Becket in her lap. "What's up?" I asked her.

"I was trying to imagine what costume she'd come up with."

I smiled, knowing that her laughter didn't hold any malice. Isadore was peculiar in her dress. She tended toward homemade shifts sewn from fabric featuring frolicking cats or enthusiastic, bleary-eyed bunnies. She wore jewelry to match, dangling kitties or bunnies with carrots. "Maybe she'll come wearing a Donna Karan skirt suit."

Pish and I headed out twenty minutes later with six tubs

of assorted muffins, most for Golden Acres and a few for the café. I dropped him off near Isadore's home, the house she had inherited from her cousin. It was a gloomy little bungalow with a dark front porch that loomed on the house like a beetle brow. He had never yet been in the house, but I knew he would keep trying to befriend her. He'd find his own way on to the bank, then back to the castle, he told me, likely with Jack McGill, who would be making one of his daily trips out to see Shilo.

I then pulled up to Golden Acres and delivered the muffins to the back kitchen, where I had made fast friends with the sole, overworked cook. It was morning snack time in the parlor, so I joined the group and sat with Doc, who was drinking a cup of premium coffee he had filched from Gogi Grace's private stock.

"It's gonna close, you know it's going to!" one old guy was stating loudly, shaking his cane at no one in particular.

"What are we complaining about today?" I asked Doc.

"Everyone's afraid the bank is going under. That's what happened in Ridley Ridge a few years back—to the community bank, that is . . . used to be the Ridley Ridge Savings and Loan—and look at that town now. Folks in Ridley Ridge, their mortgages have been sold to some big bank and they can't get ahold of no one when they need to talk. Damned shame."

I shuddered. "Was that town ever anything but a gloomy hole in the wall?"

"Sure was," Doc said. "Used to be a happening place. When I was young we went there for the church dances. That's where I met my wife in '47. Since the main bank closed up, the whole town has gone into decline. Only thing there now is a couple of ATMs and a teenie branch office of Wells Fargo."

"Pish is doing his best to keep the Feds from closing AVCB down. Maybe Wynter Castle will be the happening place now," I said, handing him his official invitation to the party. "Gogi will bring you, or Virgil will."

He grinned, yellow teeth exposed. I was curious, given his penchant for weird headwear, what he would decide to come as—a vintage scuba diver was my first thought; he would love an antique diving helmet, no doubt—but I looked forward to it.

I had other locals coming, too. Hannah, the local librarian, was coming as Clara from the kid's book *Heidi*. She is a tiny young woman confined to a wheelchair, and though she has some physical disabilities, they are overcome by her huge heart, deep intelligence, and sunshiny personality. Her parents were coming as Heidi's grandfather and Clara's housekeeper, Fräulein Rottenmeier.

So far, Hannah had not been able to convince our young teenage friend Lizzie Proctor to come as Heidi herself. Lizzie would die rather than be seen in braids and a dirndl. She would be there, though, along with her new friend, Alcina, an oddly fascinating child who flitted through my forest wearing faery wings. I assumed *she* would be coming to the party in her normal garb. The teenagers were not guests; I had promised to pay them if they would empty ashtrays in the smoking court, take coats, and report back to me any weird goings-on. It was Autumn Vale; I *expected* weird goings-on but wanted to know about them anyway. Gordy and Zeke would be my doorman and unofficial parking valet, respectively.

"Doc, have you thought any more about Melvyn and Violet, what you remember about their courtship?"

He nodded, slowly. "Seems to me Vi might still have some family in these parts. She left and moved to New

England, but her family might have kept in contact with her and be able to tell you what's what."

"Can you write down whatever you remember?"

"I sure will."

"Good. Thanks." I finished my coffee. "I'll check in with Hannah. If anyone can track them down, she can."

"Don't let that Higgins fellow take the castle away from you, Merry," Doc said, taking my hand in his gnarled fingers. "You're a good girl," he went on, patting my hand, "and Melvyn always regretted not having contact with you over the years. But your mom . . . she just wasn't having it."

"I know. I wish I knew why."

Chapter Three

�֍ ✖ ✖

I HATED SHILO'S car. It was decrepit, held together by duct tape and hope and fueled by desperation. I needed another one but couldn't bring myself to spend any of my quickly dwindling resources on something that was only going to cost me more and more as I went. When I had time, I was going to have someone come out to the castle to look at the two cars my uncle had stored in the garage—the 1940s car I remembered riding in at the age of five was still there and might be worth something to a collector—and I did hope that his 1970s Cadillac could be rescued. Until then, I had to use Shilo's beater.

I tootled along to Binny's Bakery and parked in front. This wasn't a delivery; Binny would die before she would sell something as prosaic as muffins in her shop. The girl was capital-*S* stubborn. Autumn Vale would have devoured cookies and muffins, but instead she gave them brioche and mille-feuille at cut-rate costs to try to educate their palates.

I kept trying to tell her that it wasn't education they needed; they liked her stuff *once in a while*, especially since she was selling mille-feuille at oatmeal cookie prices. But the citizens of Autumn Vale, or Valers, as I had taken to calling them, wanted the foods they were familiar with most of the time. Don't we all? It was no use; Binny was a stubborn as her father, Rusty, and that was saying a lot. The old goat had survived for months living off the land and running from imaginary Russian mobsters, with only a shed and then a tent as shelter. That takes a lot of stubborn for a seventy-something man.

So I made muffins for anyone who wanted them, with Binny's blessing. We had gotten over the hump of our early relationship when she thought my uncle had killed her father and that I may have killed her brother. Now that she had her dad back and Dinah Hooper was in jail awaiting trial in Binny's brother's murder, we were actually on friendly terms. Having found out that Lizzie Proctor, my prickly teenage protégé, was her brother's daughter had given her a boost in spirits, though Binny was never going to be a smiley girl.

I entered the bakery, which had been my first stop when I entered Autumn Vale almost two months before, since Binny lives for baking. She opens at *insanely* early hours; she figures she's there anyway, so she may as well be open. Although I was there today for green tea powder, which I could not find in any store in Autumn Vale, I was also curious about Binny's new employee. I approached the counter. "Hi there. You must be Juniper!" I said.

The girl looked up, and at first I thought she hadn't slept much until I realized that it was makeup; her eyes were ringed with dark eye shadow. It was a terrible look. I used to be a stylist to models for photo shoots—that's how I met

my late darling husband, Miguel Paradiso—and for a while
the "heroin chic" look was the style, but thank heavens that
was over. This girl had not gotten the memo.

"What can I get you?" She indicated the glass bakery
case with a lethargic gesture.

"My name is Merry Wynter," I said, sticking my hand
across the counter and examining the girl. She appeared to
be in her mid-twenties, and under the obligatory baker's
apron she wore a Def Leppard tee and black jeans. Her black
hair was restrained by a jaunty baker's cap that said *Binny's
Bakery* on it, but her dark eyes, with the kohl shadows,
appeared listless and dead. She did not shake my hand.

I dropped it and said, "I'm a friend of Binny's. Is she
here?"

"Yeah."

"Could you get her, please?"

"Okay." She turned away and ambled back to the bakery.

As I waited, I examined the teapots as usual. Binny's collection was almost as extensive as mine, but she had some
unusual pieces that I coveted. She had already given me an
adorable Capodimonte with a raised relief of a girl and
donkey that was given to her by Dinah. Oddly enough, it had
proven to hold a note my uncle had written—actually just a
snatch of Joyce Kilmer's poem "Trees"—along with some
scrawls in different handwriting, presumably Dinah's. When
I discovered a series of tree names in Becket's collar, I thought
the poem might have been pointing to some kind of mystery
my uncle had planned out. We surmised that Dinah Hooper
was working on finding the legendary Wynter treasure, and
had stolen the piece of paper from my uncle on one of her
visits, then tucked the clue in the teapot as a way of hiding it
in plain sight, kind of like in "The Purloined Letter."

We still hadn't figured out my uncle's code, though. It

was quite possible that we were overcomplicating things, but I hadn't had the time or brain energy to reason it out.

"Hey, Merry, I've got the stuff for you," Binny said, lifting the pass-through section of her countertop and joining me in front of the teapots.

I took the baggie of green powder as Juniper eyed it with a narrowed gaze. "Green tea powder," I said to her, in case she thought it was something else. She looked skeptical. Where had Binny gotten this winner? "Hey, Bin, you want to come have a coffee with me at the café? I have to go drop off some muffins."

"Sure," she said. "You can handle the store, Juniper?"

The girl nodded and slumped down on a stool behind the counter.

A brisk autumn wind had come up and swept down the lonely street. I retrieved the tub of muffins from the car and we hustled together the fifteen or twenty steps down to the café, going through the variety-store part and right back to the luncheonette. It could have been mistaken for a retro fifties diner except it was just caught in a time warp and had never been redecorated. The floor was still checkerboard tile, albeit cracked and worn, and the counter was still chrome-edged Arborite. The tables and chairs looked straight out of *Back to the Future*.

I handed the tub of muffins to the cashier, who knew what to do with them, and grabbed a seat at a table with Binny. Once we had our coffee and muffins, I asked her how she found Juniper.

"I advertised online and got a couple of enquiries, but Juniper . . . she really needed the job so badly! She'd been working in Ridley Ridge but got fired and didn't have anywhere to go."

"You hired her *just* because she needed the job," I said, my tone flat.

"Uh-huh. I let her use the apartment above the shop, too, until she gets on her feet."

"Where are *you* staying?"

"With dad, at the house. He's still not well, and until we get everything sorted out . . ." She shrugged. "He likes the company."

Her father, Rusty Turner, had been through a dreadful ordeal, hiding out in the woods with Dinah Hooper feeding him a line of bull about how the Russian mafia was after them because of some hinky dealings she had coordinated through Turner Construction. He finally figured out she was the dangerous one when she sent her son, Dinty, into the woods to kill him. By a stroke of good luck, the old guy managed to avoid harm and actually killed Dinty in self-defense. Dinah came after Rusty, furious about the death of her beloved son, and thanks to Becket I happened to be in the right place at the right time and, while escaping her capable aim with a gun, led the police to her.

It had been an eventful couple of weeks, but everything had settled down and the last month had been calm and relatively productive. "So Juniper was the best you could find?"

She made a face at me and looked away. "She needed this job so much."

Maybe it was the cynical New Yorker part of me, but I would never give a job to the one who needed it most. Shouldn't she have chosen the best candidate for the job rather than the most needy one? Not my business to encourage her to look into the girl's past a little before trusting her too much, I told myself firmly. It was a little late for a background check anyway, because Juniper had the cash desk all to herself right that very minute. I changed the subject and told Binny about my weird experience at the party shop in Ridley Ridge the day before.

"That's funny," Binny said. "I've never been there, but Juniper actually knows that guy, the one who owns the store. That's where she worked before me."

"So that's who fired her—Les Urquhart?"

"I guess."

"Did you call him for a reference?"

"Well, no. I mean, he *fired* her. He wasn't going to give her a good reference, right? Juniper said he harassed her."

"Uh, Binny, did you check *any* references?"

"Not really."

I took a deep, cleansing breath. If she wanted to put a complete stranger in charge of her till, it was Not My Business. I'd have to make up a tune and keep singing in my brain, Not My Business. I took another deep breath and let it out. I was working hard on not interfering in other people's lives. For some reason, that's difficult for me. Pish says I'm a compulsive empath, but I disagree. Isadore Openshaw came though the front door right then and strode to the luncheonette. She approached the clerk and said something.

The woman shook her head. Isadore hammered on the counter, and shouted, "But I need a job! I'll wash dishes, or clean floors." Her voice was reedy, and she seemed on the edge of tears.

I ached for her, even though she was the single most difficult woman to help that I had ever met. The store manager came in response to the ruckus and escorted Isadore out, hustling her through the tables of coffee drinkers and breakfast eaters. Binny and I were silent for a few moments, both of us looking down at our hands, but I couldn't stand it. I rushed after them, and said, "Hey, don't be mean to her. She just needs a job."

The manager, a dour-looking woman in her sixties with iron gray hair in tightly permed curls, said, "Don't care. No shouting in the café. Folks are trying to eat."

Isadore wouldn't meet my gaze and allowed herself to be escorted out. I was tempted to go after her, but from experience I knew she'd freeze me out. Instead I went back to Binny and told her that Pish was trying to help Isadore, but she was prickly. It was entirely possible that, even if she'd been home, she hadn't answered the door when I dropped him off that morning. Binny looked shell-shocked. "Gosh, if I didn't already have Juniper, I'd give the poor woman a job."

I sighed. I was having to remind myself not to interfere *a lot* this morning and was only having moderate success. I *wanted* to tell Binny that the last thing she needed was a secretive, morose, oddly dressed middle-aged woman selling her goods. Of course, right now she had a secretive, morose, oddly dressed twentysomething doing the same, so it would be trading laterally.

We parted ways, and I headed down the street to Crazy Lady Antiques and Collectibles. Janice Grover, wife of Simon Grover, the embattled bank manager of Autumn Vale Community Bank, owned the store. She's a passionate hoarder who got into the junk business to try to clear out her home. At one point a few weeks before, she hadn't even been talking to me, convinced I had railroaded her husband into trouble. We had since mended our acquaintanceship, and she was a valuable source of "stuff," all the ephemera one needs to make a place like the castle decent.

She had, in her off-site warehouse, granite urns, wrought iron planters and outdoor furnishings, statuary, garden boxes, and lengths of ornate fencing. In the store she had chandeliers, candelabras, settees, tables, Persian rugs, and a host of other things that were slowly converting the castle to a place to some warmth. She and Pish had actually become even closer than she and I, since they shared a love of opera and period costume dramas. She was flamboyant and weird and invaluable.

I sidled into her store past a shelf loaded down with junk and let my eyes get used to the dimness. "Janice, yoo-hoo!" In the time it took to say that, I noticed a cute marbleized Formica dinette set I couldn't use in the castle, and about a dozen bibelots I couldn't use either but would likely buy anyway.

"I'm coming." When she came into view, she was radiant in a fuchsia caftan and dream catcher earrings. She was also wearing a tiara. "Hey, kiddo! How's it hanging?"

"Low and to the left," I said. It had taken me a while to get her sense of humor, but by now nothing fazed me in Autumn Vale. I had begun to think there must be something in the water. Whenever I left the town to go somewhere else—Rochester, Buffalo, even just nearby Batavia—it felt a little like waking up from a dream, one of those odd ones where the bizarre seemed completely normal while you're in it. "How is Simon doing?"

"Not bad. Pishy is taking good care of him, but poor old Simon is finding it hard to catch up with all the regulations he ignored for years."

Simon Grover had been a lazy and ineffectual bank manager, content to sit in his office and roar for coffee while reading the paper and doing the Jumble puzzle. Dinah had blackmailed Isadore into several infractions of rules that Simon had signed off on without fully understanding, and they had fallen between the cracks of a complex system in a difficult banking atmosphere for a year or more. The Feds were investigating, and Pish had helped hire a professional management team from New York in his effort to save the bank for Autumn Vale. If Simon could get up to speed, he might save his job, but it was hanging in the balance.

Pish talked about banking a lot, but much of what he said was beyond me. He talked about "regulatory burdens," "syndicated loans" and "sticky deposits" (which sounded like something to be handled with an SOS pad, to me) along with other such junk about which I knew little. I'm not stupid, just bored by the whole thing. My dear, dapper friend is a passionate defender of diversity in the banking industry and has said, in his serious moments, that the history of small-town America has often times been the history of its locally owned bank. He was very *It's a Wonderful Life* about it.

"I saw Isadore this morning," I said to Janice, letting my gaze roam over the store to see if there was anything new I just had to have. "She's trying to find a job."

"She's cooperating with the Feds, but she still can't work at the bank, not after what she did," Janice said, her expression serious for once. "They've got a professional in there right now doing the work while they look for someone local. If Isadore gets out without being prosecuted, she'll be lucky."

After a moment of silence, I got down to the reason I was there, which was to pick up a quirky piece for the smoking pit I was devising to keep people from smoking in the castle. In an outdoor corner just off the terrace I had built, with the help of Gordy and Zeke's labor, a graveled area with a few wrought iron tables and some ashtrays would make a little smoking pit. Janice brought out the piece we had spoken of on the phone.

"It's perfect!" I said. It was a papier mâché tombstone. Inscribed on it in gothic lettering was: *Jimmy knew what would happen if he smoked. His doctor said, "Coffin."*

"Speaking of which, when are you going to pick up the casket?" Janice asked.

"I've got Zeke and Gordy coming out the day before the party to pick it up."

I paid her and we parted ways. I carried the lightweight tombstone out to the car and put it in the trunk, hoping the trunk lid would stay closed; it had a fifty-fifty chance between locking tight and staying that way for the next year, or flying open at an inopportune moment. Just as I heard the *snick* of the latch catching, a sloppily dressed middle-aged woman strode toward me, her flyaway hair, back in a tight ponytail, fluttering in wisps on the breeze.

"You!" she shrieked, a string of spittle landing on my blouse as she pointed at me. "You and your highfalutin friends! You're oughta be ashamed of yourself, bringing people like that gypsy and that . . . that *man* to our town! Everything was fine until you came, and now it's awful. Go home!" She then strode away at a furious clip.

I stood on the sidewalk, mouth open, staring at her retreating backside. "Crazy!" I muttered. "This town is freaking loony tunes!" I grabbed some kind of note off the windshield of Shilo's car, crumpled it up, and stuck it in my purse, then got in and headed back to the castle, troubled by the confrontation. What the heck had I done to deserve that kind of treatment?

At the castle, I parked the car in the empty parking area and frowned; no one was there, and that meant no one was working. The party was in just a week, and I needed to get stuff done as quickly as possible. It was all turning out to be much more expensive than I had anticipated, so I needed to get moving on finding a buyer for the castle before I bankrupted myself.

The big oak doors opened easily; as always, the squirt

of WD-40 added to the hinges was the cheapest fix I had found for any problem in the castle. But when I opened the doors and entered, it was not to silence but to the gentle strains of Satie's *Gymnopédies* soaring through the cavernous great hall. I stopped, eyes closed, overwhelmed by the lovely sound, violins and harp. Tears welled in my eyes as the ache of missing Miguel ate into my heart. I sank down on the stairs and let the music flow through me.

Miguel and I had made love to *Gymnopédies* one long, lazy rainy October Sunday in New York. Slow, passionate, sweet, soft, fulfilling; it had been magic. We slept together in a heap, bedcovers tossed around us, water streaming down the window; when we awoke, I restarted the CD and we made love again. I never felt so beautiful as when I was making love with Miguel.

The following day, he had died in a horrific highway accident while driving to a photo shoot in Vermont. It had been awful, the worst thing I had ever experienced, and it still haunted me. I had been trying to ignore it, trying to silence the weeping in my soul, but the next day would be the eighth anniversary of his death.

"Merry?"

I looked up and wiped the tears from my eyes. The owner of the gruff voice was Virgil Grace; he stood in the doorway watching me, his gaze troubled. The music finished and I stood, trying to smile. "That music . . . it makes me think of Miguel. I was missing my husband." At that moment, Copland's "Hoedown" came on, the rambunctious, energetic strains filling the great hall and the clicking beat of the woodblock percussion echoing from the ceiling. The contrast was absurd, and I couldn't help it—I laughed—a little wildly, I must say.

"Merry?" That was Pish, and he emerged from the hallway toward the kitchen. "I *thought* I heard you!" He stopped and cocked his ear. "Isn't it *grand*? I picked up the last bits and bobs I needed in town and *just* finished installing the music system for the party!" He charged for me, grabbed the crook of my arm in his, and we did a hoedown, twirling in abandon on the marble floor. Shilo darted out, having followed Pish, and she grabbed Virgil, who did not comply so readily, though he allowed himself to be hauled around by my slim and vigorous friend until the last, triumphant *duh-duh-duh!*

Panting, we laughed and I hugged Pish to me, tears still streaming down my face. Thank heaven for wonderful friends. I'd be *so* alone at the castle without them. I shook my clothes into place and turned toward Virgil. "I'm assuming you came here for something other than a barn dance?"

He just stood and stared at me wiping the last of my tears from my cheeks with my sleeve until I felt a little uncomfortable. There was something in his eyes, dark and shadowed by his thick brows, something that disturbed my insides. Maybe it was the vivid reminder I had just experienced of Miguel making love to me, his hands, his body, his breath warm on my cheek. Virgil's eyes, like Miguel's, were dark, a mellow brown like milk chocolate, though in almost every other way the two men were so very different. Or were they? Something to ponder.

He shook himself and blurted out, "I, uh, the federal agents want Mr. Lincoln to call them. They tried calling his cell, but—"

"Let me guess; it didn't go through. We seem to be in this weird cell-tower dead zone," I chirped. "It's only when I really want to make a call that it doesn't work."

Pish and Shilo looked back and forth between us, and Shilo got this funny secretive smile on her face. Pish said, "What on *earth* could they want now? I *just* spoke to them an hour ago, and we were good to go, I thought." He headed off to the kitchen.

"Want a cup of coffee, Virgil?" I asked to cut the zinging tension. I retreated to the kitchen, assuming Virgil would follow, and he did.

Becket sat on the kitchen table, against all health codes and my remonstrance to the two guilty parties, Pish and Shilo, who both constantly let him in. When I first got Uncle Melvyn's ginger tabby to move back into the castle—he had been wandering the woods since my uncle's death—I found that the tag on his collar had a paper insert that slid out and unfolded in accordion pleats. Pish and Shilo had it open on the table, spread out on a pad of paper. Pish's neat handwriting was evident in a list he was creating from the cat tag enclosure. He finished something up as I entered and gave me a bright smile. "I think we've got it, sweetie."

"You've cracked the code?" I put on a pot of coffee.

"Perhaps. . . . Could it truly be as simple as being a list of the trees we need to follow to find his hidden loot?" Pish asked me.

"Maybe we've been overcomplicating it all along." Given that we had been investigating the Latin names and trying to find some kind of cipher in the list, that was likely. I explained the list to Virgil as I looked over Pish's work. I'd have to talk to my friends about it later.

"Shall we move into the parlor? I'm not supposed to let Becket sit in here," I said, glaring at Shilo and Pish, who looked innocent and slightly hurt.

"I'd better call the agents," Pish said, retreating to the sitting area near the fire, where the best landline phone was hooked up.

"And I'm doing laundry," Shilo said, melting away, her vanishing act being one of her gypsy tricks, as she called them.

So I was stuck with an uncomfortable Virgil Grace for a half hour as we chatted about his mother, Gogi, and her work at Golden Acres, and how the case against Dinah Hooper was shaping up. He left with an obvious sense of relief, and I stormed off to clean something with the uneasy feeling that I was using work to replace something more fun.

The next morning I awoke knowing it was going to be a tough day. *Eight years ago today . . .* those were the first words I heard in my brain. But too many anniversaries had passed with me holed up and crying all day, drying my tears on a soft old shirt of Miguel's. That was not helping me progress with life, and I was not going to do the same now that my life had changed so dramatically in every other way.

Instead, I got moving with renewed determination to get the castle cleaned up and back on the market, with "word of mouth" being the most likely way I was going to sell an eighteenth-century mill baron's folly, a castle too big even for the hundreds of acres it was set upon. As usual I was first up, so I put the coffee on to brew and let Becket out the front door to do his business. He preferred au naturel to the litter box I had so kindly provided for him. Something caught my eye, and I stepped out onto the terrace, as I had taken to calling the wide flagstone patio that lined the front of the castle and wrapped around on one side.

"Blast! What the . . . ?"

All of my carefully placed and potted planters had been dumped, dirt all over, fall chrysanthemums ripped out and torn up. I wrapped my housecoat around me, and as Becket followed me, curious, I circled to see if there was more damage. Spray painted along the side of my beautiful, mellow gold stone castle were the words *Go Home!*

Chapter Four

"IT'S TOO BAD," Virgil said, arms crossed over his manly chest. "It's really too damn bad."

"Too *bad*?" I screeched, ready to tear my hair out at his casual choice of words. Someone had spray painted my castle! "Too bad? That's all you can say about the defacement of a beautiful landmark?" Pish didn't help much. He snorted even as I made ineffectual snuffling noises of fury. Why did my interactions with the sheriff amuse him so? "I called *you* to investigate," I said to the sheriff, shivering in the cold wind that whipped around us as we stood staring at the defacement.

"I will certainly do that. It sure seems that you've made someone mad. Can you think who that might be?"

I sighed and went over the list in my mind. Junior Bradley, the former zoning commissioner I had exposed as incompetent and lacking in the appropriate education, despite his claims to the contrary? Isadore Openshaw, who likewise had lost her job and might be facing federal prosecution because of me? Simon Grover . . . well, likewise on the federal prosecution if he didn't toe the line from now on. "You know all the obvious suspects." I suddenly remembered my tense confrontation from the day before, the angry woman who had told me to go home. I told the sheriff about it and he wrote down my description. "She was dressed in sweatpants and a sweater and had her wispy hair up in a ponytail."

"Sounds like half the women in town," he said. "Except for you," he added, looking over my DKNY jeans and Igigi Ishiko teal wrap top, gorgeous but practical.

"There is no reason to look slovenly, even in Autumn Vale!" I said huffily.

He let that go without comment, but there was a smirk there as he eyed the cleavage-baring décolletage of the top. "I think you ought to just stop making people mad."

I hopped from foot to foot, getting colder as we stood. Pish, who had gone inside, came back out with a gray pashmina that I wrapped around my shoulders, giving him a silent thanks. I turned back to the sheriff, and more calmly said, "That'll be a lot easier if I can just get the cooperation I need so I can sell this behemoth and go back to New York."

The smirk died and he nodded, eyeing the damage. "Merry, I'm not suggesting this as a police officer, but as a . . . as a friend." He met my gaze. "I think some people in town are afraid of your plans for the castle."

"What, you mean like selling it to someone who can make it a hotel or an inn and actually bring some much needed jobs and tourists to your weird little burg?"

He shrugged, his expression stony, his jaw hard and jutting.

I had gone too far and I knew it, especially since I truly liked Autumn Vale and *most* of the people in it. I had no defense, except that I had awoken in a sad and weepy mood and the vandalism had sent me over the edge. Wind whipped around the edge of the castle and I hugged myself. "They can't have it both ways, Virgil. This says, 'Go Home!' " I said, pointing at the offending graffiti. "But I don't have a home and won't unless I can sell the castle and get out of here."

Virgil, his thick brows knit, watched me with a considering stare. "I thought you liked it here. I thought you liked the people."

"I do. You *know* I do. I love your mother, Binny, Janice, Hannah, Doc, Zeke, Gordy . . ." I eyed him, left him off the list, then sighed and closed my eyes in weariness. "Everyone! But I can't let myself love this place. I just can't afford to keep it."

Jack's Smart car bounced up the lane and pulled to a stop next to Virgil's black and white. Like a clown car, it disgorged its passengers: Cranston, Zeke, Gordy, and the driver, McGill. They trooped up to stand beside us and stare at the damage.

Cranston, his face red with anger and his hands on his hips, said, "This is atrocious. Sheriff, what are you going to do about this?"

For an answer, Virgil opened his car trunk, pulled out a camera and took photos of the damage. There wasn't a lot more he could do, I realized as I calmed down. There were no tire prints on the newly cleaned drive, and there was no way of knowing if there were fingerprints or other evidence. The culprit or culprits had not left spray cans or anything else behind.

I had regained my equilibrium by the time Virgil was done and thanked him before he left. Cranston, Zeke, and Gordy promised to set to work on cleaning up the damage. Because the stone was so dense and hard, we hoped the fresh paint might come off with little evidence left. Zeke and Gordy had a surprisingly good knowledge of spray paints and assured me this was not professional grade, but cheap, watery stuff; we apparently were fortunate that the graffiti artist had not cared enough to buy a better grade of spray paint. I didn't ask how they came about their knowledge of the right paint to permanently deface stone walls.

Gordy's uncle had a power washer he used to clean stalls and pens that would get a lot of the paint off, so they left in Shilo's car to pick it up. Shilo went off with McGill to take his mother to some doctor's appointment and then on to meet someone for a home viewing. McGill's business, Autumn Vale Realty, was only part of his professional repertoire, since there was not enough business to make it his sole avenue of income, but he was still a darn good real estate agent.

Pish and I retired to the library to work on the guest list for the party. There were a million details to coordinate, and ten million lists on the go. The library was one of the rooms I wanted to work on but hadn't yet had the time, beyond a good cleaning. Being a turret room, there were a lot of windows, so the bookcases were lined up on the walls that backed the ballroom. My uncle had left a lot of the books on the shelves, mostly classic literature and poetry, and the rest of the furniture had been left in place. There was a mahogany library table in the middle of the room that we were using as a desk for our planning, and we had our lists and sheets of ideas spread out on its maroon leather surface.

I had tentative yeses from lots of folks, but a few who I wanted to see at Wynter Castle had been elusive, so I was amazed and overjoyed when one that we had not yet gotten to actually called *me*. The executive secretary for Percy

Channer, of Channer Hotels International, called and told me her employer was interested in my castle. Would I speak with him?

I said yes, of course, and waited for a few minutes. The bluff, businesslike boom of Percy Channer's voice was music to my ears. This was the first real interest I had gotten, and it could lead to something.

"Miss Wynter? Understand you've got a castle for sale!"

"I do. It is an amazing opportunity for the right buyer, a true one-of-a-kind American castle, built by my ancestor, a mill baron, pristine and in practically original condition. We're planning a showcase party before Halloween here in upstate New York to let potential investors or buyers have a good look at the castle and property. We would love to have you as a guest, Mr. Channer."

There was silence for a long minute, then he said, "I'm trying to locate you on a map, Miss Wynter. Am I right in thinking you are near the town of Ridley Ridge?"

"Yes, though Autumn Vale is closer."

"But Ridley Ridge *is* close by."

"We're about fifteen miles from there. Do you know the area?"

"I've traveled through many times. My son went to Cornell, which you're close to."

"We're chartering some executive buses and an Escalade limousine for those who wish to come from New York City but don't want to drive." It was cheaper to hire land transportation than to buy plane tickets, though it was certainly a long drive.

"I'll find my own way, Miss Wynter. Could you e-mail my executive secretary with the directions and details?"

When I hung up I was excited, but oddly disheartened. Selling was becoming a real possibility now, with Channer showing interest. Several "castle" hotels exist in the United States, like Castle on the Hudson, Landoll's Mohican Castle, and Oheka Castle, but whoever bought Wynter Castle with that in mind would have a big project on their hands. However, it could end up being the jewel in their crown if they had the vision.

Pish was watching me, and I looked over at him across the broad library table. "He's interested," I said. "And I don't know whether I'm more pleased or depressed."

We went on to formalize more lists and estimate the food and wine we'd need to keep about fifty people, give or take, happy. It wasn't the only party we'd be having, and probably wouldn't be the most successful. It was, in essence, a trial run, and that's why I was nervous about Channer's call. We hadn't planned on hitting any of the big-time guests until the next go-round, when we knew what we were doing. But I couldn't exactly refuse Channer, not when he'd asked to come. Hey, maybe he'd love the place so much he would bid big enough that I could offer Cranston a buyout.

By the end of the day, thanks to Cranston, Zeke, and Gordy, we were back to where we were the day before, though no further.

That evening, Pish, Shilo, and I had a quiet dinner together in the parlor at a low table in front of the fire. We made a toast to the memory of Miguel Paradiso. He was gone but would never be forgotten in the hearts of those who knew and loved him so deeply. Especially me. I cried myself to sleep, then dreamed of him all night.

The next day was going to be a muffin-baking and delivery day again, so I set my alarm, but it never had a chance to wake me up. Instead, the deep *bong-bong* of the doorbell and repeated hammering rousted me from bed. I tripped over Becket as I scooted down the stairs, bleary eyed, and to the door, which I flung open, yelling, "Yes? What is it?"

A uniformed man in sunglasses stood at the door, and asked, "Is this the Wynter residence?"

I squinted to clear the sleep from my eyes and, shivering at the cold wind coming in the door, looked up at him. It was a frosty upstate late October morning, dew heavy on the grass, a chill wind coming through the open door. "Yes, I'm Merry Wynter. Who wants to know?" Was he UPS? Or the Feds?

The fellow stepped back and indicated a dark-windowed limousine idling in my drive. "Mr. Percy Channer would like to know if this is a convenient time for him to look over the castle?"

Chapter Five

PERCY CHANNER? A convenient time? What the . . . ?

"I'm not ready for him," I moaned, hopping from one freezing foot to the other. "He's supposed to come to the party and have his look then."

"Mr. Channer likes to see things when he likes to see them. I would go along with it, ma'am, if I were you. If you turn him away right now, he won't be back."

I was furious, but I'd dealt with his kind of people before and the chauffeur was right. This was business, not pleasure, and I needed to snatch this opportunity and make the best of it. I was happy about one thing; at least the graffiti was gone. I hoped no new crap had been written on the wall overnight.

Pish joined me at the door, and I quickly explained the situation in an undertone.

"Merry, why don't you go get dressed while I take Mr. Channer to the library?" my wonderful friend said. He wore an elegant smoking jacket over his silk pajamas, and was eminently presentable.

I was grateful it wasn't Shilo who had come down first, because she likely would have asked him if he wanted his aura read or sung him dirty ditties while he waited. As Pish showed Mr. Channer to the library, I got dressed in a forest green Kiyonna wrap dress—because they were inexpensive and flattering to my body type, I had Kiyonna wrap dresses in all colors—and slipped on some bone pumps and pulled my dark hair back in a chignon. I pinned a cameo at my cleavage and hastily stuck bone-colored enamel stud earrings in my lobes. It took all of five minutes, and then five more for some makeup.

I descended, put on the coffee, and then girded my loins, so to speak, to go to the library.

Having dealt with my fair share of eccentric millionaires and the models they married, and armed with the laconic chauffeur's insight into his boss, I knew I might only have one shot at impressing him with the beauty of Wynter Castle. I was going to have to position it as a diamond in the rough, a blank slate, ready for molding into a highly polished gem. The stark exterior, no swimming pool, no formal gardens or even informal gardens to speak of, would have to be presented as a plus; this was virgin ground, ready for the imprint of a bold investor and brilliant designer. I would appeal to his ego, saying only a man with foresight could take on Wynter Castle and turn it into a finished gem.

Mr. Percy Channer was a short man, with a bulldog face and no neck to speak of. He was dressed in an expensive suit but with no necktie. I greeted him warmly, asked about his drive from New York, and offered him breakfast.

"Nah . . . we stopped at a McDonald's. Love the Sausage

McMuffin. But Brooke, my driver, might want some coffee."

"I'll have someone take him a cup of coffee, or he can come in to the kitchen and have a cup in comfort."

Pish bustled off to take care of it while I began the tour. I couldn't get a handle on the man. He followed me willingly enough, but kept bringing the topic back around to Autumn Vale and Ridley Ridge, rather than the castle. I wasn't sure if he was trying to scope out the potential for converting the castle into a romantic destination for locals and tourists alike, but I could have told him not to hold his breath as far as the locals. They were more interested in a beer at the Tap Room on Saturday night than an evening of fine dining and wine as a classical quartet played.

I didn't say that to him of course, and I was not being snobbish in thinking the way I did. I had plenty of evidence, and had even been to the local bar a few times to shoot pool. It was just that kind of community: no pretension, no polish, just relaxed and real. We finished inside and I grabbed my pashmina and strolled out to the flagstone terrace, leading him around to get a view of the distant woods and the property. I emphasized the castle's potential as a boutique hotel or even a spa retreat. There was plenty of room to build custom structures like a pool and sauna, I said, indicating the land with a sweep of my hand, or even cottages. We were, I said, protected from the outside world by forest and my uncle's arboretum, which I called Wynter Woods.

"Isolated, right? How about newcomers; how are they welcomed?"

I grimaced inwardly, as the unhappy incident with the woman in town and the graffiti on my castle had left a bad taste in my mouth. But I said, honestly enough, "Most of the locals have been very warm and welcoming. Though isolated, it's not especially insular."

He nodded with a thoughtful look on his face. "Any new faces in your town?"

I didn't know how to answer that. "Uh, not really. Mr. Channer, will you consider coming back for the party? I have locals catering, including Binny's Bakery in town; Binny makes the very best European pastries, as good as any I've tasted in Paris." I watched him for a moment, then said, "It's just that I'll have more of the work done by then, and can showcase rooms of interest. We're actually not ready for viewing yet."

Arms folded over his chest, he silently scanned the property.

I followed his lead, wondering what had him so irritable. When I'd first arrived, the property had seemed barren, but now I noticed all the subtleties. There were a few groves of trees in the open expanse, a couple of big oaks surrounded by grassy stretches. Outbuildings dotted the landscape, including a large garage and some smaller sheds, most empty, but with the reminders of their original uses for animal husbandry and tool storage.

Of course, because the late Tom Turner had dug quite a few big holes on my property before ending up dead at the bottom of one, there were large dirt patches where McGill had filled in the holes for me. This was not good; the longer we stood there staring, the more problems I saw and thought of.

Finally, Channer said, "I'm going to have a look around the area. If we decide to buy Wynter Castle and take on the rebuild, you do have clear title to the land, correct?"

I crossed my fingers, and said, "Yes, the castle was left to me, and me alone." That much was true enough. Brooke had the limousine door open for his boss. Channer strode over, climbed in, and didn't so much as glance back as the chauffeur closed the door, got in, and drove off down the lane, disappearing around the bend beyond the forest.

I returned to the house discombobulated, as Doc often put it. That was how my day started. It continued in the same hurried manner, with muffins to bake and the town to visit. I decided not to expect much from Mr. Percy Channer. If he came back for the party, then I would consider him interested.

One more odd event marked the late day.

I went to Golden Acres to visit with Gogi Grace. She is a lovely, classy, elegant woman in her sixties, and I'd always figured that though her retirement home was a business venture, it was also a way of serving her community. We got along extremely well; in other words, she could not be more different from her obstinate, grumpy son, the sheriff.

We were sipping a cup of her favorite cappuccino in her office, a warm, cluttered, happy room on the main floor of Golden Acres. It was more like a living room than an office, with bookshelves, artwork, and a sitting area at one end. We had been discussing Percy Channer's visit, and I had vented a little of my lingering mourning for my late husband. I went into my purse for a tissue and came out with a crumpled piece of paper, one I had totally forgotten about until that moment. Flattening it out on my lap, I read it, and the surprise must have showed on my face.

"What's wrong, Merry?" Gogi asked.

"It's this note I found on my car the other day," I said, explaining to her the confrontation with the frowsy woman and the note I had found on my windshield. "I didn't read it until just now."

"What does it say?"

"Well, it's scrawled, really, like it was done in a hurry. It says, *Your not welcome here. What will it take to make you leeve?*" I handed the note over to her. "Why do people want me to leave, Gogi? What have I done wrong?"

She put on her rhinestone-studded cheaters and read the note. She handed it back to me. "Give it to Virgil."

"He's not doing anything about the vandalism; what could he do about a crank note?"

"You don't know he's not doing anything about the vandalism. And the note could be connected. In fact, it could all be just one person, like the woman who yelled at you."

"Virgil says some people in town are worried about what I'm going to do with the castle."

Sighing, Gogi said, "Unfortunately I heard that at book club just the other day. Helen Johnson expressed a concern about your party. She wondered if you would be inviting the 'wrong kind of people' to Autumn Vale."

"Helen," I mused, thinking it sounded familiar. "Oh! I met her about a month ago or so. A church lady, right? And she's friends with Isadore?"

"As much friends as Isadore has, and more because Helen feels it's her duty to be kind to the downtrodden, as she puts it. We all belong to the same book club. But in truth, Helen is just a little old-fashioned. She doesn't mean anything by it, and I know for certain that she wouldn't be your vandal."

I remembered a tidy little church lady in tweed capris and pearls. I couldn't picture her with a can of spray paint, nor did I think she would misspell *you're* and *leave*, as the writer of the note had. "No, this doesn't seem like her. Has anyone else said anything?"

"I've heard that Minnie, the post lady, has been gossiping quite a bit about Shilo and Pish, calling them weirdos," Gogi said, with an apologetic shrug.

"She doesn't like you, either, though," I said.

"Oh, I know!" Gogi said, with a chuckle. "She keeps telling people I murdered both my husbands!"

"I guess I won't worry about it," I said, folding the note and putting it back in my purse. "If I can sell the castle, it won't be any of my concern anymore."

"Will you stay in Autumn Vale? You could buy a house here with the proceeds from the castle and still have a lot of money left over."

I shook my head, regretfully. "Even if I sell the castle, I'll have to find work, and there doesn't seem to be anything for my particular skill set here in this town." I touched her arm, then stood up. "I'll miss so many Valers when I leave."

"You'll always have a place to visit," she said. We hugged, and I headed home.

The days passed, and October continued its lovely procession, the woods surrounding Wynter Castle taking on the umber shades of autumn. It was so beautiful. Though I had a lot to do, sometimes I just needed a sanity break from my two well-meaning but demanding friends. Pish was full of expensive, if lovely, ideas for the castle, while Shilo wanted to talk nonstop about her day, which usually involved trips with McGill to see friends, or visit his mother, or help stage a house he was selling. I actually missed her presence and worked hard on not resenting the real estate agent's demands on her time. We had made no progress on the mystery of the hidden loot, my uncle's little game, but I knew we would once we had the party stuff out of the way. All of our excess time was spent fixing up the castle.

However, I did walk in the woods a few times, accompanied by Becket, who loved racing ahead on a path, then jumping out at me when I least expected it. Though he's just an ordinary marmalade tabby, his personality is quirky and intelligent with a liberal dose of independence. He made a good companion on my rambles, since neither Pish nor Shilo were into it.

Occasionally I came across Lizzie Proctor and her friend Alcina. Alcina had a talent for constructing faery gardens in the woods—little gnome homes and faery rings—which I would happen upon during my walks. Lizzie photographed them, as she did everything, and then showed the pictures to me; some of them were very good.

A few days before the party, I just couldn't stand being inside anymore. Pish was directing Zeke and Gordy on some of the decorations that needed to be hung, and Cranston was in the way, as usual, offering suggestions I trusted Pish would not listen to. McGill and Shilo were in the kitchen doing some of the grunt work associated with such a large party, and since it involved a lot of whispering, kissing, and laughter, I felt like a third wheel. McGill insisted on helping out a lot, his way of justifying the fact that he was still the agent for the property and would write the contract and help me through all the intricacies of a sale, along with the lawyer, Andrew Silvio. McGill would be in for the biggest payday of his life if I sold the castle, but I knew he was conflicted. He was a good guy and a good friend, and I liked him a lot.

So I had delegated; now it was my turn to get out of the way and let my friends do what they wanted to do, how they wanted to do it. Later I had to go into town, but it was too early to do that. It was a gorgeous day. I needed some fresh air. Those two things meant a long walk. I put on boots and a jacket, since it was beginning to get cold, especially in the depths of the woods where the sun would not pierce the gloom. I surveyed my property as I walked across the grassy expanse toward the path into the woods. Zeke and Gordy had done a great job of mowing the land and keeping it mowed, so the turf resembled real grass more than the weedy hay it had looked like when I first arrived.

As always before plunging into the woods, I paused, turned, and looked over my property. I got a chill down my back every time. It seemed too much, this vast abundance, and the superstitious part of me swore I'd pay for being the Wynter heir in some way. Maybe that's what all the harassment and vandalism was about.

What would become of the Wynter estate once I sold it? Most of the outbuildings would probably be torn down. I had explored every one of them and most were sturdy, but only one would be useful to whomever bought the property. The garage, built from the same stone as the castle, was a beautiful building now that the glass in the gothic arched windows had been repaired and the weeds cut down from around it. It had originally been stables, no doubt, but had been converted for motor vehicle use sometime early in the twentieth century as horseless carriages replaced the kind that needed hay. The garage's structure was so good that a future owner could even make it into a suite of rooms. I had seen that done at country inns before, where it would be given a classy name, like The Carriage House.

I turned to look at the castle itself. It was mellow gold in the midday sun, hard autumn light gleaming against the newly cleaned arched windows. Set in a wide open space with a flagstone drive curving up to it, it was surrounded on all sides by a wall of forest. I scanned the far edges of the woods. So far I had only walked though the arboretum, but I did know that the other sections of forest were natural, not planned. I had been told by locals that there were a couple of natural spring-water streams and ponds and other features I'd love to explore in nicer weather. Gogi had even told me my great uncle Melvyn and grandfather Murgatroyd Wynter had planned a fairy-tale-themed park many years ago and had begun to build it in one part of the forest. I'd have to find it. *If* I had time before I sold the castle.

I had to keep reminding myself that it was not for me to concern myself with all of this land, what to do with it, and how to manage it, because there was no way on earth I could keep it. Becket melted out of the woods and joined me, just sitting patiently, waiting for me to step into his world, the place where I had first seen him almost two months before.

"What am I going to do, Becket?" I said, a catch in my voice, as I stared at the castle again. "I love this place, but I just can't keep it. It's going to hurt to leave, but I couldn't stay in Autumn Vale after selling and watch someone else rip this place to shreds and make it over into a commercial hotel. Even though that's the only use it could possibly have in this world."

He rubbed against my leg, and I leaned down to pet him. "I know you love it, too. What's going to happen when I leave? You'll *have* to come with me, but it might kill you to leave here."

He looked up at me, his beautiful golden eyes full of sympathy, then set off into the woods. I followed him but kept to the paths even as he galloped into the thick shrubs. I wanted to see if Alcina had made any new faery structures. Lizzie had told me some of her friend's story, that her mother was often sick and confined to home and didn't have a lot of energy to worry about Alcina. Shilo, now friends with Emerald, Lizzie's mom, had learned even more. Emerald, who was still trying to figure out how to deal with her daughter's new family, Binny, who was Lizzie's aunt, and Rusty Turner, her grandfather, welcomed Alcina in their home. The girl had told Emerald that her mom had come back to

Autumn Vale to die, sick with some incurable disease. It wasn't said out loud, but the implication was it was cancer. Emerald and Lizzie tried to keep Alcina busy and happy, and I appreciated that about them.

There were dozens of species of wildlife in the woods. I had made something of a hobby of spotting and identifying them: raccoons, squirrels (both the regular kind and little cute red squirrels), groundhogs, skunks, possums. I had even seen a porcupine. One of my most exciting views had been of deer at the edge of the woods and bounding across my property. Pish had binoculars, and I had taken to using them from my window to try to catch a glimpse of the shy animals, the ones spooked by my presence that I only "felt" when I was in the forest.

I've been a city girl my whole life. Who knew I'd be so woodsy?

As I approached the latest faery art installation, I got an uneasy sense that I wasn't alone. I knew there were coyotes in these parts, and had actually seen one along the edge of the arboretum. It worried me to death that Becket might get picked off, but he was wily and had lived on his own for the better part of a year until I had come along. As a precaution, though, I made him stay in the castle at night, no matter how much he bellyached.

This time my sense that I was not alone had nothing to do with an animal. It felt like there was someone human nearby, a feeling that Becket seconded in his alert: bristly fur and obvious caution. His ringed orange tail puffed up like a bottle brush. I rounded a bend in the forest path and saw someone bending over the latest faery house, a structure set in a stump. Was it Alcina? Or Lizzie? But no, this girl was wearing low-riding jeans and had a whaletail above them, the infamous top of a thong showing above her jeans.

"Hello," I said loudly, and she jumped, whirling around.

"You scared the crap out of me!" she shrieked, almost losing her balance.

I examined her with interest, from the bleached fuzz of hair piled upon her head to the sharp-toed boots that I knew at a glance cost about nine hundred dollars. This was no Valer, I'd wager. From her blue glittery makeup making her look like a nineteen eighties Madonna wannabe to her crystal-studded jeans, she'd stand out by a mile in our town. "I'm sorry, but I didn't want to just walk up on you. What are you doing in my woods?"

"*Your* woods? Aren't woods just there? I mean, no one owns them, right?"

I didn't think she was willing or able to have a philosophical conversation on the concept of ownership of the earth and its resources, to argue from a First Nations viewpoint that no one owned the earth and that we traveled on it as companions to the woodland creatures—a view I sympathize with, by the way, but am not sure how to support in our modern culture—so I tackled it pragmatically. "Yes, woodlands are owned, and this one happens to be owned by me. Who are you?"

"My name is Zoey Channer."

Chapter Six

※ ※ ※

I PAUSED A beat while it sunk in. Zoey Channer; she was infamous, the wild-child daughter of Percy Channer, hotelier. "I think your father is looking for you."

She nodded. "Yeah, right? He doesn't like that I'm out of his control now."

"So he knows you're in this area," I said, not as a question.

This explained why Percy Channer had called me, why he wanted an excuse to roam the area, why he had asked so many questions about Autumn Vale and Ridley Ridge, and why he had gone to the town after leaving Wynter Castle and talked to many people there. I had heard about his time in town but shrugged it off as the control-freak billionaire's way of checking out the neighborhood, so to speak, before buying the castle. I had even, bless my naïveté, seen it as a sign of his interest. It was well known in the financial world,

Pish had told me, that Percy was fierce about every detail of his hotels.

But why hadn't he just asked if I had seen her? Had that simple approach not appealed to him? "Why are you here?"

She shrugged. I eyed her with skepticism. The fashion industry attracts its share of celebutantes, and I had heard about Zoey Channer's antics: walking through the woods in Prada boots did not fit her MO. "You're in the area with someone," I surmised. "Who?"

"Just a boyfriend." She looked around. "I guess I'd better get going," she said, and started to walk away from me down the path toward the highway.

"Wait! Why are you *really* in the woods?" I shouted.

She threw over her shoulder: "Maybe I was heading to your castle to case the joint. Ever been robbed?"

She strode away, and I was not about to follow her. What good would it do? I figured she had a car, and I was assured of that when I heard the roar of a powerful motor—some kind of muscle car—on the road beyond the woods. Why *was* she in my woods? Where was this boyfriend she mentioned, at the wheel of the getaway car? It was unlikely I was walking in the woods at the only moment she happened to be there, so how much time had she spent in my forest, and why? Had she been spying on us all?

I felt an uneasy sense of intrusion on my privacy, though that was silly. I wasn't exactly living in a glass house. My peaceful, contemplative mood ruined, I called Becket and returned to the castle, the cat racing ahead of me. I told Pish about my experience. He wanted me to tell Virgil about what sounded, in retrospect, like a threat, but I was tired of telling Virgil anything, and what could he do anyway? I suppose I could have called Percy Channer and told him about meeting his daughter in my woods; it might even have gained me brownie points with a wealthy, powerful hotelier, but to heck with him, I thought. If he couldn't be forthright and just ask about his daughter, then it wasn't up to me to hook him up.

Instead of doing anything about it, I headed into town for a few last-minute errands before the party in two days. I chose a weekday to host my little soiree for two reasons. First, this was business. And second, all of the folks I invited had busy social lives on weekends, and this was fairly short notice. A weekend date would be hard to squeeze into their social calendars, I reasoned, so a week night worked out best for everyone. It was only the first, after all, and for future events I could give invitees more time to plan. Enough people had said yes to the invitation that the ballroom would be full.

Autumn Vale is a town like many in our country; it has suffered through a dreadful recession, fighting a losing battle, in some cases, and winning the day only occasionally. Main Street looks like a fighter's mouth missing teeth, with several dark gaps where there used to be quaint stores. But it had not yet descended into the grim drabness that was Ridley Ridge, and might not if Pish could save the bank from closure, since the bank drew people to Autumn Vale, where they then spent a few of their hard-earned dollars. It was truly the economic heart of the community.

I tried to patronize the local establishments as much as I could, and on a selfish level I think it worked somewhat; most of the locals are polite on the surface, at least, barring the occasional verbose lunatic and Minnie the local post lady who had decided, as Gogi had told me, that I was a snob and too big for my britches. I am *not* too big for my britches. Actually I like them tight fitting but not indecent. I dropped in again on Gogi at Golden Acres just to make sure she and Virgil were still coming to the party and bringing Doc with them, then I headed down to the library.

Hannah, the wheelchair-bound librarian, was a special friend to me. When I first met her, she was mourning the death of Tom Turner, the fellow I'd found at the bottom of one of the holes on my property. I felt for her; losing the one you love is the worst pain anyone can experience. She was still sad—she loved him with a romantic intensity suitable to the twentysomething she was—but with the attention of Lizzie and I and Tom's sister, Binny, she was beginning to come around. I would be seeing her at the party, but she had called me the night before to tell me she had some information she wanted to share on the possible antecedents of Cranston Higgins. Even though it was a Sunday, she wanted me to meet her at the library so she could show me or tell me what she had found.

The little Autumn Vale Public Library is on a narrow side street, and if you don't know it's there, it's easy to miss. There's a hand-painted sign that hangs out over the sidewalk and a wheelchair ramp built by the late, lamented Tom Turner. The inside is a little gloomy because the windows are set too high in the cinderblock walls to let in enough light, but it was improving, infused with Hannah's book-loving personality. I had promised her the boxes of books I had had in storage for years, if they weren't too musty. Since a lot of them were my mother's and grandmother's, the mix was eclectic, from mysteries to feminist philosophy to classic literature to poetry. I hadn't gotten to that yet—the boxes of books were sitting in a vacant room upstairs—but I promised myself I would after the party.

The library was only open three afternoons a week. The rest of the time Hannah took books to Golden Acres for the folks who live there, and also to the local schools. The library was rarely empty on the days she was open, and even though it was Sunday, today was no exception. Word must have gotten around that Hannah was going to be there for a few hours, because Isadore Openshaw was perusing the shelves, and so were a couple of other patrons who I didn't know. Isadore was a voracious reader, from all indications, and I would have talked to her about books, except she avoided me, perhaps seeing me as the author of her misfortune. It was troubling that she was becoming increasingly isolated—a layer of blame from the locals over the bank's troubles and her own quirky, aloof personality were having the expected effect. She was being shunned, but if she wouldn't loosen up and talk to people, what could anyone do? If she wouldn't even let Pish help her, then she was in a sorry state indeed.

I greeted Hannah, and sat down in the chair beside her wheelchair. "So, what's up?" I asked, after we had chitchatted about the upcoming party.

"I found some old references to a woman named Violet, and she may be the one Cranston is claiming as his grandmother," she said, retrieving a file of old newspaper clippings from her desk drawer. She opened the file and laid it flat. "Look here, Violet Flores . . . it's a 1942 notice that she's leaving Autumn Vale and wishes her friends will come visit her and her older sister, Dorothy, at the Vale Variety and Lunch for an informal tea."

I checked the date, and it coincided with what Cranston had said about his grandmother leaving Autumn Vale. But would a girl who was sneaking out of town because she was pregnant have a going-away party? "I should just do the DNA test and get it over with," I mused, still undecided over Cranston's claim. "But once that's done, there's no going back. I guess I'm looking for some way to ease into it, to get an idea of what to expect."

"What happens if it turns out he is who he says he is?"

Hannah asked, her wide gray eyes fixed on mine with a wistful expression. "Would that change anything?"

"No," I said, knowing that she was actually asking if there was any way we'd all be able to stay in Autumn Vale. "In fact, it would probably speed things up, because Cranston is pressing for us to sell. Mind you, he has some unrealistic expectations of the real estate situation." I made up my mind then and there to go ahead with the DNA test. "May I use your phone?"

I got the information I needed and hung up, then borrowed the phone again. "There," I said, with a false brightness, as I pressed the End button. "For better or worse, I've made an appointment for two weeks from tomorrow at the hospital in Rochester for both Cranston and I."

"Why a hospital?" Hannah asked. "Why not one of those at-home DNA tests?"

I shrugged. "If we're going to do this, we may as well do it right. I've been told the test has to be administered at a hospital for legal purposes."

"You shouldn't have done that, Merry," Hannah said, her eyes shining with tears. "I don't want you and Shilo and Pish to leave, ever!"

I hugged her. "Avoiding this wasn't going to change anything, sweetie. I can't stay indefinitely without a proper source of income."

"I know," she said. A customer came to the desk, and Hannah signed some books out for her, then turned back to me as the patron hustled hurriedly from the library.

"But let's not think about that!" I said. To change the subject, I told her about my encounter in the woods with Zoey Channer.

"Oh, I know about her. I see her picture in *People* and *EW*!"

"What have you heard lately? I'm trying to figure out why she's hanging around here and not Hollywood or New York."

For the next few minutes, she regaled me with stories of Zoey Channer's exploits. First Paris Hilton had taken her under her wing, but then the two had a spat and ended up as frenemies. Zoey tried to get a reality show deal, but someone died on the set and the whole thing was canceled. She did a stint in rehab, then jail on a drug charge. Then rehab. Then jail. A theme was developing.

"So what is the latest?"

Hannah did a web search and came up with the most recent headlines, which were that Zoey had met someone through her cell mate in jail, and was going out with a "bad boy," a guy named Dave Smith who had done time for fraud and robbery. Uneasily, I thought of her joking about casing the castle. Maybe it wasn't a joke. She was currently out on parole.

"I think I'm going to call Virgil and just have him keep an eye out for Miss Channer and her sketchy boyfriend." I got up to leave.

"I'm really looking forward to the party, Merry." Hannah gazed up at me, her luminescent gray eyes gleaming with excitement. "It's going to be my first."

"Your first party?" I asked with amazement. "Didn't you go to prom, or . . . or something?"

She shook her head. "I was a pretty good student but got bored at school, so my mom and dad took me out and I was homeschooled from then on. We belonged to a home school association and they had a prom, but they didn't have it at a place I could get to. This party is going to be epic!"

For once she sounded her age instead of like an old soul. I had a sudden realization of how Shilo, Pish, and I coming to Autumn Vale had opened up her world, in a sense, beyond the scope of her beloved books, and how much she'd miss us when we left. I reached down and hugged her, not able to tell her we'd stay, but sure I would always stay in contact with her. "I'll give you a personal tour of the main floor of the castle. It's going to be a great party."

The next day was unbelievably busy from dawn, when the temporary wheelchair ramp was delivered and affixed to the door off of the butler pantry so Hannah could get into the castle, through the food deliveries, to the arrival of Zeke, Gordy, and a crew of extra Valers, who helped in every aspect. I had a meeting with Lizzie, Alcina, Emerald, Juniper Jones, and Binny. We walked around the castle and I explained the party layout, which mostly covered the ballroom, the great hall, and the parlor, which I was making into a ladies' room for fixing makeup, in the old tradition. It doubled as a coat area as well, and I had a couple of portable clothes racks and a few dozen wooden hangers set up, thanks to Janice Grover.

"Lizzie, you and Alcina . . . Alcina!" I repeated, trying to get the girl's attention. She had spun off and was examining a teapot, one with butterflies all over it, her long, thrift-shop skirt dragging while her faery wings threatened to knock over anything too close by.

Lizzie caught my eye and shrugged. Emerald bit her lip and smiled. I had Lizzie's mother there not because she'd be helping out at the party—she was coming as a guest only—but because I was making an effort to include her in her daughter's life. She had had a rocky road as a single parent but had finally come to terms with her mother on where Lizzie lived—wherever she felt like that week, her mom's or her grandmother's—so things were starting to settle down in that respect. Now that Lizzie's paternity had been exposed, Emerald and Binny were becoming friends;

in Tom, both had lost someone who, though difficult to deal with on occasion, had been doing his best to become a more responsible and reliable grown-up.

Emerald tried to shepherd Alcina back to the pack, but the girl just smiled and drifted away again. Emerald told me Alcina's parents, including the fatally ill mother, were advocates of the "unschooling" philosophy of learning, so Alcina did not go to the local school. The parents apparently had a farm and sold vegetables at the roadside all summer; what they did for sustenance in winter I did not know. However, what I *did* know was that Alcina not only had no ability to focus on anything for more than a few minutes, but she was also frightfully ignorant of even the basics of literature and, I was afraid, could not yet read properly, even at thirteen.

The fact that she did not need her parents' permission to help out at the ball was even more scary. In theory I thought that unschooling could work, but I didn't think it was doing Alcina any favors. Maybe that said more about her parents than unschooling, and it may have had a lot to do with her mother's health problems. The girl was certainly creative and talented, a gifted artist of the faery genre, but I worried for her future in a world that was hard on dreamers. I settled for explaining to Lizzie what I wanted from them. I wasn't going to be too hard on Alcina, not when she had so much going on at home.

I heard a vehicle pull up outside the open front door and left Binny in charge. Dashing outside expecting another delivery, I was startled to see a pickup truck with a bunch of guys in the back.

"Can I help you?" I asked, striding toward them. I shaded my eyes with my hand and looked them over.

"You sure can," one fellow in a torn Budweiser tee said. "Hear you're having a party tomorrow night. What time?"

"I beg your pardon?"

Another of the guys said, "Can't hear very well, huh? *What time?*" He shouted the last, as if by virtue of being nearly forty I was also hard of hearing.

"Why does the time matter to you?" I asked, beginning to get an uneasy feeling.

"We wanna know when to show up. Duh!" yet another guy said, shaking his shaggy hair back out of his eyes and jamming his hat down over curls.

"But you haven't been invited," I replied, beginning to feel a little desperate.

He looked puzzled and adjusted his ball cap so the duck-bill was pointed sideways. "But it's a party."

"That requires an invitation to attend," I finished, staring up at him.

The guys looked puzzled still, and exchanged looks. Was the concept of a party to which you needed an invitation so foreign to them?

"We'll bring a case, if that's what you're worried about. We aren't stiffs, you know."

"I'm sorry guys," I said, keeping my tone light, "but this is a 'by invitation only' party. It's business, you know, just to showcase the castle. You'd be bored to tears." I regretted adding the last part immediately, because it implied I was only *not* inviting them to save them from boredom.

Budweiser T-shirt guy knit his brow, and said, "Okay. We thought . . . Never mind."

The driver gunned the motor, reversed, spun around, and roared back down the lane. I hoped I wouldn't have any trouble with them. They hadn't seemed violent, just a little clueless.

I got through the endless day, fell into bed exhausted, and awoke the next morning knowing that I was going to be even more tired by the end of the night. I would need to be fortified by lashings of hot coffee and the good sense of my friend Pish. He has thrown a hundred parties and thrives on the chaos, the utter anarchy, of the party atmosphere, whereas I prefer order and calm. Shilo and McGill were supportive, too; they had some work to do at a house he was selling but put it on hold just to help me get the place ready.

By six thirty PM, just before my helpers were to arrive, I stood in the great hall and surveyed the decorations. There was a comforting blaze in the grate of the great hall fireplace, with the massive screen I had found in Janice's warehouse guarding it, and beside it a set of tools. It was McGill's job to make sure the fire was safe through the evening; I wasn't taking anything for granted, enlisting the most responsible person among us. I wasn't even using real candles, figuring battery-operated flameless candles were more expensive but a lot safer.

Along the railing of the grand split staircase—it started as one wide sweep and then split to arc up to the gallery by two separate staircases; think the Titanic staircase, only without the handrail in the center—I had swooped swaths of maroon and gold material. In the middle of the great hall on a low table was the casket I had rented from Janice. A couple of borrowed five-foot-tall candelabras stood by it with flameless tapers flickering. In the casket was a mannequin dressed in an old tailcoat with his eyes wide open. That was my nod to Halloween, a few days away.

Just then the music started, chamber music with a very gothic feel. Pish's sound system worked beautifully. He would switch to some light jazz once all the guests were there and we began to serve snacks. I had hired two real bartenders, fellows who could help with crowd control if the unforeseeable happened, and two cocktail servers, one woman and one man, all from Buffalo; they were coming with a busload of party attendees and had told me over the phone what to set up for them. The bar was in the ballroom. Juniper would be circulating with trays of hors d'oeuvres and helping out in the kitchen, where a couple of local women would fill trays and do other tasks. I didn't want to hire Juniper, but Binny had pled her case—the girl needed to make some money after a couple of months unemployed—and I caved.

The party was expensive, but Pish was excellent at wheeling and dealing. He had called in some favors, too, and I was grateful to my excellent friends. I had rescued a few bottles of Uncle Melvyn's best wine, but I was saving that for the richest of guests. Yes, I was discriminating, but I needed to schmooze. My stomach was in knots as I finally ran up to get ready for the party.

In choosing a costume for myself, I wanted something I could wear all evening, something I could move in, and something attractive—no hideous witch costumes for me. I was the hostess, and I wanted to stand out. Janice Grover was once smaller than her present abundance—in other words, she was once my size—and had, from her days as a New York hostess before her husband had been consigned to the management of a backwoods bank, a store of costumes from parties of the past. Honest to goodness, the woman had never thrown anything out in her life.

From her hoard I chose a beautiful brocade Victorian gown of sumptuous purplish material that was surprisingly lightweight and loose enough on me to be comfortable. It wasn't meant to portray any actual person, nor was it Halloweenish, but if forced to answer *Who are you?*, I would be happy to tell them Christina Rossetti. I expected that would elicit little more than blank stares, but I had become accustomed to that in Autumn Vale. To be fair, I would have received the same blank stares among my New York acquaintances.

I stared at myself in the mirror and evaluated my costume, running my hands down over the lovely fabric. The proper undergarments, vital for a woman of my figure (which is "plush-size," according to Shilo), had transformed the sagging dress into a proper regal shape with the additional help of a few safety pins. I had wound my dark hair up into two knots at either side of my head, and I draped a gold embroidered shawl over my shoulders. Pish had wanted me to dress as Cleopatra, while Shilo had suggested I go as a queen, any queen, because she said I'd look "splendiferous" in a crown, but this was good for me.

As I descended, the door gong sounded. Pish opened it to a crowd of locals, and from then on the evening descended into chaos. Organized to some extent, but still chaos. I had gotten a one-time permit to serve alcohol, but it was important that everything be done to adhere to the law, so I had been extremely stern with Lizzie and Alcina; if I caught so much as a hint that they were drinking the wine, or even carrying it, they would both be chauffeured home. Their jobs were to show folks where to hang up their coats, help Juniper with the trays of hors d'oeuvres, assist in the kitchen in any way they were asked, and check the smoking pit for full ashtrays or burning butts.

Gogi Grace came as Sarah Bernhardt, the legendary actress, dressed as La Dame Aux Camélias from the famous poster. Nobody was going to get that, either. I wouldn't have, except she had told me in advance. Virgil, looking embarrassed but handsome, came in a cape coat and deerstalker hat, carrying a pipe and a magnifying glass. Sherlock Holmes; how perfect!

Doc English trailed them. I cocked my head to one side

as he bowed before me, and I tried to figure out if he was wearing a costume or had just randomly plucked things from the lost and found. He wore an oversize pinstripe suit jacket and a weird beige colored wig on backward, so the hair all fell forward, and carried a cracked leather briefcase. He told me he was Donald Frump. It was hilarious and brilliant.

Emerald was dressed as a cocktail waitress; her costume was going to hopelessly confuse people, because the female cocktail server I had hired was going to be dressed similarly. Simon and Janice Grover arrived as Tweedledee and Tweedledum, though she insisted they were Tweedledum and Tweedledummer. I knew which was which, in that case; I didn't have a good opinion of the bank manager's intelligence. Cranston was costumed as Doctor Frankenstein, with thick glasses and a lab coat and carrying a severed hand. Binny was adorable as the Pillsbury Doughboy. At first I couldn't figure out who Isadore Openshaw was, but Janice, who had been trying to make up to the woman for making fun of her for years, whispered to me that the fluffy knitting gave it away: she was Miss Jane Marple, an easy costume to pull off in that it resembled her usual dress.

Shilo wore a tiered skirt and an off-the-shoulder peasant blouse with a scarf holding back her abundant dark hair, while Jack had on black pants tucked into knee-high boots with a white shirt, and he also had a colorful scarf over his head. He sported a clip-on earring in one lobe and carried a fiddle. They were gypsies, suitable, since Shilo always said she was half gypsy and half Irish traveler. Pish was dressed as the fifties version of that most hedonistic of all heterosexual males, Hugh Hefner, with a velvet smoking jacket and silk pajama pants and carrying a pipe and a *Playboy* magazine, the Marilyn Monroe issue. Not everyone would get the joke, but anyone who knew my good friend well enough would.

Zeke and Gordy, dressed in tailcoats and white gloves, were to check names at the door against the master list I had given them and park cars for those who had not been chauffeured. I didn't have the kind of insurance I would need for true valet service, so they couldn't *present* it as such, but they could help folks out if they asked. There wasn't much they could get in trouble with, as far as cars went—I hoped—since we were in the middle of nowhere.

I personally supervised Hannah's arrival at the pantry door, where the wheelchair ramp had been installed. Her Clara costume, a white blouse, pink striped dirndl and shawl, was adorable on her slight frame, and her parents, dressed in cute Tyrolean costumes rented from some shop (definitely not the Party Stop in Ridley Ridge), were Grandfather and Fraulein Rottenmeier. Once they had seen the ground floor, I left them to their own devices. Juniper Jones arrived dressed as a French maid, though her sour expression did not seem very service oriented. I crossed my fingers and hoped she wouldn't throw a tray of hors d'oeuvres at a guy if he pinched her butt or did something equally heinous, like saying hello or smiling at her.

The stretch Escalade and the tour bus arrived, as did other chauffeur-driven vehicles. The Westhavens, a couple from a family of famous hoteliers, had come as Zelda and F. Scott Fitzgerald, which I appreciated even if no one else got it. They were friends of Pish and attended as a favor to him. I didn't expect them to be interested in the castle as a purchase; they just loaned élan to the whole affair, and I thought I might be able to pick their brains later regarding who might be interested in buying my castle.

I had also invited a couple of society-type newshounds, hoping the party would warrant a small notice in the *New York Times* or the *Daily News*, or at least some social media buzz. The bartenders did their jobs, and the two servers circulated with glasses of wine, threading in and out of the ballroom and the great hall, as Juniper carried trays of hors d'oeuvres and pastries. Once I judged everyone to be lubricated but not drunk, I went to the stairs and took the microphone that Pish had set up with his PA system. I cleared my throat and said, "Good evening, everyone. Welcome to Wynter Castle. My name is Merry Wynter, and the fellow in the casket is *not* my late uncle; he is the ghost of Wynters past!"

Chapter Seven

�֎ ✖ ✖

EVERYONE TITTERED AND applauded politely, then I stated the reason for the soiree. "We have gathered you all here to give a first exclusive look at the Wynter estate, a property that not only holds this wonderful eighteenth-century castle, but also has seven outbuildings, including a garage holding a genuine vintage Oldsmobile, and various sheds. There is so much more here, though, than meets the eye.

"More than fifty years ago, my great uncle Melvyn Wynter planned and planted an arboretum that holds hundreds of species of native flora. The whole property is several hundred acres, and I believe this place would be perfect for a retreat or a spa, or a country destination inn like the world famous Castle on the Hudson or Oheka Castle. Please enjoy your drinks and the snacks provided by local businesses, such as Binny's Bakery in downtown Autumn Vale, and ask any one of the waitstaff where the washrooms and smoking area are set up. Please see me for information about the castle."

"Or me," Cranston said, stepping up on the stairs beside me, grabbing the microphone and waving his hand around. "I am Cranston Higgins, the grandson of Melvyn Wynter."

I held my temper; this was not how we had talked about the intro, but I wasn't going to get into family—or faux family—business in front of the crowd. "Please see me *personally*," I said into the mic, "so we don't get confused about who is thinking about what, okay?"

As I drifted from the great hall to the ballroom and back, I overheard Cranston bragging about his roots in the area. There was no real way to stop him, not without creating an unpleasant scene, so I ignored him, chatting with my guests about Wynter Castle and its potential. I had prepared a few pieces of interesting history about the area and the Wynter family, but I didn't know enough. I needed to correct that before the next party.

Some of the folks on the list would never be investors or buyers of the property and had been invited simply because I wanted gossip to get out. This would be the beginning of creating buzz, as marketers say, so I had tried to capitalize on many of my past connections. This unfortunately meant inviting some of my former friends in the fashion world, and it seemed like every single one of them felt the need to give me the latest scoop on Leatrice's continued descent into lunacy.

One former model, who was now a talent scout for Leatrice's agency, followed me around as I mingled, telling me that my former employer had gone through four assistants since my hasty departure, and had called the police on three of them. "Everyone knows she trumped up that crap about the necklace, Merry. You should come back to New York! So many of the girls could do with your stylist skills."

"I'm so far out of it fashion-wise," I told her. "I don't think I can do it anymore."

She didn't continue on that line, thank heavens, and instead wanted to know what Shilo was doing hooking up with a local yokel. I watched Shilo and McGill whirling down the ballroom to the barely heard music, her skirts and long, dark hair, headscarf apparently abandoned, flaring out around her. "Jack has been good for her. I've never known her to feel like any place is home, but here, she seems to feel . . ." I paused. I was about to say *safe*, but I didn't know why I was thinking that. "At home," I said instead. My former "friend" looked at me like I'd lost my marbles, then walked away, shaking her head, to rejoin the fashion crowd that huddled as far away from the food table as they could.

Home. Had Shilo found that in Autumn Vale and with Jack McGill, real estate agent and jack-of-all-trades? It was an elusive concept, home. I hadn't had one—not a true home in every sense of the word—since Miguel died.

Pish approached and took my arm. He was one constant in my world, and his kindness had been my most homelike experience for some time. I leaned against him as we observed the chattering, circulating mob, gowned and costumed in an array of gaudy outfits. It sure seemed like there were a lot of people. I had kept the guest list down to what I thought we could comfortably hold, but the ballroom was crowded.

"Does this seem like a lot of people to you?" I muttered to Pish. The babble of noise was growing in volume, and the jazzy music was barely audible over the chatter.

He looked around uneasily and nodded. "I'm seeing people I don't know, and I knew everyone on your list. Did you see the hooker in the Mardi Gras mask and the cowboy?"

I shared his concern. "There's one guy here with a wild wig who is either the Barber of Seville or Sweeney Todd, it's hard to tell which. I don't know who *he* is. And there are *three* Draculas, though I thought only one of our guests was coming as a vampire." I was glad a fair number of our important guests had opted not to wear costumes, because at least I recognized them. Percy Channer, I noted, was not among the attendees, unless he had managed to elongate and thin out his barrel shape. But I had this uneasy sense that there were people avoiding me, vanishing onto the terrace or into the great hall as I moved toward them. I was pondering that, trying to figure out what had led me to that belief, when Pish stiffened beside me, on the alert.

"Who are the ones dressed like a football team?" Pish asked, pointing across the room.

I eyed the group. It was all men, and they were having a wonderful time drinking wine and talking to the girls. One slung his arm over Juniper Jones's shoulders, almost upsetting her tray. I was about to cross the ballroom to intervene, but she ducked away from him and continued on with the hors d'oeuvres, a frown etched permanently on her face. "I don't know who that is," I said, but then remembered the truckload of guys I had turned away the day before. I shared my hunch, and Pish agreed I was probably on the money. "What are Zeke and Gordy thinking, letting them in?"

I started toward them, trailed by Pish, but was waylaid by Melanie Pritchard, an amazing New York real estate agent I'd met while I worked for Leatrice Peugot. I had invited her to get an honest critique from her viewpoint on how likely it was that I could market the castle to New York entrepreneurs.

She was angry, and I knew there were few things that infuriated her. "Merry, what the hell is going on?" she griped, tugging her suit jacket down over her hips. She was not costumed, and I hadn't expected she would be. "First of all, my flight was delayed—some kind of bomb scare—so I had to rent a car instead of catching your bus. Then those goons at the door tell me I'm already here!"

I exchanged a glance with Pish. "I'm so sorry, Melanie. I'd better sort this out," I said, and headed out of the ballroom to the great hall and toward the front door. I was stopped often on the way, sometimes by well wishers, sometimes by folks actually interested in the castle, but twice by other people who'd had the same experience as Melanie. I was getting more and more annoyed with the boys.

"Merry, have you seen Binny?" Emerald asked, stopping me with a hand on my arm.

"No, why?"

"I'm worried about Juniper," she said, chewing her lip and looking around. She said something else, but the noise level was worsening in the great hall as folks were posing for photographs with the dummy in the casket. Uncle Mortimer, as Pish had begun calling him, was a popular fellow.

"I couldn't hear you," I hollered. "What did you say?"

Emerald came closer and cupped her hand near my ear. "I *said*, Juniper was talking to some dude, and he had his hand on her arm, and she looked upset. I wanted to find Binny to get her to ask Juniper what was wrong. Last time *I* tried to talk to that girl, she gave me a look that would freeze Satan in his tracks."

"If I see Binny I'll tell her. Or I'll tackle the girl myself;

where *is* Juniper? I saw her heading this way, but she's disappeared on me."

Emerald turned and searched the boisterous crowd around the casket. "I don't know. She was talking to that guy, the one just heading back into the ballroom," she said, pointing to a blue-jeaned figure wearing a cowboy hat.

I was torn; find Juniper or talk to Gordy and Zeke? "Look, I saw Juniper just a few minutes ago and she *seemed* fine . . . as fine as she ever is, anyway. But I'll see what I can do," I said. "Are the girls doing all right?"

Emerald grinned, her eyes lighting up, the great hall fire giving her face a soft glow. "Lizzie is having the time of her life! But Alcina? Who can be sure what that girl is thinking?"

We parted ways. When I finally got through the crowd to the front door and exited the castle, there was no one on the front terrace. That was not right; one of the two guys was supposed to be there at all times.

Pish followed me out a moment later. "Where are they?" he asked.

My answer was not as eloquent as usual. The explanation soon presented itself, as Zeke and Gordy, in their rented tailcoats, came galloping around the side of the castle and along the flagstone, followed by Becket, who was howling furiously.

"Get that cat away from me!" Gordy yelped. "It's got weird eyes. Get it away from me!"

A couple of girls in sleazy/sexy hooker getups, followed by another girl also disguised in sleaze but with a feathered glittery mask instead of elaborate makeup, trotted around the corner, laughing. As soon as they saw me, they skidded to a halt, their eyes wide behind the masks. The third girl retreated.

"Who are you two?" I asked pointing at them. "I don't remember inviting you, whomever *you* are."

They backtracked, giggling and hooting, and their laughter was joined by some male rumbling laughter around on the ballroom terrace. Ten to one they were with the football players. Followed by Becket, I stalked over to Gordy and Zeke who were conspicuously checking their clipboards and conferring. "Hand it over," I said, my palm out.

Gordy handed me his clipboard, and I checked it in the weak light of the outdoor sconces, running down the list of names. Some had two check marks against them, and one of those was Melanie Pritchard. "If you can tell me how one person can arrive twice, I will let you both off the hook," I said, pointing to the offending names.

Zeke shrugged. "How are we supposed to know what these folks look like?"

"So who were those two girls?" I said, hitching my thumb in the direction of the two gigglers.

"Uh, Melanie Pritchard and friend," Zeke responded, his eyes wide. Gordy nodded in agreement.

"Neither one of them is Melanie. How did this happen?"

Zeke shrugged. "When she came—the taller one . . . they came together in a taxi from somewhere—she laughed and told me if I could guess who she was I'd get a kiss, so I said Miss Melanie Pritchard, 'cause she looked like a Melanie, and she said, yes, that's exactly who she was. With a friend. And Gordy checked her off."

"And she kissed us both!" Gordy added.

I thought I had covered everything with them, but apparently I forgot to tell them to engage their brains and not their groins in the ID process. "Okay," I said, looking over Gordy's clipboard. Every name had been checked off with the exception of Les Urquhart, the owner of the Party Stop, and Percy Channing. "So why did you start letting a *second* of each of these people in?" I asked, indicating the double checkmarked names. "Why didn't one of you come get me?"

Both shuffled their feet and shrugged. I heard some boisterous noise through the open doors and uneasily wondered if things were getting out of hand. I sure hoped not, or this whole idea of introducing Wynter Castle to the world via parties could be done before it began. Pish appeared concerned, too, looking over his shoulder into the great hall. "Okay, no one else gets in," I told Zeke, thrusting the clipboard back at Gordy. "I'm trusting you guys. I understand that you didn't know who was who this time, and I'll make sure you're better prepared next time." If there *was* a next time for them.

The evening wore on. I knew I should be schmoozing the potential investors, but there were too many other things going on, and I ended up stomping out social fires like a flamenco dancer on Red Bull. One of my fashion friends, Zimbabwe Lesotho (not her real name, and I only ever called her Zee), mortally offended Isadore Openshaw by cornering her and trying to give her fashion advice. I took Zee aside and told her that Isadore was a bit prickly; besides, what she was wearing was supposed to be a costume, though it was how she usually looked. My friend then had the good grace to apologize, complimenting Isadore on her "cool old-lady costume," which opened up a whole new can of worms.

Doc English got tiddly and told a couple of my friends, "You're fired!" They thought he was hilarious and launched a drinking game with the old guy. I was too busy looking for the football geeks and their girlfriends, a couple of whom had been seen heading upstairs. I didn't find them, but I did find an angry Becket, who now sat teetering on the railing howling down on the gathering. "Becket, why don't you hide in my room if you hate this so much?" He just hissed at me and stalked along the railing, leaping down to the floor and crawling away to a dark corner to grumble.

Cranston was, oddly enough, a saving grace. He was gently humorous, a hit with one and all. He circulated, making sure folks had drinks and something to eat, encouraging people to try one of Binny's pastries and extolling her skills. In short, all the things I ought to have been doing if I had the time. It was good to have him there.

At some point in the evening, the casket containing Uncle Mortimer disappeared from the great hall while Pish and I talked to a group of interested investor types in the ballroom. I thought I knew who had taken it—the football team—so I wasn't concerned. If it got ruined and I had to end up paying Janice for it rather than merely renting it, then so be it.

Finally it was over. The Westhavens were already gone, and I couldn't help but feel that the boisterous footballers were to blame for their early departure. I had wanted to talk to them, to get their professional input on Wynter Castle, but that would have to wait. The other chauffeur-driven folks left fairly early, too. The danged footballers and their giggly girlies—only the two; the third had disappeared—were also gone, probably to some raging bush party that was hopefully not in *my* woods. Then the big tour bus and the stretch Escalade took off with their loads of New York and area investors.

Finally it was only locals remaining, except for one particular friend of Pish's, who had a summer place nearby and so had driven himself over. Pish's friend happened to be one of the Feds who was looking into the Autumn Vale Community Bank fiasco, so Virgil was hanging out with the two men as they talked about legal aspects of the banking business.

I had already checked upstairs and no damage had been done, I was pleased to see. Locking our personal rooms *seemed* to have kept folks out. Shilo's bunny, Magic, was peacefully munching on a fresh carrot in his cage in her room. My room and Pish's were exactly as we'd left them. Becket was asleep in a corner of the gallery overlooking the great hall.

I trotted back downstairs and checked the kitchen, which was a mess. "Wow, this is awful," I said, surveying the piled up dishes, bags of trash, and food everywhere. The local helpers had not been paid to clean (I couldn't afford to pay anyone to do what I could do after the party) and were already gone, as were the bartenders and servers, aboard the charter tour bus.

Shilo skipped over to me and hugged my shoulders, while McGill, who was drying dishes, smiled after her. "Don't you worry about it. It's not as bad as it looks, right girls?" she asked of Lizzie, who rolled her eyes, and Alcina, who yawned, gently flapping her faery wings in time to some internal rhythm. I hadn't figured out how she worked her wings and didn't care to know. Let it be one of the mysteries of life. Emerald and Binny were washing dishes, laughing, and talking, perhaps about the evening. Emerald turned, and said, over her shoulder, "Shilo is right, Merry. It looks worse than it is. I'm going to help clean up, then get the girls home."

"I'm staying to help get everything back into shape," Binny added. "Has anyone seen Juniper? I was supposed to give her a ride back into town before heading home."

There was a chorus of *no*s, and Emerald said to me, with

a worried frown, "I haven't seen her for quite a while, not since before I caught up with you and asked if she was okay."

I shrugged. "She must have found some way back to town and didn't want to bother anyone." Or be cajoled into helping clean up. "Anyway, I want to thank you all so much," I said, clasping my hands in front of me in a prayerful salute. "I know this was a lot of work."

"But it was fun!" Binny said, her eyes shining. "I've never been to a party like this before!" She worked so hard that this was not surprising.

"I have to go and tend to a few things, but I'll be back," I promised. I felt guilty about leaving them to it, but I could hear Gogi in the butler's pantry helping Hannah and her parents get ready to go, and I wanted to be there. Gordy, a good and careful driver, had backed their specially equipped van into position at the butler's pantry door for Hannah's father, who was worried about doing that kind of maneuvering in the dark. Then he and Zeke opened the van doors to get ready for the wheelchair. I rushed to say good-bye to Hannah as her mother tucked a shawl around her shoulders.

Her thin face was wan and gray with weariness, but she smiled up at me with delight in the weak illumination of the overhead pendant lights. "I had such a good time," she said, grabbing my hand.

I shared a worried look with her mother. "You're not overtired?"

"*Please* don't fret about me. I truly have had such a good time tonight, and people were so kind to me! Your friend Zee introduced me to a whole bunch of people, and when I told them what my costume was and what I do, they all sat down with me, and we talked about the books they loved as kids. *Goodnight Moon* and Harry Potter and Nancy Drew and the Bobbsey Twins. Then we talked about classic literature and new books and . . . and I drank some champagne! Zee said every girl should drink champagne at a party." She giggled, then hiccupped. "Pish and I danced. I had so much fun."

I hugged her, not letting her see the tears in my eyes. Zee was going to get a special note of thanks. I loved Hannah so much; she was like a cross between the sister I never had and the daughter I probably never would. It was going to be so hard to leave Autumn Vale once the castle sold. I had thought leaving New York was difficult, but this was going to be worse, and I wasn't quite sure how I had become so deeply entangled in such a short time.

They left after Hannah's mother hugged me hard, whispering a heartfelt thanks, and said good-bye. I asked Zeke and Gordy to clean up out front and make sure there were no live cigarette butts anywhere out front or in the parking area. They would come back and do a more thorough job in the light of day. As Gogi and I strolled in through the pantry door, she yawned and told me she was going to find Doc and sit down somewhere with him until Virgil was done with my friends.

"If you want to go right now," I said, threading my arm through hers, "I can wrest Virgil from Pish and his friend."

"No, dear, please don't," she said, undoing a barrette and loosening her wig. "I can wait another half hour, and Doc is probably already asleep. Virgil so seldom has anyone to talk to about work. Being the boss, he's used to giving orders, but none of the PD staff are up to his level intellectually." She stopped, so we stood in the dim, quiet hall, with just the sound of the girls' laughter from the kitchen echoing softly to us.

"Maybe I shouldn't say that," she continued, "but being his mother, I suppose I'm allowed a bit of bias. You know, he worked for the Rochester Police for three years, and then he was going to join the FBI. He applied and was accepted for training, but when I got sick, he came back to Autumn Vale to look after me. The Autumn Vale sheriff died, so Virgil took over and stayed on." Gogi had had breast cancer but was now cancer-free after a radical mastectomy and treatment. Virgil, her youngest son, had been the one to look after her through the ordeal.

"I know he's a good man, Gogi—you don't have to sell him to me," I said, one hand on her shoulder.

"He likes you a lot, you know," she said, searching my eyes in the dim pendant light of the back hallway.

"And I like him," I replied, gently. "I'd better look over the rest of the castle. I have to track down a missing casket and Uncle Mortimer." I squeezed her shoulder and rustled away down the hall and through the kitchen, holding up my skirts so I wouldn't trip. How could I tell her that I was not in the market for a boyfriend, and anyway, all Virgil ever did was criticize me and my approach to life in Autumn Vale?

McGill was putting out the fire in the great hall with an expert hand, and I thanked him, then strolled past the men and through the ballroom, out the open doors, and onto the terrace. It was chilly, so I was glad of the long sleeves of my dress. I walked the length of the terrace to the smoking pit, the stench of cigarette butts alerting me to their presence. I didn't want to take Lizzie's word for it that she and Alcina had checked for live cigarettes. I was sure they had done their best, but they were kids, after all. From the lingering odor of butts, I surmised that they may not have emptied the ashtrays like I'd asked, so I was glad I checked.

I retrieved the can I had put in the corner for the butts, and set it on the wrought iron table. Given that October evenings are chilly in upstate New York, I had rented a propane heater for the smokers. It was still on, so I reached up and turned it off, then noticed something out of the corner of my eye. I squinted into the darkness just beyond the edge of the terrace. Crap, was that the casket? Yes, it was. I sighed. Was Uncle Mortimer still with it?

I gathered my skirts and stepped off the terrace, thinking to move it back up onto the flagstones and off the gravel. In the dimness, I lifted the lid, which must have slammed shut while they'd moved it. I squinted; was that the mannequin still there? Must be, I figured, but it had been dumped onto its side. Damn footballers! I tried to move Uncle Mortimer onto his back, but he felt heavier than last time and not as rigid.

The mannequin was dressed wrong, too, in suede fringed chaps, blue jeans, and a leather vest; who had I seen dressed like that? The cowboy slouching around the party! I had made a mental note to figure out who he was, but I never got around to it and then he'd disappeared, so I had forgotten about him. Had he dressed Uncle Mortimer in his clothes as a prank?

I picked up the battery-operated lantern that was sitting, still lit, on the wrought-iron table and brought it over to the dummy, held it up, and looked down. "Oh, for heaven's sake!" I said out loud. It wasn't a dummy; it was the dang cowboy. He must have gotten wasted and fallen asleep in the casket. Now what were we going to do with him? All the cars and buses had left.

"Come on, you, wake up!" I said, grabbing his shoulder and shaking him. I was going to have to give him a place to sleep it off, then get him to Rochester the next day to catch a bus or a train home. Why hadn't his friends looked after him? He had been with others, another guy and a girl, when I'd seen him, hadn't he? "Come *on*!" I said, shaking harder. Why wouldn't he wake up?

I gasped and knelt by the guy, putting my hand on his chest and my face near his mouth. His shirt was wet; what from, I wondered? There was no breath, no heartbeat. No . . . no life!

That's when I dropped the lantern and started screaming.

Chapter Eight

❋ ❋ ❋

I KIND OF heard the sound of footsteps, but entrenched in horror, I just stood staring, my mouth open. The pool of light flickered from the lantern on the damp, yellowed grass and I wavered, dizziness sweeping over me.

"What's going on, Merry?"

That was Virgil behind me. I turned and threw myself at him, grabbing hold of his muscular shoulders, his solidity reassuring. "It's a . . . It's a . . ."

Pish followed Virgil, then stepped off the terrace and picked up the lantern from the ground. He stepped into the shadowy dimness where I pointed, and approached the casket, the lantern swinging and sending an arc of light back and forth. "It's a man wearing a mask. What is he doing in the . . . ?" He knelt beside the casket. "My God," he finally said. "He's dead."

"Who is it?" I asked, trembling.

Pish stood, wiping his hand on his jacket and shaking

his head. Virgil, oddly equipped with a pocket flashlight—did Sherlock always carry a torch?—pushed his deerstalker cap back, and clamped his meerschaum between his teeth, then bent over and directed the light on the body's face, pulling up the Lone Ranger–type mask. I was watching Virgil and saw his body go rigid.

He said something unrepeatable and staggered back, letting the mask drop. "It's Dinty Hooper!" he exclaimed, huffing like a sprinter.

"That's impossible!" I blurted out. Dinty Hooper was already dead, having been identified from his unfragrant and decaying remains in my forest—Lizzie and I had found the body, and we eventually discovered that Binny's poor old dad had killed him in self-defense—so I was on pretty firm ground there.

But Virgil had his cell phone out and muttered some sharp commands to whoever was on the other end. His colleague from the Feds, an older man, had come out to the terrace and was assessing the situation in a calm manner.

"Who is it really, Virgil?" I asked, shivering and clinging to Pish. It was dark and cold and I was near tears.

He looked over at me, then to Pish. "Take her inside; she's cold. Make sure she has something for shock, but not booze. I need her clear."

"I am not a child, Virgil Grace!" I said, stomping my foot to make that perfectly clear. "Who *is* it?"

"I told you," he said, his voice gritty, "that he *looks* like Dinty Hooper."

I could hardly make Virgil's face out in the shadows, but he sounded ticked off. I had nothing else to say, except, "How did he die?"

"I don't know. The ME and my team are on their way.

Go inside and make sure the kids don't come out here, but don't let anyone go home. This is a crime scene."

"Okay," I said, still clinging to Pish.

"And Merry . . . I'm going to need a guest list and phone numbers of every person who was here tonight."

I started to shake and covered my face with my hands. It wasn't exactly an answer to "How did he die?" but it told me a lot. It was murder. "Not again!" I wailed, my voice muffled. At this rate the castle was going to get a reputation. *I* was going to get a reputation. That shouldn't have been my first thought, but I just didn't want to ponder the poor dead soul—whomever he was—lying so fittingly in the casket I had rented.

"Take her inside!" Virgil barked to Pish.

"Of course, Virgil, right away," Pish said, tugging me toward the open terrace doors. His hands were shaking and his voice was weak.

I pulled myself together once we were back in the dimly lit ballroom. "Pish, wait! We need to talk about what we're going to tell the others." I couldn't see his narrow, clever face very clearly, but I could feel him thinking, and I did the same. "We'll tell them there's been an accident," I said, slowly. "We can't let them go home, so we'll have to tell them some of the truth, but I don't want them to know everything yet."

"We'll keep it bare bones," Pish said. "But I think Gogi can know everything, or as much as we know."

I nodded and went to find Gogi. She was in the turret breakfast parlor and had her feet up on another chair, her head back; she must have dimmed the lights a little, because it was subdued, just the wall sconces on low. She was dozing, as was Doc, who was sprawled on a settee by one of the windows, snoring loudly. I knelt by Gogi and touched her arm; she awoke immediately, alert as always. She put one hand to her elaborate, frizzed coiffure—a wig, of course—and smoothed it back with a self-conscious chuckle. "I guess I'm not as young as I once was. Can't party with the best of them." She sat up and shook herself awake. "Is Virgil ready to go?"

"Gogi, something has happened," I whispered, crouching beside her as if at a confessional. I told her everything and enlisted her help to keep the worst from the girls. I gathered them all, including McGill, who had been wandering about somewhere. I asked them to come to the breakfast room, which was a little brighter now with the chandelier—a smaller version of the one in the great hall—lit.

Binny, Emerald, Lizzie, Alcina, Shilo, and McGill sat around the round table. Gogi still sat on her chair with her feet up, her lovely lace Edwardian gown drooping around her. Lizzie and Alcina had their heads down in their arms and were facing each other, making funny faces and giggling wearily, *beyond* tired, no doubt, after such a long evening. Emerald looked worried and picked at her manicure, tugging her lace French maid's cap off her glossy hair and tossing it down on the table. Zeke and Gordy, hunched on the settee at Doc's feet and whispering to each other, both seemed a little frightened, but Doc English snored on, oblivious.

"There has been an accident and someone is hurt," I said, trying to smile around the table. I was very aware of the young police deputy who had been posted just inside the door. "We all have to stay put for a while until Virgil decides what to do."

The girls asked what was going on, but I just shrugged, then Pish, Binny, McGill, Shilo, and I tried to make conversation about the party. It sounded stilted and fake, and we trailed off eventually. I could hear officials arriving, the heavy thrum of an ambulance and police cars rattling the windows, flashing roof lights casting weird moving illumination across the breakfast parlor walls. Nothing happened for a long time. The ME arrived at some point, I presume, made the pronouncement of death and took a stab at the manner, and then the rest of the team descended upon us. In this weird case, Virgil had witnessed much himself, so he directed the investigation without interviewing us all first.

A while later he appeared at the door sans deerstalker cap and greatcoat. His plain white shirt was rolled up at the sleeves and his buff trousers were tucked into riding boots. He was a handsome man, even weary as he clearly was, his thick eyebrows two angry slashes angled over his chocolaty eyes. He beckoned to me and Pish, and we followed him out of the room.

"Is there somewhere we can talk?" Virgil asked as a couple of uniformed officers searched every corner of the great hall with the aid of their own brilliant lights, collecting bits and pieces of detritus.

I led them up to my uncle's office, a tiny airless room tucked between the bedrooms upstairs, and unlocked it. Virgil followed us in and shut the door behind him. I turned on the green banker's lamp atop the desk, content with that faint, gentle illumination on my weary eyes, then sat down with Pish on a leather ottoman along the wall.

"What's going on, Virgil? How can that poor man be Dinty Hooper?" I asked.

"He's not."

"Okay, I *know* that. But who is it?"

Pish put his arm around me and squeezed, trying to comfort me.

Virgil slumped down in a vintage wood office chair that screeched at his weight. "We think it's Dinty's twin brother, Davey Hooper."

"He had a *twin*?" I shrieked.

"Will you keep it down?" Virgil said, jumping up, pacing to the door, and looking out. Becket slipped in before he shut the door again.

"Nobody downstairs is going to hear me. The walls in this place are two feet thick." I digested the news. "What the heck was *he* doing here?"

"I was just going to ask you that."

"Like I'd know?" I said, staring at him.

"Hush, children," Pish said, in his most paternal tone. "Virgil, you know Merry could not possibly know Dinty Hooper's twin brother, or even that he had one. It's ridiculous."

"Okay, all right," Virgil said, threading his fingers through his hair and jamming it back, though it just flopped back over his forehead when he was done. "We're not one hundred percent certain about that yet, but when we did a search, we came up with Dinty having a twin, and I'm almost certain that's this guy, or it's an eerie coincidence, given that he looks just like him."

"It has to be him," Pish agreed. "It's too big a coincidence that someone looking just like him would come here."

"You're right," I said. "So what did he come here for . . . revenge?"

"Because of his brother dying, you mean?" Pish said. He looked perturbed and took my hand, cradling it in his. "But why sneak into the castle? It was Rusty Turner who killed Dinty."

Virgil held up both hands. "First things first; did you notice the cowboy, assuming he was the only one dressed like that? How did he get in to a private party? I thought this was by invitation only."

"He was the only cowboy; that's one thing I'm sure of. I did see him, but only from the back." Then I told him about Zeke and Gordy's shoddy doorman act, and that I could give him the guest list, but it wouldn't help him a whole lot.

"At least with the list I'll be able to track down folks who were here and talk to them, ask them if they noticed anything about the cowboy: who he was with, what he did, who he talked to."

I perked up. *Who he talked to?* "I know one person he talked to: Juniper Jones."

Virgil looked interested. "Okay, that's good. Where is she, by the way?"

"I don't know. She was supposed to stay and get a lift to town with Binny, but she must have hitched a ride into town with someone else. Probably didn't want to get stuck helping with cleanup."

"All right. Good." He looked from Pish to me, his expression grave, as he stood. "Before I even ask you two any questions, I need you to do something for me: while your memories are fresh, write down a description of all the folks you noticed who didn't belong, those you didn't invite. I have to go and talk to the team, but I need this info stat."

He strode from the room, and Becket jumped gracefully up onto the chair Virgil had vacated and settled, his paws tucked tidily under his white bib. I got a clipboard—one that already had a list of all the reasons I had to sell the castle on it—and a fresh sheet of paper. Pish stuck out his hand.

"What?"

"Give it here, kiddo," he said, waggling his long fingers. "Even a cryptologist couldn't figure out what you've written."

"All right, Mr. Hefner, whatever you say," I said.

We made quick work of the list of those who'd come to the party without an invitation:

1. The footballers, though we couldn't figure out how many of them there had been, because they'd kept milling around.
2. The sleaze twins and their shadow, meaning the two giggly girls and the other one, who'd followed them out to the terrace. I had a feeling the one who'd trailed them wasn't with the other two.
3. Sweeney Todd. Pish said the Demon Barber seemed to have been following him, and he didn't know why.
4. Extra Draculas, at *least* two.
5. And the cowboy, now tentatively identified as Davey Hooper.

"Is that it?" I asked, glancing over the list, penned in Pish's neat cursive.

"As far as I remember."

Pish's tone was odd—a little aloof, as if he was thinking of something else—but I dismissed that as the same disturbance I felt at the memory of a dead body lying downstairs. How long had he been dead? Had anyone seen what happened?

I grabbed another sheet of paper and began jotting down random bits and pieces. I made a note of Zeke and Gordy's checkmarks; that should at least pin down how many extra people they'd let in, but, come to think of it, I already knew there were not enough extra checkmarks for the football team. I looked over at Pish. "I wonder if those guys dressed up in football uniforms are friends of Gordy and Zeke's?"

"Good thought. Maybe the boys let them in, thinking it wouldn't hurt. If so, they may be able to identify some of them."

I sighed and jotted down a note about the truckload of guys who'd thought a case of beer would get them an invitation to my party. They were my top suspects for the football team, since they went away far too easily. A wave of anger washed over me, and I threw down the pen. "I can't *believe* this is happening again."

"Too, *too* coincidental, for sure," Pish replied.

I eyed him, knowing the thoughtful look on his face meant something. "If it's Davey Hooper, then this is not a random killing and not a coincidence. He didn't come here by accident."

"True." He paused, his expressive mouth drawn down in a frown, then said, "This is going to get out to the press, my darling child."

That could be a public relations disaster. As much as I shouldn't be thinking of that in the face of a murder on my property, self would intrude. "Unless we handle it swiftly."

"Handle it?"

"Figure out who killed Davey Hooper."

"I was afraid you were going to say that," Pish replied.

"Afraid or hoping?" I said, knowing my friend too well.

"A little of both," he admitted.

A ruckus outside the door erupted. "No, I want to see her!" came Shilo's "hysteria" voice, a tone I know too well. "Why have you got her locked away?"

The rumble of a masculine voice that came after was a puzzle to me, until I figured out that Virgil must have posted a police officer at our office door. The jerk! What did he think I was going to do, slip away into the night, never to be seen again? Did he have someone at the ground beneath my window, too, fearing I'd crawl out of the tiny window like an overweight Rapunzel and scale down the wall using my hair as a ladder? I crossed the room in two steps and jerked the door open. "It's okay, Shilo," I said in a calming tone.

"Why are you locked up in there?" she asked, her voice shaking, tears forming in her eyes. McGill was holding her to him, his eyes betraying his worry.

He had never yet seen this side of Shilo, the frightened child she managed to hide most of the time. "I think the sheriff is just being cautious about who talks to whom," I said. The tall, solidly built officer shrugged. I wondered if Shilo had been more affected by our last adventure than I knew. Her life before modeling had, I surmised, been a series of frightening events. For my dear friend I stood in place of family, and I was all she had, she often told me. I brushed it off, but I believed she's serious when she said it. I turned to the officer. "Why are you here?" I asked the young cop. I wasn't going to stand for any foolishness.

"The sheriff just told me to keep an eye on everyone, ma'am."

Oh lord, I was a *ma'am* to this fresh-faced young man. I was ready to cross the great divide between flirtable chick and respectworthy older lady, or . . . oh, who was I kidding? I had already crossed it, at least for a fellow this young. "You tell the sheriff to get his butt up here now," I demanded. "I am not going to be sequestered from my friends like this."

"He's . . . uh, he's busy right now."

"I know that," I said, softening my tone. This was not his battle; he was just doing his job. "But I don't want to stay up here all evening. We've done what he asked us to do. Please let him know that." I turned to my friends. "Everything is okay, Shilo, and I'm sure I'll be downstairs in no time. McGill, please take Shilo back downstairs. Pish and I were just helping the sheriff by making a list, and he wants to be aware of where everyone is in the castle. Until it's thoroughly searched, it's all a crime scene to him." I was actually making sense, and proud of it.

"Okay, Merry. You know I'll take care of her." He encircled Shilo with his arms and gave me a look that spoke volumes about how he felt.

I knew what he meant. He hadn't done it yet, but he was going to propose to my friend. He had fallen swiftly and hard for the girl, and though they had only known each other a couple of months, I had a good feeling about their relationship. He led her away, murmuring to her as she nodded and whispered back.

Pish smiled over at me. "Good work, my darling," he murmured, and took my hand, squeezing it.

The young cop had radioed something to his superior, and as my friends disappeared down the stairs, he said, "Sheriff Grace said he'll be right up." His expression held something like awe, and I wasn't sure if he always looked like that or he was impressed that my request had an immediate result.

Virgil was as good as his word. To my surprise, instead of a curt word that we could join our friends, he came into the office and closed the door behind him. We sat down, and given that Becket had taken his chair and didn't look ready to give it up, he rested his tush on the edge of the desk, folding his arms over his chest. He had undone the top button of his shirt and was showing a dark swirl of chest hair. He was, in the words of some of my friends at the party, swoonworthy.

"I want to bring you up to speed regarding what we've learned in the last half hour or so," he said. "We're sure this is Davey Hooper. Authorities at the jail where Dinah Hooper is being held, awaiting trial, asked her about her son, Davey. She claimed she had no contact with him, but that was a lie, because she has had phone conversations with him in the last month. We're reviewing those tapes now. When she was told about his probable death, she collapsed. We'll be matching Hooper's prints; his fingerprints are on record because he's served time for fraud and uttering, and we even have photos of a couple of his tats. They match."

"Uttering?" I asked, loath to interrupt him since he was being so forthcoming, but I was confused.

"A type of forgery, my dear," Pish offered.

"Oh! I've heard the phrase *uttering a forged document*. Is that what they mean?"

"Kind of a redundancy, but yes, that's the case."

"Davey's done time," Virgil continued. "But not a lot. We don't know why he was in Autumn Vale or why he was here at the party."

"It has to be connected to his brother's death, right? And his mother's arrest?" I asked.

"Too early to say. Can't speculate." Virgil clamped his mouth shut and pushed himself away from the desk. "You can go down to the kitchen or that other room—whatever you call it, the one where the others are."

"The breakfast parlor," I supplied.

"Yes, there, if you want. Do you have the list?"

I handed it over to him and explained about the footballers. "They aren't checked off on the list, so we thought Zeke and Gordy might know them. They *may* be the same guys who showed up here yesterday expecting an invitation to the party. I turned them away. They're about the same age, anyway—thirtyish—and might be friends or old schoolmates of the boys. The sleazy girls looked like they were with them."

Virgil looked at the list, his dark brows drawn together, wrinkling his forehead. "Sweeney Todd," he said, his voice hollow.

"Does that mean something?"

Virgil and Pish exchanged a look, then Pish turned to me. He took both my hands in his and rubbed them, thumbing my palms in an intimate fashion. "Darling, there was an *awful* lot of blood. I'm glad but *surprised* you didn't see it. It looked to me like the cowboy—Davey Hooper, if it's him, and I suppose we must think it is—had his throat slit. If the Demon Barber was carrying a straight razor, it would have made a dandy weapon. The fact that we don't know the person dressed as Sweeney Todd is troubling."

"Slit his throat?" My voice broke and I shivered. "What an awful way to go."

"Yet who would have thought the old man to have had so much blood in him?" Pish quoted from the Scottish play.

"Except that he wasn't an old man, but a young one," I amended, as tears welled and began running down my cheeks.

Virgil's jaw flexed. "We'll get whoever did this, Merry, I promise," he said.

And I believed him.

Chapter Nine

EVENTUALLY, DOC, BINNY, Emerald, and the girls were allowed to go home. Binny gave Gogi and Doc a ride, as Virgil was going to be busy for the foreseeable future. It took the rest of the night, but the police officers finally cleared the castle room by room—they never did find the murder weapon, though, I was told—and my friends and I went to bed. The federal agent was going to stay the night in Pish's suite. Pish had one of the more spacious rooms, one with a sitting room attached, because he insisted on paying me top dollar, and I wanted him to have the best. He had a pullout sofa bed for guests.

The next morning was astonishingly, weirdly normal, as long as I kept my mind off the body I had found and the police officers who still lingered. I hadn't slept well, but lying awake thinking all night had its benefit. I realized that Davey Hooper dying where he did might not mean anything about me. This could have been a convenient place for him to meet someone, or maybe he just wanted to see where his brother had died. It was even possible that he had come intending to cause trouble but had been followed or stalked by someone with an ax to grind. Or a straight razor to use. Whoever had killed him, they were long gone now.

"Who do you think did it?" Shilo asked, yawning and scrubbing her eyes as we drank our morning brews at the table in the kitchen.

The Fed was already up and long gone. I deduced that from the absence of his sleek black car from the parking area, which I had noted when I let Becket out that morning. Pish hadn't come down yet.

"I wish I knew. Did you notice anything weird at the party last night?" She gave me a look and I rolled my eyes. "Okay, so that was a dumb question. There was a lot of weird going on. But you must have seen stuff that I didn't." We had already discussed who the cowboy was, and how odd it felt that he had been milling about our guests and then had been murdered. At my lovely party! I truly felt awful for Davey Hooper, and despite how horrible she was, I even pitied Dinah. I had to keep reminding myself that these people had freely made the choices that brought them to where they now were. "Did you notice the cowboy particularly?"

"I saw him a couple of different times but didn't think anything of it. I was mostly catching up with some of the New York crowd." She flipped her long, dark, tangled hair out of her eyes. "Did you hear? Leatrice has signed up to be a guest judge on some modeling show."

"Good luck to the producers," I said in all sincerity. Keeping Leatrice on schedule and sober/straight had been my job for too long. "Anything else catch your attention last night?" I said, trying to keep my flighty friend on track.

"Other than Virgil staring at you longingly?" she said, casually watching me.

I sighed and got up to make some breakfast muffins, setting raisins to soak, then getting out a wooden cutting board and grating some carrot. Everyone kept trying to shove Virgil and me together, but I hadn't noticed any sign that he was truly interested. Nor was I. "Those football players, for example. Did you see them talking to anyone at the party?"

"Mostly they kept to themselves, except one or two of them kept trying to get girls to dance, especially our model friends." She drank some of her herbal tea, a blend McGill's mother, who I understood was an herbalist, had recommended.

"Did you see the two girls who were dressed provocatively? They were party crashers, too."

"I thought there were three of them?" she asked as she yawned and stretched.

As I blended the oils and eggs with the sugars for some Morning Glory muffins, then chopped some apple and got down the glass jars with sunflower seeds and shredded coconut, I pondered my sense about the group. I liked to cook while I thought; it helped. "That's the thing," I finally said in answer to her question. "There were three similarly dressed, but I felt like there were two who were following the footballers around, and then one other who wasn't really with them, even though she followed them sometimes."

Shilo frowned down at her peeling manicure, chewing on her lip as she thought. "The third one, the one alone, did she have frizzy blonde hair peeking out under a black wig, and was she wearing Manolo Blahnik Kahika floral cutout boots?"

I was taken aback at the precision of her memory, but I

shouldn't have been. Shilo's eye for the very best in couture was puzzling to me, since she was content with boho/hobo chic most of the time. Her odd costume at the breakfast table was a case in point: she wore a long, floaty skirt, a peasant blouse, a man's vest, and cowboy boots. It was her eye that had made her a good model; she knew clothes, even though she didn't care to be fashionable all the time. Like a lot of models, once she knew what the customer wanted, she could turn it on and crank it out. "Uh, maybe," I said, not sure what the Manolo boots she was talking about looked like. My memory pinged on something. "Did you say she had frizzy blonde hair under the dark wig?"

"Yup."

"And wore expensive boots?"

"They were black cutout boots that came up—"

"Got it! Expensive boots." It *had* to be Zoey Channer, with that combination of frizzy blonde hair and expensive footwear. So she had gone from observing to sneaking in; I hoped none of my guests were missing anything, because I did not trust her one little bit. That was something I needed to tell Virgil, because I had completely forgotten to call him to tell him about Zoey Channer hanging about in my woods.

Pish finally joined us, and after popping the muffins in the oven to bake, I shared my thoughts. "I knew after finding her in my woods that the only reason her father came here was to look for her. So why didn't he show up at my party? I don't get it."

Pish nodded slowly, getting a cup of coffee. "Also, why did *she* sneak into the party? And why do you think she was following the other two girls all night?"

"At first I had the impression she was trying to blend in with them. That could still be true, but there may be something else. I have got to remember to tell Virgil about this."

"What does it have to do with the murder?" Shilo asked.

"I don't know, but anything might help."

"Might help what?"

I jumped and turned. It was Cranston, who had the annoying habit of just walking into the castle whenever he felt like it. "How did you get in?" I asked.

"Brought Zeke and Gordy up to work," he said, affably sidestepping my question. He did that often, answering another question instead of the one asked. It got irritating very quickly. "You said there's a lot more to do, and the boys seem anxious to get back to it," he added.

I sighed. It was useless to reprimand someone so cheerfully obtuse. "Have a coffee, Cranston. Oh, by the way, you'll be pleased that I'm finally moving forward."

"Moving forward? What do you mean?" he asked, grabbing a mug off the stainless steel counter and filling it. He liked his coffee black and strong. He sat down by Pish, who gave him a look and got up to leave. Pish wasn't crazy about Cranston, but my possible cousin was, as I said, either cheerfully obtuse or willfully ignorant of people's dislike.

"I've made an appointment for us to have our DNA tests done." I told him the date. "We have to go to the hospital in Rochester, so I figured I'd make it a shopping trip, too. Want to go, Shilo?"

"Maybe," she said, dreamily.

When I glanced back to Cranston, his eyes were wide and startled looking; he sat, mug in hand, like a tribute statue honoring the benefits of caffeine in promoting alertness. "What's wrong, Cranston? It's what you wanted, right?"

"Yes, of *course*. It's just . . . I didn't know . . . I didn't think . . ." He shook his head and took a sip of coffee, putting the mug down. To my embarrassment, he got up and came around the long trestle table to me, leaned over, and hugged me hard. "You don't know what this will mean to me," he finally said as he released me, more serious than I'd ever seen him. He clasped his hands in front of him. "It's *more* than the castle, Merry. I've never had much family, and if it turns out we're cousins, how cool will that be?"

I was moved that that was how he saw it, and I reached out to touch his hand. "Thanks, Cranston. I hope we're really cousins, too." I paused a beat and looked over at Shilo, who was unresponsive to our touching family scene. "I have to go into town in an hour or so. Let me know if either of you need anything."

Cranston was still staring at me with fervent hope. "My granny Violet is smiling down on you from heaven, my dearest," he said.

His voice was choked by a sob that was ruined for me by Shilo rolling her eyes. I had to restrain a snort of laughter, not an appropriate reaction to a man talking about his late, beloved grandmother. I understood Shilo's reaction, even though it was unsuitable; everything about Cranston was larger than life. He wore his fervid emotions on his sleeve and expected to be taken seriously even while saying things nobody's said since the nineteenth century. "I'm sure she is," I said to Cranston while giving Shilo a stern look behind his back. She stuck her tongue out at me, the brat! She then bounced off to clean Magic's cage, which, the way she did it, could take the rest of the day.

Cranston left, heading off to wherever it was he went. I didn't know if he had ever worked, but he didn't have a job right now, that I knew of. He had vaguely talked about being lucky in finance, and I pictured a situation much like Pish's, My dear friend had done well enough to retire early but for a few clients he still retained.

Once Cranston was gone, I went outside to talk to Zeke and Gordy, wrapping my sweater around me to ward off the late October chill. They were busily tidying up the terrace outside the front door, picking up cigarette butts and random bits of paper and the occasional costume piece that couldn't have been seen in the dark the night before. The rest of the terrace was off-limits, as the police were keeping a perimeter around the scene of the crime. Both fellows studiously avoided my eyes, and I knew them well enough to know what was up. "Hey, guys, come here," I said.

They trudged over to me and stood, identical hangdog expressions on them both.

"I just wanted you to know that you are not to blame for what happened last night."

Zeke, a shocked look on his face, looked me in the eye finally, and said, "That murder? Course not!" His Adam's apple goggled in his throat like a fish rising to bait.

"I think it was a hit," Gordy whispered, his gaze slewing between the lane and the forest. "Weird folk been hanging around hereabouts lately."

"I wasn't talking about the murder! I meant it wasn't your fault that stray, uninvited guests got into the party. I didn't equip you properly, so I'll rethink our system, I promise." Both looked relieved, but I wasn't done. "However, the football team is another matter. You didn't even *try* to account for them on your list. How come?"

They exchanged guilty glances.

"Are they friends of yours?"

They shook their heads. Gordy swiped a hank of wispy hair out of his eyes. I thought he was going to say something, but he didn't.

"Well, then, who were they? I know you know them."

Zeke sighed. "It's just . . . those guys were from our high

school, back in the day. They . . . we . . . you don't understand." He choked to a stop.

But I thought I did. Everyone has known a group of guys who were the kingpins of their school, the elite, the top dogs. And what did guys like Gordy and Zeke do? Placate. *That* was likely why they let them into the party. Old habits die hard. The football uniforms probably took Zeke and Gordy right back to their spot on the bottom of the pecking order. "But you've been out of school for what . . . twelve or more years now?"

"Maybe that matters in New York City, but in Autumn Vale, things kind of freeze around high school." Zeke glumly stuck his hands in his pockets as Gordy nodded in agreement.

"Were they hanging out with two girls or three?"

Zeke glanced over at his friend, then said, "We were talking about that, and figured we ought to tell you the truth. We weren't sure at first, but we were when we saw them again. The two girls were Candy and Sylvia Frobisher. They're twins." His tone was worshipful, and I knew who those girls were, though I'd never met them. They were the girls every guy in school wanted to date. They were the prom queens, the cheerleaders, the social butterflies. They were probably still coasting on their looks and would until life offered them a wake-up call.

Neither guy knew who the third girl was, and they weren't even sure they had let her in. It was one of the Frobisher twins who had impersonated my friend, Melanie Pritchard—I had a feeling that, despite what Zeke said, the boys knew that when they let them in—but the two were not with the third girl at that point. This was not good. It seemed some of the crashers could have come by way of the terrace door through the smoking-pit area, bypassing the doormen, such as they were. That was going to complicate Virgil's job, no doubt, but I was sure he had already thought of that.

I went up to my office, the one in which Pish and I had spoken to Virgil the night before. It would eventually become a storage closet, being too small for anything else. I mostly preferred working in the library, which was gloomy but would be better once I had the draperies dry cleaned and the windows properly washed. The primary attraction of my uncle's tiny office was that it had one of the two working landlines in the castle, the other being in the kitchen.

So I spent the morning making calls of thanks to friends and asking if they'd enjoyed the party. Universally, the ones I managed to connect with said they had a good time, and some went so far as to assure me that they were going to rub Leatrice's nose in the fact that I was now living in and owned an honest-to-goodness castle. I sincerely begged them not to, but I doubt they listened. That part of my life seemed so over, and I didn't want to even think about Leatrice, much less hear about her.

My next task was to contact those who I thought might actually be interested in the castle as a hotel or retreat venture. That was less successful, as I couldn't seem to get ahold of anyone and had to leave messages with secretaries, assistants, and, in one case, a wife. That's about when the phone began to ring off the hook. It started with a call from a TV station in Rochester. I thought it was a joke at first, because the young woman on the other end asked me about my role in the haunted castle murder. "I beg your pardon?" I said.

"You are the owner of Wynter Castle, right? Merry Wynter? What happened? Was the dead man a guest? Who do you think killed him, if it wasn't you?"

I got my wits back, said I had no comment at this time,

and slammed the phone down. Which then rang again. I couldn't ignore it, because I had people calling me back. I stared at it for a moment, then picked it up. "Merry Wynter," I said, with trepidation.

"Hello, Mrs. Wynter. My name is Shawna Potters, and I'm with the *New York Daily News*. I heard about your party, and I'm interested in talking to you about it."

"Wonderful," I said, not bothering to correct her misuse of the honorific. So, maybe someone was actually interested in the castle as a real news story! "What would you like to know?"

"I understand that after the party you found a body gruesomely murdered and wearing a grim reaper costume. What did you think when you found it?"

I said, "No comment," and hung up. Grim reaper? Really? She didn't ask about the truly gruesome part, that his throat had been cut, probably by a prop from someone else's Sweeney Todd costume, and that he'd been stuffed in a casket I had thoughtfully provided. It seemed that all the details hadn't leaked out, and I was not going to fill folks in. From then on it was all junk calls: newspaper reporters, pranks, and cranks. I checked out some social media on my spotty cell reception, and sure enough, word was traveling fast: we were trending, touted as "a place to be seen at Halloween" on Facebook and every other social media platform. Someone had gotten ahold of an online newspaper account—from the *Ridley Ridge Record*, no less—of the dead body being found; given the Halloween tie-in, it was becoming the most forwarded item.

Great. How had people found out so quickly? All of my out-of-town guests had been gone by the time I'd discovered the body. I looked online further . . . Darn! We had already been named one of the top twenty places to see on a blog called Weird Upstate New York. My poor, beautiful old castle! It had been nicknamed the Ghastly Gothic Pile, and a file photo had been used. I knew it was an old picture because there was no ivy on the castle.

I switched on my answering machine so I could weed out the cranks and went downstairs for lunch. A young officer came to the kitchen and informed me that, because of the social-media buzz, there were cars cruising the area back roads looking for Wynter Castle. The only thing saving me from being found, ironically, was the township/county propensity for renaming roads in the area and neglecting to make changes on the maps.

Virgil had borrowed a few police officers from the Ridley Ridge force to take care of gawkers and make sure they didn't come up my lane and disturb us. I was grateful that the castle was not visible from the road, and I hoped the furor would die down quickly.

Meanwhile, the smoking pit was still off-limits to everyone, and the police had an officer posted there to make sure it *stayed* off-limits. I had Shilo take the poor fellow a cup of coffee and some of the breakfast muffins, then got down to seriously considering what work needed to be done if I was ever going to sell the place and move on. Wynter Castle is magnificent, but I, like other inheritors and/or buyers of gothic monstrosities, was quickly finding out how expensive mansions and castles are to heat, light, and maintain. No wonder Melvyn died virtually broke. The property taxes were paid up for the next year, at least, and there was some money for incidental upkeep expenses, but I just couldn't keep it. In my more irrational moments, I wept over that fact, but it remained just that: a fact.

So I had to suck it up and figure out how best to market the castle. The conversations I had had last night and on the phone that morning had pointed out how desolate the place still felt. I had done my best with the fabric and decorations to make it feel fuller, but it was still dusty, dank, and virtually unlivable, except for little pockets of sanity created by Shilo, Pish, and myself. My uncle had not been a decorating wiz, so it was some kind of miracle that he had at least done something right in the kitchen.

Pish joined me at the table in the kitchen, and we ignored the ringing phone while I made lists, one enumerating things I still needed to do before I could sell the castle, and another of the more achievable suggestions folks had for me. I ignored many, including Zee's idea that I should make a dungeon in the cellar so I could rent the place out to S&M enthusiasts. Zee has always seen things from a slightly different angle than anyone else I knew. The only use I was putting the cellar to was its current one, as a wine cellar.

"So, this is what I have so far," I said, showing Pish my list of things I needed to do.

He put on his close-up glasses and read the list out loud, only complaining once about my terrible handwriting. "One—Rooms not open have to be aired out, furnished at least minimally so people can see them. Two—Exterior gardens still require a lot of work. Three—Zoning needs to be nailed down. The problems with Junior, the former, now-fired zoning commissioner have complicated things. Four—The inheritance needs to be tied up, and if that includes paying off Cranston, we'll need to figure that out." He laid the list on the table. "That's all true," he said.

"And?" I could tell there was more. He seemed distracted, and it worried me. "Pish, is there anything wrong?"

He shook his head. "No, not at *all* my dear." He took a deep breath and looked at the list again. "Let me think on this," he said, tapping it with one finger. "But why don't you, at the same time, explore options for *keeping* the castle?"

"Are you out of your mind?" I stared at him. He was serious, I could tell. It was a horribly impractical suggestion, especially coming from a financial wizard. "It would never work, Pish. I just can't keep it. What am I going to do, open a hotel? It would need hundreds of thousands in renovations. Maybe even millions. And I'm not a hotelier; never was, never will be."

"Maybe a hotel isn't the *only* option."

"If you have other ideas, spit them out."

He reached across and put one warm hand over mine to calm me. "Let me think it over, dearest. *Then* we can talk."

I eyed him, a little worried at his continuing distraction. "Pish, truly, if there is something wrong, don't think you're worrying me, because I can handle it. I'm a big girl. You just seem . . . I don't know. Distracted. Not quite yourself."

The doorbell sounded; that loud *gong-gong* sound took a little getting used to, but it was necessary in such a big place. I jumped up and hustled to the front door with Pish trailing behind me. I found Virgil standing on the terrace with Zeke and Gordy watching. "Hey, Virgil," I said. "I'm glad you're here. I've thought of some stuff, like . . . I should have told you about Zoey Channer showing up in my woods, and then we think she was maybe at the party. This whole thing is freaking me out, and I was hoping you'd be able to give us an update."

His expression was grim, and he eyed Pish warily. "Mr. Lincoln, is there somewhere we can talk?"

"Did you hear any of what I just said, Virgil?" My gaze slewed from the sheriff to my friend and back. "Why do you want to talk to Pish? What's this about?"

Another cop got out of the cruiser and joined the sheriff at the door. Virgil sighed, and said, "Mr. Lincoln, we *need* to talk."

Pish was silent.

"What is this about, Virgil?" I asked, my concern ratcheting up at the weird vibe I was getting from everyone. "You need to say something, and *now*."

His mouth twitched and his ears got red. He turned to Pish and said, "I'd prefer to do this somewhere private, but okay. Mr. Lincoln, would you like to tell us about your connection to Davey Hooper?"

Chapter Ten

❉ ❉ ❉

PISH GRIMACED AND sighed.

"What the hell does that mean?" I asked. Both Virgil and the officer remained stone-faced.

"Maybe I'd better speak to the sheriff in private, Merry," Pish said, eying Virgil with what seemed like trepidation.

"Uh-uh. Nope. No way. You are *both* going to tell me what is going on." I noticed Gordy and Zeke still watching, goggle-eyed, rakes in hand. I grabbed Virgil's shirtsleeve and pulled him in, then said to the other officer, "You, come in. Go to the kitchen. We're all going to have a little chat."

I put off the talk as I made more coffee and set out a basket of fresh muffins—anything to let Pish have a chance to gather his thoughts. I had no clue what Virgil was talking about, but given how distracted my friend had been in the last twenty-four hours or so, it worried me.

"Enough! Merry, if you insist on staying, then sit down and stay quiet," Virgil barked. I bristled and was about to retort, but he had already turned to Pish, and said, "Mr. Lincoln, what is your connection to Davey Hooper?"

Ignoring the sheriff's command to sit down, I watched my friend from my spot at the counter. After a moment of silence, I opened my mouth to speak, but Virgil sent me a warning glance. This was between Pish and him.

"That's just it, I *don't* know him," my friend said, unhappily. "Or I don't think I do. But when I saw him—when I saw his face—he looked vaguely familiar. I just don't know *why!*"

The sheriff exchanged a look with his subordinate, who was taking notes. "You didn't pull his mask up when you looked at him, correct?"

"No, of course not!" Pish said.

I was getting an uneasy feeling about this, and it put me on the defensive. "Virgil, why does it matter if Pish knew him or not?"

He ignored me. "Mr. Lincoln—"

"Stop *calling* him that!" I exclaimed, pushing away from the counter, my gaze flicking back and forth between the two men. "You were calling him Pish yesterday. Why are you suddenly—"

"Mr. Lincoln, does the Cayuga Correctional Facility ring a bell?" Virgil raised his voice to talk over me, an effective way of getting me to shut up. I glared at his profile, but he ignored me.

Pish started to shake his head, but then stopped and knit his brow. "Well, yes, as a matter of fact. I've been there. But Davey Hooper? I just don't remember the name."

"Why would you visit a jail?" I asked him as I sat down across from him at the table. "And why would you remember someone from there?"

He sighed and met my gaze. "Dearest, you remember *Cons, Scams, and Flimflams?*"

"Of course. That's the book you wrote on financial scams, the scammers, and the victims who fall for them," I said, pretty much quoting the press release blurb. Becket had followed us into the kitchen, and I was agitated enough that I didn't shoo him out and even let him jump up on the long worktable.

Pish turned to Virgil, his manner calm and his eyebrows raised. "I went to Cayuga—as well as several other facilities all over the country—to interview men and women incarcerated for financial cons. It was research for my book." He sat back in the Windsor chair—one of the mismatched set I used in the kitchen—crossed his legs, and tilted his head. "Are you telling me I actually interviewed that young man?"

Virgil nodded. "It's on record."

My friend shrugged, a casual gesture that belied the tension I could feel radiating from him. "All right, so I interviewed him."

The deputy, who sat just beyond Virgil, jotted down some notes.

"Did you recognize him? Was he here to met you?" Virgil asked. He leaned forward and continued, "Did you talk to him, Mr. Lincoln?"

"No, no, and no," Pish said, a hard note in his voice. I only ever heard that when he was angry and being very blunt. "Sheriff, I interviewed over *two hundred* scammers for the book as well as hundreds of their victims. I may have notes on my conversation with Mr. Hooper, and I can find them for you if you want—in my New York condo, of course, not here—but I did not see him nor did I speak with him last night."

"Is that the story you're going with?" Virgil said.

I was astounded at his insinuation that my friend was lying and leaped to my feet, startling Becket. "That is enough, Virgil Grace. This interview is over. Pish, you are going to call your lawyer and you're not going to say another word until you speak with him."

"Merry, sit down," Pish said, that hint of steel still in his voice. "I do not need you to mother me like you do Shilo."

I looked over at him, hurt.

"I'm sorry, my *darling*," he said more gently, reaching out and touching my arm. "I know this frightens you; it does me, too. But you need to calm down. I can take care of myself."

I did as he said.

"I do not take Sheriff Grace for a fool," Pish continued, eyeing the man. "And only a fool would think I would kill the fellow when I had no motive. I don't even remember him. Something about his face—the jawline or his mouth—looked vaguely familiar, but that's all."

"Does it happen so often, then?" Virgil said, watching Pish.

"Does *what* happen so often?" I asked, frowning across the table at the sheriff.

Virgil glanced at me, but his gaze returned to Pish. "Mr. Lincoln, do you get sued for sexual harassment so often that you don't even remember the men who sue you?"

I gasped.

Pish's eyes widened and there was a subtle change in them. Now he remembered Davey. I could tell that, but Virgil wouldn't understand his expression as I did.

"Ah, so *that's* who he is. Was. His last name wasn't listed as Hooper, though, was it?"

Virgil said, "No, he was David Isaac Smith. Hooper is Dinah's last name by her second husband, but Dinty and David had their father's last name, Smith. They used Hooper, but it wasn't their legal surname."

"*That's* why I didn't make the connection when you said his name," Pish said. "You must realize that a dead body, with his throat slashed and wearing a Lone Ranger mask . . . well, it doesn't make a good visual cue for the living man."

The young police officer was scribbling madly, his whole face red.

Virgil's expression was blank, and I couldn't tell anything from it, not if he believed my friend or didn't believe him. "So, I repeat . . . do you get sued so often you don't even remember who sued you?"

"You have no right to speak to him like that," I said, my voice controlled but trembling.

"Merry!" Pish's tone held warning. He gave me a speaking look, and his expression assumed a professional blankness, very much like Virgil's. "Remind me of the details, Sheriff, if you please."

Virgil looked down at his own notebook, now open flat on the table in front of him. "The complainant said that during the interview you attempted to touch him inappropriately. He claimed that you suggested that when he got out of prison, he might like to come to New York and stay in a fancy condo in Manhattan."

My friend's expression hardened into distaste. I was reeling from the information, but he calmly said, "I remember now. It was ridiculous, as there was a guard present the entire interview. The fellow filed the complaint after attempting to blackmail me with his spurious claims."

"I didn't know about this." I watched his expressive face, his mouth twisted in a grimace from the memory.

He turned to gaze at me fondly. "I don't tell you about sordid details, my dear. You've had enough to deal with in the last eight years or so. This has happened twice in my life." He turned back to Virgil, a subtle change in his demeanor that troubled me, though I couldn't pinpoint why. "I have nothing to hide, Sheriff. I'm open about my life, and I'm relatively wealthy. Some see that as an invitation for chicanery. I reported him for the blackmail attempt, which is why he tried to sue me. I say 'tried' because the suit was dismissed, and the fellow was warned that another nuisance suit would land him in trouble or delay his release. I had the impression he had been a thorn in the prison warden's side for some time."

"So you never gave him money or any other gift?"

Pish stayed silent for a long moment. "I don't like the tone of this conversation. I think I am done talking, Sheriff."

It did not escape me that he didn't actually answer the question, and I was afraid it didn't escape Virgil, either. His next words confirmed that. "Mr. Lincoln, if you could take my deputy to fetch the costume you wore to the party, I would appreciate it greatly." He then turned to me and added, "Merry, we'll be taking your gown, too."

His face didn't give away anything, and I complied, tight-lipped. They were going to test our clothes for blood.

After, Pish stayed up in his room (which had already been searched as part of the investigation, as had mine and Shilo's) to work on his current book, as Virgil and his minions spent more time investigating the scene. Eventually the sheriff returned to the kitchen, where I was doing prep work for the next morning's muffins. As he entered, I kept chopping nuts, my knife flashing in the bright light of the halogen bulb I had put in the pendant over the stainless steel countertop.

Virgil stood near the door. I felt his steady gaze on me. It made me want to shrug my shoulders, anything to get rid of the weird feeling of being watched, but I didn't.

After a long moment, he said, "Merry, I know you're mad that I'm investigating Pish."

I whirled and shook my fist in his direction. "You're darn right I'm angry! Pish Lincoln is the sweetest, gentlest man you will ever meet, and he is no more capable of slashing someone's throat than I am!"

His thick eyebrows climbed his forehead, and he looked pointedly at the knife in my fist. "I have no opinion on this, Merry, believe me. But when I come across a piece of evidence like that, I can't and won't ignore it. Someone killed Davey Hooper, slashed his throat in a brutal manner. Until I figure out who, everyone is a suspect."

I DIDN'T MUCH LIKE ALL THE GRUNT WORK ASSOCI-ated with getting the castle ready. I cleaned when I had to, but it didn't make my day. Unfortunately Pish and Shilo were pretty much the same. We were gradually getting through all the dusting, washing, laundering and scrubbing associated with bringing the castle up to snuff. There was so much else to do, it was slow going. I was just grateful for the inexpensive and enthusiastic outdoor help of Zeke and Gordy, but Pish and Shilo . . . they pitched in for nothing. I had no idea how I was going to repay my wonderful friends for all their help, but I was going to have to come up with something substantial.

Fortunately, I *do* enjoy decorating, and that includes painting: walls, trim, cutting in, everything! There was a lot of it to do if we were going to hold another soiree to try to market the castle. Some of the advice I received from friends who had visited was that any buyer would want to see more finished rooms, so that their imaginations would be sparked by the potential displayed. To that end I was fixing up some of the bedrooms.

My great uncle Melvyn had done work, but it must have been decades ago, and he'd had atrocious taste. Jack McGill insisted that my uncle had had a vision for the castle, but if that was so, it was the vision of a color-blind hippie squatter. One of the rooms was done up in seventies turquoise and yellow with cheap rattan furnishings spray-painted white. It looked like the sunroom in a Florida retirement home. Another was a hideous eighties mishmash of dusty rose and ruffles, and chrome and glass; and a couple of others were all hunter green, burgundy, and faux wood finishes. Horrible!

At least he hadn't touched the bones of the rooms, though, so we could work from there. Of course, in twenty years someone would likely be complaining about my design esthetic, but I was starting over with some of the best rooms, meaning the turret bedrooms and the luxury suites, particularly the ones that had already been fitted out with private bathrooms. At least Uncle Melvyn hadn't installed the bane of any decorator's existence, colored bathtubs and toilets.

Shilo was a willing and energetic participant, so we were beginning that morning in the west turret bedroom, the one that had been painted dusty rose. We were using a glossy white for the trim. Perhaps painting trim doesn't sound like much work, but picture an octagonal turret room with many windows soaring to ten feet or so, and all the trim that entails. It was a daunting task. Melvyn's dusty rose mess just ate up all the sunlight in the afternoon, so I had to figure out another color for the walls once we were done with the trim. I had called a designer friend in Manhattan, and he'd asked for photos, for which I had enlisted Lizzie's help. We had sent him a ton of pictures, not just of the turret room but others as well. He was fascinated, but I explained that I had little money and didn't want to decorate everything in sight; I just wanted a few choice rooms in which to use the antiques already available to me and needed to paint or wallpaper them on a strict budget.

The result was that when Pish went back to the city for a couple of days at the end of September to retrieve some belongings from the condo he shared with his mother, he helped our mutual designer friend box up some samples and paints suitable for the space and brought them back with him. The designer had come through so magnificently that I had paint and fabric enough for at least a couple of rooms. I had stroked several different colors on the wall in bars to see how the light affected it, and the winner for the turret room was a pale yellow called "straw," a delicate but rich tone that accepted the afternoon light and filled the room with a gorgeous glow. I would have loved to pair it with natural wood trim, but it would take forever to strip the baseboards and other woodwork, and I didn't have that kind of time. We were taking the easy road.

Shilo and I spent the rest of the afternoon painting trim and finished late that night. The next morning was going to be busy, so no more painting for the day. I tumbled into bed exhausted but had trouble sleeping for worrying. Was Pish in trouble? He had avoided me for the rest of the day by working first on his book, then on the bank's problems. He then went with his federal agent friend to the Grovers' home for dinner and an evening of talking opera with Janice. He wasn't home when I went to bed.

The next day was going to be a busy one. They were having a Halloween party at Golden Acres, and I was supplying treats for it, as was Binny. I was also supplying some cookie-and-square platters to a meeting at the Brotherhood of the Falcon meeting hall, which was going to be a new client for me. I awoke early and baked a few dozen muffins as well as several batches of cookies, chocolate chip and peanut butter. I made lemon squares, too, a simple and delicious addition for those strange beasts who don't like chocolate or peanut butter.

I actually had a new muffin recipe that was so good, it was sinful. I worked it out to honor Hubert Dread, one of the old guys at Golden Acres who had told me a long story about his meeting with "the King" in some kind of undercover operation. He claimed that Elvis was actually an undercover agent for the FBI. It was clearly one of Hubert's highly embroidered and fanciful tales, but fun. My own knowledge of Elvis, which was sketchy, related mostly to his food preferences; I knew he loved peanut-butter-and-banana sandwiches. So I baked a couple dozen Fit for the King muffins, which were peanut butter, banana, and chocolate chip. Delectable! I also made a batch of Pecan Pie muffins and, while I was at it, a couple of batches of bran and carrot.

That took a couple of hours, but it was still only midmorning when I arranged a few baskets of muffins and platters of cookies and squares, then loaded the rest in plasticware. I had a couple of stops to make, and the first one was going to be interesting. The Brotherhood of the Falcon Hall was on the outskirts of town, but the meeting was not a Falcon meeting. It was kind of a town hall deal, with a few local politicians and interested townsfolk. I piled the stuff in Shilo's rust bucket—she was still sleeping and would be for the foreseeable future, given how much and how late we had worked the day before—and headed down the lane.

I had driven past Brotherhood of the Falcon Hall, as the Falcons' boy fort was called, so I knew where it was, on a

side road off Butler Lane/Wynter Line, whichever you
wanted to call it, or depending on the day of the week and
which local body of government had the upper hand. The
Brotherhood members may as well have posted a sign that
said *No Gurlz Aloud*, because they were a very cliquey bunch,
every last one of them frightened to death of his wife, I'd
be willing to bet, judging from the couple of members I
knew. Simon Grover, bank manager and brotherhood
member, was completely cowed by Janice, and I suspected
that lawyer Silvio was the same. Mrs. Silvio was a Latina
with exotic looks, long red fingernails, and ferocious clothing tastes. I had only seen her in passing, and I didn't want
to stereotype her based on her heritage or appearance, but
she certainly interested me.

I had learned that on the agenda that day was a discussion
of the mess left by Junior Bradley, the former zoning commissioner, and what was to be done about every single bit
of business he had conducted in the two and a half years
since he had taken over the job from the retiring zoning
commissioner. This concerned me, since some of those zoning decisions had been made about my uncle's plans for the
Wynter Castle property.

However, I knew I was barking up the wrong tree if I
thought to bust in on the meeting that day. There was a strict
"no girls allowed" policy at the Brotherhood Hall, clearly
unconstitutional and certainly out of bounds if they were
holding town council meetings there. Normally I'd be up to
fight that, but I wasn't going to be in Autumn Vale long
enough to worry about it, and if they didn't want to be
dragged kicking and screaming into the current century, or
even past the middle of the last one, that was not my business. It was a job for other local ladies.

If I was completely honest, I hoped that the zoning

problems with the castle were not a worry, because *past* zoning was not an issue. Melvyn and Rusty Turner had been working on zoning for creating a development of homes on the Wynter property, but I didn't see that as a viable option. I felt we had a strong case for asking them to clean the slate of past requests and to propose rezoning the castle to include its possible future use as a hotel or resort. I could handle that by speaking to whomever took over Junior Bradley's position or possibly to someone at the town clerk's office.

I pulled up at the Brotherhood of the Falcon Hall, where several cars were already parked in haphazard disarray in the gravel parking area. The hall was a bland box of a building on a parcel of land set in the middle of the woods. As I already noted, it was located on the Wynter Line, now Butler Lane. I was beginning to get used to the dual nature of road naming in Abenaki County, since the county, the township, and the town were constantly at war and made changes whenever they felt like it. If they ever hoped to have any kind of tourism industry, that could become a problem, but they seemed blithely unconcerned that they were shooting themselves in multiple feet while they do-si-doed among themselves.

I eased into a spot next to a big black car I recognized as the Grovers' vehicle and grabbed the platters of treats and tubs of muffins from the seat next to me. I found the back door and entered, balancing the food awkwardly in my arms, to find Janice arguing with another woman.

"You and I need to get together and put those men in their places, Sonora, or they'll keep running things in the same boneheaded way they've been doing for the twenty years I've lived here!" She was talking to the woman I recognized as Mrs. Silvio, Andrew's wife. Janice turned and said, "Back me up on this, Merry. Town Council should not be meeting at the Brotherhood Hall, not when they have a discriminatory policy against women!"

"Okay," I said, trying to pull the door closed behind me with my foot. "So, burning bras at dawn? Or we march on the hall with salad forks and brûlée torches?" I had imagined Janice was the kind of woman who didn't give a rat's patootie about such stuff, and here she was advocating social action. She was my mother redux.

Janice gave me a look, but Sonora laughed gaily, her head thrown back, her dark, glossy hair a wild tumble of curls. She was dressed, however, in a sober skirt suit of taupe, with plain black pumps . . . very conservative as befit, I supposed, a lawyer's wife. The bank manager's wife, on the other hand, was gowned in a fuchsia muumuu, one of her hundred or so such dresses. Janice grabbed a platter from me and slammed it down on the counter as I set another beside it. I put the stack of muffin tubs and the other platters down, too, and glanced around the room. We were in a barren-looking kitchen fitted with commercial-grade ovens, two refrigerators, and little else. Pitiful.

I refocused on my friend. "Don't look at me like that, Janice," I protested. "As a matter of fact, on my way here I was just thinking it was extremely weird that Town Council would be meeting here, where women are not welcome. Why is that?"

"The Town Council building was condemned; black mold. Had to be torn down, it was so bad," Janice said, rolling her eyes. "And nobody since has had the cojones to make a decision on a new town hall."

"Oh. Well, I'm not really an Autumn Valer, so I wish you luck, but I don't see what I have to say about it."

The two women exchanged looks. The lawyer's wife shrugged and turned to get milk out of one refrigerator.

"Merry, this is Sonora Silvio, Andrew's wife," Janice said huffily. "She's helping me get these sorry dopes organized, and I'm staying for the meeting whether they like it or not. I was just trying to convince Sonora to stay, too."

"I'm sorry, Janice," Sonora said, her voice colored with a faint accent, probably Cuban. She poured milk into a couple of pitchers and put them on a tray that already held sugar bowls, sweetener packets, and cutlery. "I have to go to my son's school for pizza day. Petruchio likes me to be there."

"Merry?" Janice said, turning to me. "What about you?"

I considered it; I really did. For a few seconds, at least. "I just can't, Janice. I'm sorry. I have a million things to do, among them dropping off muffins at the café and some other baked goods at Golden Acres." I smiled at her as I unpacked my tubs, then tried to change the subject. "Did you have fun the other night at the costume ball?"

"Sure," she said as she scooped coffee into the huge coffeemaker, then set it to percolate. "Dumber and I had a grand time."

"Did Pish have anything to say last night at your place?"

"You mean about Virgil accusing him of killing that idiot who got his throat slashed, as if Pish Lincoln would do anything of the kind?"

I was happy Pish had staunch support in Autumn Vale other than from Shilo and me, but Sonora was frowning over at Janice, then at me. I shouldn't have brought up the subject. I mentally shrugged; pretty soon it would be all over the place anyway, so better to present it in the best light, as something patently ridiculous. I briefly described what was going on with the murder investigation but did not get into the specifics of my friend being under suspicion. She had already heard much of it.

"My daughter Giuletta heard from a girl in her class that the dead man was dressed like a cowboy. Is that true?"

I nodded, wondering if her daughter's school friend was Lizzie.

"I wondered," she said. "That explains a lot."

"What do you mean? Did you see the guy?"

She nodded. "I saw him, I think, along with two others on his way to Autumn Vale from Ridley Ridge. I was coming back from doing some shopping, and they cut me off. I followed them to give them a piece of my mind, but I couldn't get them to stop."

"Your lucky day," I said. "Given what happened later, I mean. I believe he was killed by someone he knew, maybe even someone he came with. Who else was in the car?"

She frowned and tilted her head, staring up at the stained ceiling as she pondered. "I did not get a perfect look, you understand, but there was someone with what looked like a black wig and someone else in the backseat."

"Hullo, hullo, what are you little ladies doing here?" a voice boomed.

A tall gentleman, probably in his mid-seventies, stalked into the room and rubbed his hands together. "Gabbing, huh? Gossiping? Ah, gotta love the ladies."

"I have to go," Sonora said, and hopped toward the door, waving good-bye. "Talk to you all later!"

Darn! I wanted to ask her more questions and tell her to let Virgil know what she'd seen. I would have to be sure to pass her name and story on to him myself; I made a mental note . . . a car with three people in it, one with a black wig. Now, who was this fellow? I observed with interest.

Janice smiled up at the man. "Elwood Fitzhugh, just the fellow I wanted to see."

He sidled up to her and put his arm over her plump shoulders and squeezed. "You finally ready to leave that old tub o' lard for me, sweet missy?"

I thought she'd deck him for talking to her that way, but instead she smirked up at him. "Poor Simon. You're too hard on him, El. No, I wanted you to meet Melvyn's great niece, the one who inherited the castle! Merry, this is Mr. Elwood Fitzhugh, the zoning commissioner before Junior Bradley was hired."

"Well, now, aren't you just the spittin' image of your mama!" he said, staring at me and nodding.

"You saw the picture Melvyn kept," I acknowledged.

"Not at all, not at *all*," he said. "I met your mama!"

"You met my mother," I said, stupidly repeating that startling statement.

"I surely did. Don't you remember me? I guess you were such a wee scrap of a child, and pretty tuckered. I was heading to Rochester to get some information on a builder who had done some work in Autumn Vale. I was about to head out of town when the cab driver from Ridley Ridge—the one who your mama called, you know—flagged me down."

He turned his long, lined face up to the ceiling, squinting, then looked back down at me. "If I remember right," he said, waggling his finger, "his cab blew a tire and he needed someone to take you and your mama to the train station in Rochester. Would I do it? he asked. I said sure, didn't mind the company, and so I took you both to the train station, and your mama and I, we chattered the whole way, hour and a quarter—or more, the way I drive. She was a fumin' the whole time over Melvyn and how bullheaded he was."

I stood for a long moment staring at him, stunned. When I was very young, not long after my father died, my mother and I had made a trip to Wynter Castle, but the visit lasted only overnight. My mother and Melvyn argued, and we left abruptly. But it seemed that Mr. Fitzhugh had talked to my mother just after the fight. I had a vague memory of being moved from the cab to another car, which must have been his.

What had she said to him, I wondered? In the heat of the moment, had she spoken of issues she never would talk about later? I wanted to talk to him at length, but there was one burning question that, if answered, would give me some perspective on all that came after. "Mr. Fitzhugh, did my mom say why she and my uncle fought?"

"Oh sure," he replied. "Your mama was a spitfire, I will say. She was mad at Melvyn because he wanted you both to come and live at the castle."

Chapter Eleven

❈ ❈ ❈

I HAD BEEN hearing the noise level increase from the room beyond the kitchen but hadn't paid much attention to it until that moment, when I heard a loud *bang-bang-bang*, like a hammer on wood. Elwood's ears perked up and he half turned toward the open door.

"Meeting's starting. Gotta go."

"No, wait!" I cried and grabbed his shirtsleeve. "Mr. Fitzhugh, please . . . Why was my mother angry that Melvyn wanted us to come live at the castle? We were broke by then, and it would have been a lifesaver."

His brow wrinkled and his long face held a puzzled expression as his gaze strayed back to the babble of voices from beyond the kitchen door. "Can't remember, offhand. Seems to me there was more, but . . ." He shrugged.

I could tell his attention was more on the meeting beginning in the other room. "Mr. Fitzhugh—"

"Call me Elwood!"

"Uh, Elwood, could we meet to talk this over? I have so many questions, and you're the only other person in Autumn Vale, besides Melvyn, who saw my mother."

"Well, sure, missy. How about I come out to the castle? Curious to see what you're doing out there."

"Would you come out tomorrow for lunch? I could show you around and tell you my plans. Since you were the former zoning commissioner, I'd be curious to know what you and my uncle talked about." And what my mother told him, I thought, but did not say.

He agreed, and then headed in to the meeting with one more saucy wink and grab at Janice.

"I'm going in there. Are you coming with me?" Janice said.

I was still stunned by meeting someone who had seen my mother in Autumn Vale, but Janice's plight tugged at my civic concern. She was right that someone needed to confront the bozos who thought it was okay to exclude women from a town council meeting, and if she was going to do that, the least I could do was support her. "I can't stay, but I will go in there with you as a show of support."

She sailed—like a majestic barge, I must say—through the door into the hall—a dimly lit, smelly cavern of masculinity—and I followed. It was dismal. There were no open curtains, so the place was dully lit by some dusty pendant lights dangling over a big, open hardwood floor, where rickety folding chairs, half of them occupied by men and the rest empty, straggled along in haphazard rows facing a lectern. Another row of folding chairs arced behind the lectern, and these were occupied by Andrew Silvio, Simon Grover, Elwood Fitzhugh, and some other locals I knew as the elected town supervisor and two councilmen. I hadn't actually met the men, but as they spent every morning at

Vale Variety and Lunch swigging coffee and acting like they were solving the problems of the United States of America, I had seen them many times. I supposed the men in the rows of chairs were Brotherhood of the Falcon members, and maybe some of the others were locals.

Simon was at the lectern blustering about how Junior Bradley had fooled them all, and how he would need to be replaced while they considered pressing charges against him, and how Simon didn't know how this had happened and the councilmen would need to take ownership of their part in the fiasco. While he was yakking, Janice and I calmly took seats at the end of the front row and stared at him until he trailed off, looking confused.

"Uh, what do you ladies want?"

Janice stood and turned to face the men in the audience, her bearing queenly and her expression stern. "What we want is an equal say, and that means coming to town meetings as a citizen of this town, even in your little boys-only club. And if you are going to continue holding Town Council meetings at the Brotherhood Hall, then I move that the hall should be open to women at *all* times to foster an atmosphere of inclusiveness."

Simon turned red and hammered on the lectern, shouting, "Janice, you can't make a motion; you're not a member."

I was getting confused, so I said, "This isn't a Brotherhood meeting, though, is it?"

"Well, no, but . . . but . . ." Simon trailed off.

Elwood stood and said, "I say we go along with the ladies. This is a new century, boys, and the old ways are gone, much as we might mourn them. For myself, I say the ladies would add a bit of interest to Brotherhood meetings that are stale." He winked at me as murmurs of approval drifted through the seated gentlemen, and Silvio nodded. It appeared that Simon might be the only Brotherhood member who was still for the boys-only rule.

Simon had regained his poise, such as it was. "Of *course* ladies are welcome to any town meetings held at the Brotherhood Hall, but as to the Brotherhood of the Falcons, well, we'll have to discuss it amongst ourselves at another time."

Janice nodded. It was good enough for the moment, but I didn't think she was done. Her husband had proved himself to be the doofus she had long suspected, and now he was reaping the rewards.

"I have to go, Janice," I murmured. "Are you good here?"

"I am just fine," she murmured. "Come by the store another day and I'll show you some stuff I've got for the castle."

Just before I exited, I turned and saw Janice survey the gathering, then turn toward the men behind the lectern. She said, in a booming town council voice, "I want to ask what we're going to do about development in Autumn Vale? There are too many empty storefronts, and we need to encourage folks to move here if we're ever going to revive our economy. I say we start by making one of those vacant buildings downtown our new town hall, and move meetings there! And another thing—with elections coming up, we have to consider who best will help our town and township move ahead, rather than stagnating like Ridley Ridge."

Atta girl, I thought, as I left. I thought I may just have witnessed the birth of a local political superstar. I'd have voted for her, if I'd had a vote, for town supervisor.

I dropped off muffins for the Vale Variety and Lunch, then headed to Golden Acres, a modernized and expanded manse in a pretty section of town. It was the soporific hour after breakfast but still an hour or so before lunch; many of the old folks had toddled off to their rooms for a nap, while others sat dozing in the sunny front parlor. I had set Doc a task and wondered if he had come through. I had asked him to write down anything at all he could remember about the mysterious Violet and my great uncle.

After delivering the muffins to the kitchen, I went through to the front of the retirement home, where oldsters snoozed and gabbed on cool autumn mornings. Gogi had set up a kind of honor bar for senior ladies and gents. It was a buffet with stacked teacups and mugs and two giant urns with coffee and tea in them.

She said if folks paid their twenty-five cents, it was good, but if they didn't, she was fine with it. The price of a cup of coffee or tea was worth it to see the smiles it induced. It gathered folks in one place who might not normally come out of their rooms or their shells. Something for free, or next to it, was a great lure for those on fixed incomes. Old age is all about connections, Gogi had stated. These folks had seen friends and loved ones die far too often, and so any new friends they could make to fill the void were welcome distractions.

I found Doc there on a sofa in a shadowy corner by a bookcase, his feet up, a book on his lap. It somehow didn't surprise me that he enjoyed Carl Sandburg's poetry. Doc may have appeared to many as an odd duck, but I saw the piercing intelligence in his twinkling eyes, and our conversations had ranged over a wide variety of topics. He cracked jokes, sometimes willing to appear as the crazy old dude, but his intelligence was formidable. His opinions of the world at large had been formed at home, then broadened by his time spent overseas in the war, when he and Melvyn were young bucks looking for adventure. His vigor suited Sandburg.

"How'd you like the party the other night, Doc?" I asked, sitting down beside him.

"Huh? Oh, hello, Merry. It was a good one. Met some interesting folks, 'specially your buddy, Pish. In my day we woulda called him a swish, but I don't say that no more. He has a way about him. I like him a lot."

"I like him, too," I said. "What did you think of the final event of the night?"

"You mean the dead body?"

I nodded.

"You know, I saw that fella a coupla times in the evening."

"The guy dressed as a cowboy?" Hooper had been the only cowboy, a stroke of luck for the investigation.

"Yeah. He was talking to a girl dressed kinda hoochie, with some frizzy blonde hair stickin' out under a dark wig. Looked like they were arguing."

Aha, so we had a connection between the two, the cowboy and the hooch, aka Zoey Channer, and an argument. Interesting. I remembered what Sonora Silvio had said about the cowboy and someone with a dark wig in a car, and I wondered if they had come together. So many questions, so few answers. "Did you hear what they were arguing about?"

"Nope. Damn music was too loud, and that Cranston, your maybe cousin, he talks a blue streak and was trying to yak over the music."

"What did you see, then?"

"That girl . . . first he tells her off over something and walks away, then she comes up to the cowboy and shakes her finger in his face. He turns away, but she grabs his arm, and he shakes her off. Then he storms off toward the terrace, with her following like a raft in his wake."

I mused on that. What connection could there be between Zoey Channer and Davey Hooper? Was it really them in the car together? "Did you see anyone dressed like Sweeney Todd?"

"Sweeney what?"

I was about to explain, until I saw the glimmer in his eyes. "You *know* who Sweeney Todd is . . . wild hair, barber coat, etcetera."

He frowned down into his cup and twisted his lips into a grimace. "I did see him, but only early on, then he disappeared. Why does he figure into the tale?"

I shrugged.

"Carryin' a straight razor," Doc said, and nodded. "So that's how the cowboy was done in."

Excellent guess, as was often the case with Doc. "You mustn't share that with anyone!" I cautioned, glancing around. Not that any one of the half-dozen dozing seniors would be listening in, but still. . . .

"Doctors keep a lot of secrets," he said, with a nod and a wink.

My head was swimming, but I seemed to have reached the last of the information Doc had about the party. "So, what have you got for me?" I asked, wondering if he had remembered his task.

I should have had more faith. He pulled a couple of lined sheets from the poetry book and handed them over, then watched me as I unfolded them. His scrawl was as bad as any doctor I had ever known, so it took me a little time. I knew that Doc had gone to school after coming back from the war and had become a doctor on the GI Bill. He told me that Melvyn had taken advantage of another part of the program, low-interest loans for servicemen, to start improvements on the castle.

I read what he'd written:

Violet (can't remember her last name) was a pistol, a redheaded firecracker. She and Melvyn started going out when we were all in high school, and everyone thought they'd get married right after graduation—set up house at the castle—but then Pearl Harbor happened and me and Mel enlisted. Him and Vi had a fight of some kind, but we had to go off to training, and he didn't have time to make it up to her. He wrote, but she never wrote back. We came back to Autumn Vale after basic, but only for a few days because we were being deployed.

I don't know what happened while we were home. Mel was going through some crap, but so was I. My old man was sick, and everyone knew he was dying. I was the oldest in my family. My old man wanted me to look after my mother. I didn't know whether to go or stay, but I couldn't stay, not since I had enlisted, so I tried to help my mom out as much as I could.

God, we were just kids.

I looked over at Doc, thinking how much that interjection told me. Do we all get that sense of pity and overwhelming sympathy for our younger selves as we get older? I wasn't that old, but I felt it coming on, the sense that if I could only go back and speak to a younger me, I'd give myself a stern lecture and a big hug.

Then I thought of Sandburg, and his admonition to "live not in your yesterdays, nor just for tomorrow, but in the here and now." He was right, and I would learn from that and move on, understanding that the young woman I had been then had to go through what she had to become the wiser woman I now was. If that made any sense. Doc was bent over his book, reading the poetry.

I continued:

Anyway, when Mel and me got back together to go off, he wouldn't talk about Violet, and I just figured they

*hadn't made up, or they had . . . I don't know. I was too
full of my own worries.*

*That's the last I remember about Violet until we got
back. We were kind of busy for a while there. Anyway,
when we got back, we heard she up and got married to
some 4-F guy right after we left. I never heard about a
kid. Her folks moved, too. . . . They went somewhere. I
don't know where.*

And that's pretty much it.

Well, it wasn't very helpful, but there was something
there. "Doc, you said you all went to high school together.
Did you guys do yearbooks back then?"

"Sure. They were carved on stone, but we had 'em."

I chuckled. "Do you happen to have a copy?"

"Nah. Why would I keep old crap like that?"

He was indeed the embodiment of Carl Sandburg. I
thought for a moment, and something occurred to me. He
might not have a yearbook, but I knew someone who just
might: Hannah, my favorite librarian in the world. I said
good-bye, surprising him with a kiss on the cheek that had
everyone staring, and headed to the library.

Hannah was open for business, but there wasn't a soul
there, for a change. Inevitably, we had to talk more about
the party, but as we did, she appeared to be avoiding mention
of the dead man. I knew her sensibilities; she is like Beth in
Little Women, focusing on the beauty and light in humanity
rather than the depravity, which, though she acknowledged
it, did not touch her. However, I wanted to know what she'd
noticed or seen, regarding the crime that happened just yards
away from us all. She is intelligent and from long habit
notices what others are doing, even those who eschew her
company.

"Hannah, did you notice anything that night to do with the fellow dressed as a cowboy, or the girl with the feathered Mardi Gras mask on?"

She met my eyes and nodded. "He was interesting. Before Zee got me caught up with the group talking about books, I watched him for a while as Mom and Dad went to get some drinks and look around the castle more. I thought . . ." She frowned down at her slender hands, her delicate fingers threaded together. "I had a feeling he was looking for someone."

"Looking for someone," I repeated. "Did he find that person, do you think?"

"I don't know."

"You said he was interesting; why?"

She frowned and turned her face up to the light that filtered in from the small windows that lined the upper portion of the library wall. Her gamine face had filled in some in the month I had known her, and yet she was still painfully thin and faerylike. Thoughtfully and slowly, she said, "He wasn't just chatting and eating and looking around like everyone else. He seemed to be looking for someone specific, like he was there to meet someone. I don't know if he met that person, but I just felt like he was tense, you know? And anxious. He wasn't there to enjoy the party."

Davey Hooper would certainly not have been there to enjoy the party. There was only the most tenuous connection between me and Dinty, his late brother, but Binny had been at the party, too, and it was her father who had killed Davey's brother, albeit in self-defense. Could she have been his quarry? He had not approached Binny at all that evening, though, to my knowledge. It didn't seem like revenge was his purpose. And I would have thought that if he was after

Pish, then he would have approached him at the party, but he hadn't.

Or had he? Pish was hiding something, I was afraid. He tries to protect me, no matter how much I tell him I don't need protecting. It goes back to the time right after Miguel's death, when I was so fragile that just the mention of death or sorrow cut me like a Ginsu knife through a paper heart.

"You know now who he was, the cowboy." It was a statement, not a question. The whole town knew who the cowboy was, in one sense.

She nodded. "The fellow who died, and the brother of Dinty Hooper. I heard from Zeke."

"Zeke comes in here?"

She smiled. "We went to middle school together, before I started homeschooling. He was left back and I skipped grades, so we weren't far apart. When he began to have trouble in high school, I tutored him in literature and English. He's . . ." She hesitated. "He doesn't like to admit it, but he's dyslexic, so reading comprehension takes him longer."

Suddenly some things made sense. Zeke always let Gordy, who was not really as bright as he was, do a lot of the tasks that required reading. "It won't go beyond me, and if he never brings it up, I won't mention it." It gave me an idea for how to organize the lists for the next party. "Would it help Zeke, do you think, if I matched photos with the names of folks on the list for the next party? Would that make identification easier? It actually makes sense for a whole lot of reasons, and Zeke's dyslexia is only one."

Hannah approved. "It's easier for him to remember names, especially unusual ones, if he has a picture to go with it. That's how he got better in history. He's smart; he's the one who helped me install the computer and Internet here in the library, and he always takes care of any problems I have that way."

"Okay, I'll do it that way next time. Now . . . you said you don't know if the cowboy found who he was looking for?"

She shrugged. "I haven't a clue. I saw him talking to several people, so I suppose any one of them could have been who he was looking for. He spoke to Cranston and Emerald, as well as the Mardi Gras girl. And Juniper . . . he spoke to her, too." Hannah paused, then went on. "Juniper looked unhappy."

"How is that different from her usual look?"

"The same but more. Does that make sense? I just had a feeling there was something *more* wrong that evening for Juniper." She paused, then glanced over at me and asked, "Binny says Juniper lived in Ridley Ridge before here?"

"That's what she says. Why?"

Hannah just shook her head. I knew she'd be thinking about it—whatever *it* was—and when she had something solid she'd call me. I changed the subject, bringing up my conversation with Doc. I shared his note. She read it over and her eyes lit up when I asked about yearbooks.

"I do have a stack. I've been working on getting the whole set of Ridley Ridge High School yearbooks from the beginning, in the twenties."

"I'd need . . . let's see . . . nineteen forty or forty-one, I think."

She moved the joystick on her wheelchair and zoomed expertly around her desk to a shelf at the far end of the room. I followed, and she clicked along the tidy row of yearbooks, the slim leather-bound volumes all kinds of dull colors from gray to brown to maroon, until she found what she wanted. She put a finger on the top of one and slid it out from among its brothers. "Here we go, nineteen forty-one. Let's look for your uncle first. When we've done this, I have some stuff to show you."

"What did you find?" I asked, excited. "Is it about Violet? And my uncle?"

"Not now, after," she said firmly.

She held the book on her lap with one hand and worked the joystick with the other. We went back to her desk, and she laid the book on the surface. Her gray eyes sparkling, she looked up at me. "I feel like we're uncovering a mystery, you know? Like Nancy Drew and her friends."

"*You* can be Nancy. I think I'm more Jessica Fletcher than Nancy Drew."

She pulled her gooseneck lamp down, closer to the book—the library was a little gloomy; it could use better lighting—and opened it. We scanned through it together until we found the senior class section and located Melvyn Wynter's oval portrait; he stared out at me from the page in all his teenage skinniness. His expression was bland, but I swear there was a twinkle in his eyes that made me think he was the jokester I had been told he was by Doc English. I made a mental note to look back to the previous grades for my grandfather, Murgatroyd Wynter, a character even less well known to me than my uncle.

On the seniors' welcome page, titled "Class of '41," Melvyn was listed, to my astonishment, as the class poet. There was a better photo of my great uncle, his gaze brooding, his hawklike profile very much what I (barely) remembered of my father. Was there any of Cranston in his appearance? I did search, but Cranston had a bluff, friendly appearance, not the hatchet face of Melvyn. Maybe if I found Violet I'd see the resemblance. Hannah and I both searched but didn't find a Violet among the senior class, nor the juniors. Was Cranston's whole story a hoax or a lie?

I just didn't know. After all, Hannah *had* found the reference to Violet Flores's "leaving town" party in the local newspaper archives. In such a small place, how likely was it that there woud be two Violet's leaving town at about the same time? If Violet Flores was indeed my Uncle Melvyn's Violet, then perhaps she had left school early, though no one had said so.

Hannah looked thoughtful for a moment, then pulled up a search on her computer. She softly said, "Aha!" and turned the screen to me. I saw a list of other versions of the name Violet and there, under Spanish, was Yolanda, one of the names of the girls in the senior class.

"Yolanda is such a pretty name; why would she go by Violet instead?"

Hannah hesitantly said, "It made her stand out. Maybe in 1941 she didn't want to sound foreign, you know . . . Spanish or Mexican."

I nodded. She had a point. In the America of the time, with all the uncertainty of a world at war, blending in may have been a priority. "So this may be Violet; we don't know."

But just then I saw something else, a random photo of a group of kids from the senior class hanging around the football field. There, his arm slung over Yolanda's shoulders was my uncle, Melvyn Wynter. "That's her!"

Chapter Twelve

❊ ❊ ❊

HANNAH SQUEALED EXCITEDLY and clapped. "You're right!"

We read the caption: *Melvyn Wynter, our local poet, takes a moment with his friends and Yolanda Flores, the lucky young lady who has caught his eye.*

"Well, that certainly suggests Yolanda is Violet," I said.

She nodded, thoughtfully. "I wish we had Cranston's locket here so we could tell if this is the same woman as in the photo." She glanced over at me. "What do you think of that?"

"What do I think of the locket?" I shrugged. "A sweet gesture on Melvyn's part, the kind of thing a young fellow would buy his girl, right?"

Hannah frowned down at the page, then turned back to her computer, her tiny fingers flying over the keyboard then clicking her mouse. "Here," she said, turning the screen toward me. "This is a file I made of pictures of lockets from the nineteen forties; click on the arrows to scan the photos. They look a lot like Cranston's locket. During World War Two the government shut down gold mining, so anything made of gold got more expensive or was just impossible to get. That could be why the locket is gold filled, or some cheaper alloy, or it could just be that he was only a teenager, after all, and couldn't afford anything better. But it's something else that has me puzzled." With a click of her mouse, she brought up photos of the *insides* of the lockets. "Do you notice anything that makes these different from Cranston's?"

To humor her I looked at the photos. I'm ashamed to say it took me a solid three or four minutes of examining the photos before I caught on. By then I had prodded her a few times just to tell me, but she wouldn't and watched my eyes instead. Then it dawned on me. "Oh. Wow. Of course! Why didn't I get this before?" It was staring me in the face the whole time. "If Melvyn gave Violet a locket, then he would put in *his* photo, not hers."

She clapped her hands. "Very good!"

I smiled over at her, thinking what a little teacher she was. The photo was certainly something to consider and to ask Cranston about. "Was this what you wanted to show me?"

She nodded.

"There may be a logical reason," I warned.

"Of course. But it's something, right?"

"It sure is. You are one smart girl."

Some patrons came in just then, but I had to leave anyway. Hannah whispered that she was going to search through some local archives next and try to find any references to Melvyn and Violet among them. I told her about the trunks in the attic and how I hoped to search through them for any photos or anything related to Melvyn and Yolanda/

Violet. I was full of questions, including what had been going on between Melvyn and his parents and with my grandfather, Murgatroyd, during this time.

I headed out, down the little side street on which the library lived, and out to Abenaki, then down to Binny's Bakery. I wanted to ask Juniper about being accosted by the cowboy, Davey Hooper, and what he had wanted. She had no doubt been questioned by the police by now, but I would never know what they had learned from her.

I entered, only to find a harried Binny simultaneously looking after the counter and tending to her ovens in back, where she was making a hundred creampuffs for a wedding-shower order. I zipped behind the counter and helped her clear the backlog of customers, after which she slumped down on a stool and pulled off her baker's hat, wiping her forehead of sweat, her curly dark hair, so like her newly discovered niece's, sticking out in spiky fluffs.

"So where is your new helper? I wanted to talk to her about the party, to see if she saw or heard anything."

She sighed, heavily. "She was here this morning, for all the good she was."

"What do you mean?"

"I mean she wouldn't stop crying. The cops talked to her yesterday, and she came in this morning babbling about how mean they were. I tried to calm her down—told her they had asked everyone at the party the same questions, probably . . . I know they did me—but I was busy. Virgil came in at one point and asked if she could come by the police station again after work."

"What did he want?"

"He didn't say. Why? Is it important?" Binny asked.

"I don't know; probably just more questions."

"Yeah, I guess. He asked me the weirdest stuff, like did I see Pish with the dead guy at any point." She eyed me. "What's that all about?"

"I don't have a clue," I said, thanking my lucky stars that not only does Binny not listen to gossip, she is the least curious person I have ever known, solely focused on her baking business and now her family; otherwise, she would have put two and two together. "What happened then?"

"Then she went out for a smoke break and just never came back." Binny fluffed her erratic bangs until they were even worse. "I'd have more luck hiring Isadore."

"Frying pan into the fire pit," I said. Isadore Openshaw did not, in my opinion, belong in the service industry. Some folks just don't. "Juniper was seen talking to Davey Hooper the night of the party. I wonder if there's some connection there." I was willing to entertain any notion that would distract attention from Pish's past with the victim.

"Could be. That would explain why she's so upset, I guess," Binny mused. "I don't think she knew who the dead guy was until the cops told her during questioning."

"When did she leave the party that night?" I asked. "And how? She was supposed to stay, and you were going to give her a ride home."

"She just took off. I don't know *how* she got back to Autumn Vale. I forgot to ask, I've been so busy. Right now I've got a hundred creampuffs that I need to box, and I'd better get back to it, because I've only got half an hour. Thanks for the help, Merry."

I took the hint, left the bakery, got into Shilo's rust bucket, and headed out of town toward home, climbing out of the Vale. But I then had a fateful brainstorm and changed direction. The day was turning gloomy, and the wind tossed the tops of the trees, sending showers of golden and red leaves fluttering across the highway, swirled into torrents by the car. That should have been the harbinger of evil to come, but I blithely crossed a river ravine on a low truss bridge, turned onto a wider highway, and was soon in the depressing environs of Ridley Ridge. I was going to go to the Party Stop, but thought I'd make another stop first.

I parked on the main street and got out of the car. Shilo's dilapidated rattletrap, groaning and griping as it shuddered to a stop, seemed peculiarly at home in this gray, sad town. A faint misty rain was blowing across the street, and one person hustled into the little café, the place I had entered to ask the waitress about the location of the Party Stop. The same pudgy, texting waitress was working, this time pouring a cup of coffee for the newcomer, who had taken a window seat. Why anyone would want a window seat in Ridley Ridge I could not say. Any other seat, maybe one of the ones next to a faded travel poster with a photo of Greece, would have been preferable. I turned up my sweater collar and ran across the street to the café, entered, and approached the waitress, who was already slumped down on a stool at the lunch counter near the cash register, texting madly.

"Hi," I said, sitting down on the stool next to her and taking off my damp sweater.

"Uh, hi," she said, jumping up. "You want coffee?"

"Sure. Is the owner here?" I asked.

"No. Joe only comes in on Saturday to sign paychecks," she said, slipping behind the counter and grabbing an almost empty coffeepot.

That was good, because she was the one I wanted to talk to. I took the cup of coffee, though I could tell it was old, burned, and awful, with a visible oily sheen on the surface. I cradled it in my hands; at least it was hot, and I was cold. "My name is Merry, and I bake muffins. I was wondering,"

I said, eying the glass cake cover with a pile of sugary donuts under it, "do you think the owner would sell my muffins here?"

It was a simple question, but she stared at me like I had asked if he would sell crystal meth if I cooked some up. "I don't know."

"Can I have Joe's phone number? I'll just ask him, okay?"

She readily agreed to that and wrote his name and phone number down on the back of an order slip. I stuck it in my purse, then sipped some of the wretched coffee, choking it down with difficulty. "You lived here long?" I asked, setting the cup down and pushing it away. "Susan," I added, glancing at her name tag.

"All my life." She was starting to get more comfortable with me.

"I came here a couple of weeks ago looking for the Party Stop, remember?"

She nodded.

"Do you know a girl named Juniper Jones? She's working in Autumn Vale now, but said she worked at the Party Stop before moving on."

Susan rolled her eyes. "I know her. She's a special kind of crazy, I'll say that."

I kept my expression blank but felt a little jiggle of excitement in my stomach. Had Juniper, seen arguing with Davey, killed him for reasons unknown? Had she known him before coming to Autumn Vale? "Crazy how?"

"Crazy as in *cah-razy!*" Susan said, eyes crossed and twirling her finger around one ear. Eyes wide, she leaned over the counter and whispered, "She threatened a girlfriend of mine at the pool hall one night just for laughing."

"Laughing?"

"Yeah. Said she'd cut her pretty face into ribbons."

"That sure is a special kind of crazy," I said. *Cut her pretty face into ribbons*, eh? Sounded fairly psychopathic, and also like she'd be handy with a straight razor. "How long was she in town?"

"A few weeks, I guess."

"Where did she come from?"

"I have no idea. I mean, who would purposely move to this town?"

I couldn't disagree with her. "What about Les Urquhart; what do you know about him?"

"He went to school with my uncle Reg. Reg says Les is a sleazoid."

"In what way?"

She leaned over again and whispered, "I heard he sells drugs out of the back of the Party Stop. He went to jail for dealing, you know."

That confirmed my guess about Les's side business. Maybe it was more than just pot, though. "So why did he hire Juniper Jones?"

"Who knows? He's got all kinds of weirdos hanging out at that place. I wouldn't step foot in there, even if the Party Stop *is* the only place in town to buy a Halloween costume!"

"What kind of weirdos?"

"Lately, there was this guy hanging around that no one saw except at night," she said, glancing around as if there were a crowd trying to listen in on the gossip. "He was a skinny dude—tall, lanky, long hair. Everyone joked he was some kind of vampire, like . . . he only came out at night!"

I asked a few more questions, but that's about all she had to offer. "Well, thanks, Susan," I said, laying a five dollar bill on the counter and waving off change as I stood and hoisted my purse up on my shoulder.

"Anytime. It's nice to talk to someone from the outside world," she said wistfully, staring past the lone customer out the window to the gloomy streetscape.

"Have you ever thought of leaving Ridley Ridge?" I asked.

"Where would I go?" she said with a hopeless shrug.

Into the wide, wide world, I wanted to say; a waitress can waitress anywhere, even New York City or LA. But it was her business if she was so defeated by life in the twilight burg that she couldn't even see a place beyond the town line of Ridley Ridge. I got into Shilo's car and headed to the Party Stop. The parking lot was surprisingly full, so I was forced to use on-street parking. The car idled for a moment before stopping, making a *knock-knock* sound that was not the beginning of a joke, I hoped. When I entered, it was to the noise of kids racing up and down the gloomy aisles while their mothers screeched at them to shut up as they surveyed racks of ready-to-wear Halloween costumes. Les sat at the cash desk still reading *Moby-Dick* and ignoring the chaos.

"It's Halloween tonight, isn't it?" I said by way of a greeting. I had forgotten. That had to be the result of some kind of blockage in my brain. My mind boggled at the thought of Halloween in Ridley Ridge.

He looked up and nodded. "Busiest day of the freakin' year." He sighed and put the novel down, splaying it out on the counter. "So how did your shindig turn out the other night?"

"It went pretty well, all things considered," I said with crossed fingers. I supposed a murder at your party, if you didn't find out about it until after the end, didn't devalue the whole experience, right?

"Heard about your little trouble after. Sure am sorry for you." He stood and rang up one brood, a woman with

three kids, one a baby on her hip. She bought a witch costume, a mad doctor, and a pumpkin outfit for the baby.

"Thanks. It was a horrible thing to happen, even though
I didn't know the guy."

Once the woman had exited, he leaned across the counter,
swiped lanky hair out of his eyes, and said with a smirk, "I
heard he was the twin brother of that other guy who got
murdered out at your place. You seem to have your share of
troubles."

Apparently the *Ridley Ridge Record* had made quite a
bit out of the "rash" of murders at my place. They made it
sound like I was the Autumn Vale Slasher. No wonder I was
getting a reputation, even though the killings had nothing
to do with me. "I don't even know why he was there, that's
the thing," I said.

A dad with a sulky teenage son and younger daughter
came up to the counter with an armload of costumes. He
gave me a friendly smile, and I smiled back; definitely not
a native Ridley Ridger. He fished out his wallet, complained
about the price, argued with his son, and finally left.

"Les, I'm checking something out for a friend. Did you
employ a girl named Juniper Jones?"

His look became guarded. "Why? What's she done now?"

Taken aback, I said, "Nothing that I know of. She got a
job at a friend's shop in Autumn Vale, but she left work this
morning and didn't come back. Have you seen her?"

He shook his head.

"What can you tell me about her?"

"She was trouble from the get-go," he said. "I felt sorry
for her. She just rolled into town on the Greyhound, nowhere
to go, nothing to do, so I gave her a job straightening up the
stock for the holiday season. She did squat of the diddly
variety and caused trouble all over town, so I let her go."

That corroborated the waitress's story of a troublesome Juniper. I was afraid of that. "Maybe it's a good thing if she's taken off from Binny's place." I couldn't think of anything else to say. "I'd better get going."

"Sure," he said.

"I'm just going to have a look around first."

His expression changed, and he looked shifty again, like he had the first time I'd seen him. "Uh, nothing new since last time, you know." His gaze flitted to the back and then back to me.

"I'll look, nonetheless," I said, my determination hardened by his worried look. Would I find Juniper hiding in the stock area, perhaps? I headed toward the back, past a startled mom dragging her twins from costume to costume in desperation.

I wove through the place, then around one last long shelf filled with dusty plastic totes. The back was empty, except for piles of boxes near a loading-dock door that was open, letting the cool autumn air waft in. There, sitting up on a stack of the boxes like a princess on a cardboard throne, was Zoey Channer.

"Well, hello," she said, taking a drag on a cigarette and blowing the smoke out. "Fancy meeting you here."

"Zoey! So, did your dad ever connect with you?" I asked, examining her exaggerated Cleopatra makeup and frizzy blonde updo. My voice echoed strangely in the cavernous storage area of the Party Stop. "Or are you still avoiding him?"

I heard a rustle behind me, and Les came screeching out from the aisles and skidded to a stop, eying us both. He was dressed in sagging cargo pants and an Ed Hardy T-shirt; it was hard to see what the attraction would be for a girl like Zoey Channer, but maybe that was the point. Her father would hate Les Urquhart.

"I'll take from the silence that you haven't let your father know where you are yet."

"Daddy dearest can kiss my ass," she said, and tossed the cigarette down on the cement floor.

"How many times I gotta tell you, butt it out," Les said, hopping over and stomping on the glowing cigarette end.

"Did he not fund your partying properly, or did he make the mistake of wishing you wouldn't spend so much time in jail and around jail rats?" Silence. "So, why did you crash my party?" I asked her. "I know you were there."

She shrugged, fished in her purse, extracted a package of cigarettes, and pulled a fresh one out of the pack. "I was bored to tears. Thought Daddy might show up at the party looking for me, and I wanted to see what he'd do."

Les nervously looked from her to me and back. "Zoey, why don't you take off? You, too, lady. I got customers to look after."

Despite his wish to get me out of the way, I wasn't going anywhere until I found out where Zoey was staying so I could sic the police on her. She may have seen something, given that she smoked and would have had reason to be out on the smoking terrace. "It was a wild night," I said. "Did you enjoy the party? You were following around those two local girls. I saw you."

"Fancy you recognizing me with the costume on," she said, giving Les a look. "Told you I should have gone as a vampire."

Vampire. There had been a surfeit of vampires that night, not all of them accounted for. "Did you come, too?" I asked him, wondering if he was one of the random Draculas.

He shook his head but didn't say anything. Oh, I was *definitely* going to send Virgil Grace their way. I couldn't think of any reason why they'd kill Davey Hooper, but I didn't know everything about these two and what, if any, relationship they had with Hooper. I was confused; Les *must* be the guy Zoey had met through a cell mate, I figured. Or was he? Davey Hooper had been seen arguing with/talking to Zoey Channer, so he could have been the guy she'd met, her jailbird boyfriend. Was she the bewigged person Sonora Silvio had seen in a car with the cowboy? Had they come to the party together?

One thing I felt sure of: Davey Hooper must have been the vampiric night crawler Susan the suddenly chatty waitress reported to have been staying with Les. My head swam with possibilities but no certainties, dizzying me as random threads and thoughts zipped around in my brain. I hate when that happens, especially when I don't have time to sit down and think things through. I gave myself a shake and still stared at Zoey, who was making faces at Les. Ultimately, once I had pointed Virgil in their direction, it would be none of my business. I couldn't think of any reason to keep probing, except an insatiable curiosity and a desire to find anyone to pin the murder on *other* than Pish.

Ignoring Les's antsiness—he kept glancing over his shoulder toward his shoppers, who I could hear rummaging in the shelves and dropping things, kids shrieking and mothers yelling—I asked Zoey, "Did you see anything that night? Out on the smoking terrace, for example?"

"Are you kidding me?" she asked. She lounged back and puffed on her cigarette—such an attractive look for a young woman—and smirked.

"Why would I kid?"

"Oh, I just thought you were. I don't *do* smoking terraces to smoke, that's all. I smoke wherever I damn well please."

"Such a rebel," I said mildly, sure she would not get the intended sarcasm. Les did, though, and glowered at me. I eyed him and thought, *He's trying to get in good with this girl because her daddy is Percy Channer of Channer Hotels International.* How would that feel, I wondered briefly, to know that guys would try to date you just because of who you were? Not great, I concluded. Not great at all.

I heard a rustling sound, and someone called from the cash register, "Hey, does anyone work here? Or should I just damn well help myself to these (expletive) overpriced nasty-ass costumes for my (expletive) nasty kids?"

Must be a true townie, I concluded, just happy to be alive and living in lovely Ridley Ridge.

"I'll be back," Les said, and waggled his finger at Zoey. "You behave yourself." He took off at a lope around the shelf and disappeared.

Good, a chance at Zoey alone and unhindered. "Which one is the fella of the moment, Les or Davey Hooper?"

"Davey who?" she asked, blowing a smoke ring toward the ceiling.

So that's how she was going to play it. "You came to my party just to see if your dad showed up, you say. Then why were you watching my place originally? Are you the lookout for some particularly stupid band of crooks?"

"Who do you think you are to talk to me like that?" she said, suddenly snapping out of her nonchalance. She glared at me, her face pinched into an angry expression. "What gives you the right?"

"What gives me the *right*? Oh, that's good. Let's see . . . first, how about finding you skulking around in my woods and having your father come to my place looking for you while pretending to want to buy the castle? Oh, and then?" I glared at her and spoke very precisely and succinctly. "And then, how about finding a man *dead* and *covered in blood*, his throat slashed ear to ear . . . on my terrace?"

Her face paled and she was silent. I couldn't read her expression, which had gone blank, but it looked to me like she was trembling. Now that I had at least managed to wipe the smirk off her face, I would try again. "Did you at any time see the fellow dressed as a cowb—" I was interrupted by someone hurtling through the open back door and running toward us.

Zoey cried out, and the girl—Juniper Jones, I quickly realized—flew at her, screeching, with a knife in her hand. I was stunned for a moment as the two girls fell in a heap behind the boxes, screaming and wailing. Juniper was shrieking what sounded like a steady stream of "Ihateyou! Ihateyou! Ihateyou!"

"Stop! Stop it . . . *Juniper!*" I raced toward them and tried to pull Juniper off Zoey, but she kept slipping from my grasp. Her dark makeup was streaked all down her face, but there was a look of such hatred there as she attacked Zoey, whose clothes were beginning to look like ribbons from the slashing of the knife. Blood oozed and splattered, soaking into the fabric of her sleeves.

"Call nine-one-one!" I yelped over my shoulder, my hands getting slippery from blood. I tried to grab Juniper's hair, but she whirled and fended off my hand, then returned to her victim.

Les was suddenly there. He leaped on the wailing girl, grappling her into a headlock, but Juniper, wildly powerful, struggled out of it like a greased pig. By this point I was in full panic mode; not much does that to me, but I don't do well with physical conflict. I'm sorry to report that I was jumping up and down, flapping my hands like a useless chicken. A teenage customer—clearly with a better head on her shoulders than I—came running back, cell phone in hand, dialing and then babbling into it about a stabbing at the Party Stop.

And then everything paused for one moment, like a still from a movie. Juniper, blood on her face, knife still in her hand, stared at me, her expression full of wonder and pain. She did not seem to know how she had gotten there, nor what she was doing. She looked at Zoey, and then at the knife in her bloody hand. She dropped it, and it clattered on the cement floor and skidded under a box, but she didn't appear to notice. Her expression crystallized into hatred, and she spat on Zoey, then ran out the back door, leaped off the loading dock platform, and disappeared.

Les, bloodied by the conflict, galloped after her as I thumped down on the floor on my knees and grabbed a costume another customer was holding to stanch Zoey's bleeding wound. She was sobbing, rolling around on the floor, and wailing that it hurt, not so cool now that she was in trouble.

Police erupted into the place, and I babbled out that the assailant had taken off, and Les, the store owner, was chasing her. An ambulance arrived and paramedics took over my nursing duties, as Les came limping back. Apparently his own leg had been slashed by the mad delinquent as they had grappled on the floor.

It was going to be a long day in Ridley Ridge.

Chapter Thirteen

❊ ❊ ❊

I SPENT THE rest of the afternoon in the Ridley Ridge Police headquarters being interviewed by the local sheriff, Ben Baxter, who was a lot older and not nearly as good-looking as Virgil Grace. Not that that mattered. They called Virgil for a character reference, but when the sheriff came back from the conversation, it seemed that Virgil had not been completely complimentary. Baxter implied that he had heard I was an interfering sort.

I walked the sheriff through my impulsive decision to head to the Party Stop, what I had said to Zoey Channer, and what had happened next. He asked a lot of questions, and I answered as best I could. I had a lot to think about, but my brain was not processing by the time I was done with the hamster wheel of questions, each one asked multiple times in different ways. Why had I come to Ridley Ridge that day? Who had I spoken to? Why had I asked the waitress at the café about Les Urquhart and the Party Stop? Was there a particular reason I had decided to come to Ridley Ridge that day? Were they to believe that I had just happened to find Zoey Channer in the back of the store and that was exactly when Juniper Jones attacked her? Had I been in contact with Juniper?

I kept my cool. From conversations I overheard I gathered that both Zoey and Les were still in the hospital, but their wounds were not considered life threatening. During breaks in the questioning, I thought things over. I wondered if Juniper Jones had been supplanted in Les Urquhart's affections by Zoey Channer and had come back to the store to take her revenge. Was that what she had been weeping over in Binny's Bakery, her broken relationship? I was too tired to think clearly, because some things were staring me in the face and I *still* didn't get them.

Given that I was exhausted and sitting there in blood-stained clothes, I think I was cooperative if not exactly affable, but when they let me go, it was with a warning to stay out of Ridley Ridge unless Baxter specifically asked me back. I would not only comply, I would warn everyone with whom I had contact to stay out of Ridley Ridge.

He also warned me not to interfere in their investigation into what had happened. As if I would!

When I finally got back to Shilo's car—walking, because the police officers were "too busy" to give me a lift for another hour or more—there was a ticket on the car for parking too long, over the two-hour street-parking limit. I considered storming back to the police headquarters. I had only been parked there over two hours because I had been doing my civic duty in talking to them! But the idea of going back to Sheriff Baxter gave me cold shudders, and on a day that was already too long, I couldn't face it.

I climbed into the car out of the drizzling, misty rain,

longing for a vehicle with an actual working heater. That would not be Jezebel, even on a good day, so I'd need to shiver for heat until I got back to the castle. At least I was confident that this rotten day wouldn't get any worse. But then, when I tried to start the pathetic wreck, it whined and groaned, refusing to even turn over. Like a creaky senior with rheumatism, it did not like damp weather.

I sat, head bowed, feeling alone and dejected, but I couldn't stay that way forever. I pulled my cell phone out of my damp purse and scanned the numbers. I tried the castle, but no one answered. I tried Shilo's cell and then Pish's, and then even Cranston's. Still, no one answered. I couldn't pull Binny away from her bakeshop, and Gogi had a new tenant moving in that day.

My only option was Virgil Grace. He answered promptly, was there in ten minutes, and ushered me to his sheriff's car. I got in, watched by several of the gloating citizens of Ridley Ridge, and put my hands to the heat vent, hoping I would thaw. I truly never wanted to see that town again but would need to, to retrieve Shilo's broken car. I sighed and laid my head against the passenger window of Virgil's car as he drove out of the town and onto the highway.

"Merry, I—"

"Not a word!" I said, holding up one hand. "I do not want to be chastised as if I am some delinquent teenager who disobeyed direct orders. I do not want to be chided or warned, nor do I want to be scolded or reproached. I've had just about enough today."

"I was just going to say how sorry I was that you got in the middle of that," he said mildly enough.

Suspicious of what sounded like sympathy, I looked over at him. "You've already had your revenge by warning the sheriff that I was troublesome."

"I didn't do that," he claimed.

His jutting chin, clothed by stubble, was pointed straight forward, hands on the wheel at ten o'clock and two o'clock, so I examined him in the gray light of late afternoon. He seemed sincere. My tone was more conciliatory as I said, "Virgil, I hope you know that I don't go looking for trouble."

"Sure," he said easily, then ruined it by adding, "It just seems to find you."

I magnanimously ignored that. "And, despite what you may think, I know for certain that Pish Lincoln is not guilty of murder and could never hurt anyone."

He was silent. Me, too, for a while, anyway.

"Merry, I don't *think* he did it," he finally said. "But I am in a position where I have to keep an open mind. He had a motive, but it's a weak one, since he doesn't seem to be hiding anything. That I *know* of. I'm investigating; let's leave it at that."

Given that I still feared Pish was hiding something, I knew I had to let it go. So I told him all I had learned. That Sonora Silvio may have seen Davey Hooper and Zoey Channer in the same car. I filled him in about Juniper Jones and Les Urquhart and Zoey Channer, especially the fact that Zoey smoked and had been at the party. She may have seen something in the smoking pit or even been a part of something. "The waitress at the café, Susan, told me Urquhart has been hanging around a guy who sounds a lot like Davey Hooper. There could be a connection there, Virgil."

"There could be," he said, nodding. "I'll look into it. And I mean *I'll* look into it, Merry. Stay out of it."

I wouldn't promise, not while Pish was a suspect. Instead, I said, "Well, I'm sure your buddy counterpart in Ridley Ridge will help you out."

"Not likely."

"What do you mean?"

"I don't get along with Sheriff Baxter."

I waited, but no explanation was forthcoming. "Okay, Virgil, why don't you get along with Sheriff Baxter?"

He shifted in his seat and wheeled off the road and up my drive. "I divorced his daughter," he replied and gunned it.

"What? Your ex-wife is the next town's sheriff's daughter?" I gabbled, hanging on to the hand rest at the sudden acceleration. "Who was she? What was her name? Why did you divorce?"

He parked, looked over at me, and said, "I don't talk about it. Ever." Then he got out of the car.

I would have pursued it, but I didn't have the opportunity—I was distracted by the scene in front of the castle. There had been no rain at the castle, but the sky was still gloomy. The parking space in front of the castle held, besides Jack's Smart car, a tow truck and two Cadillacs; one was the old one that had been in the garage out back, and the other was brand new and familiar to me. Caddy one had a mechanic bent over the hood, with Gordy and Zeke clustered around, and Caddy two had Percy Channer and the driver standing outside of it talking to Pish, Shilo, and McGill. I took a deep breath and let it out slowly as I emerged from the car and circled to stand next to Virgil.

"Does that bozo worry you? The fireplug guy?" Virgil muttered.

Surprised by his perspicacity, I said, "Not really, but he's Zoey Channer's multimillionaire father. I think we ought to tell him about his daughter, if he doesn't already know."

"Let me handle it."

As I stood by the police car, I looked over at Pish, Shilo, and Jack and shook my head at them, putting one finger to my mouth. We needed to let this play out without interference.

Of course, at this point, I had completely forgotten about the blood on my clothes, so I didn't get why my friends looked so alarmed. I followed as Virgil strode toward Channer, who whirled, his pudgy face suffused with dark red. The multi-millionaire was about to duck around Virgil to come at me, bellyaching about his daughter, but the sheriff put out one arm and halted him in his tracks.

The driver/bodyguard made a move to intervene, but Channer held up his hand. "It's okay," he said to his edgy employee. He adjusted his expression to one more concili-atory, even though his face was still red. He looked me over, then asked, "Has my daughter, Zoey, been here?"

"That's a good question," I replied. "You should ask her that."

His lip trembled into a sneer and his chin lowered, mak-ing him look even more like a bulldog. "I keep hearing she's been to your place, and been around that town, that Autumn Valley or whatever the eff it's called, but no one will talk to me." His anxiety was ratcheting up as he spoke, and he moved jerkily, fists on his hips, his feet apart. "What gives? You hiding her? If you are, I'll have your tail in court so fast it'll make—"

"Stop right there," Virgil growled, gripping the man's shoulder as my friends trooped toward us. "I wouldn't advise threats toward Miss Wynter."

"What do you expect?" he griped, wresting himself from Virgil's hold as his chauffeur/bodyguard trembled in anx-ious abeyance. "My daughter has been hanging around some lowlife jail scum, and I want her back where she's supposed to be, in New York."

"Lowlife jail scum?" I said. "Do you know what this guy looks like?"

"I haven't seen him," he admitted, squinting over at me.

"Hear he's got long hair. Can't stand long hair on a guy. Didn't like it when I was a kid, don't like it now. When I came here to find her . . ." He paused. "I mean, I'm looking for her everywhere. Need to keep her out of trouble."

I noticed the mistake, and I didn't think he meant the first time he barged into my castle. "You *did* come to my party, didn't you?" How had he gotten in? How had he been dressed? And why hadn't he checked in at the door? I had invited him, for goodness sake. Of course, if he'd had evil intentions, he would not have wanted to make himself known. He struck me as a guy who liked to do things his own way.

Virgil went still beside me, and I could feel tension radiating from him. Percy Channer was an unknown factor, one of the unaccounted-for guests. This could be very important.

Percy sneered. "Maybe I did get in, and maybe I didn't; you don't need to know. But you oughta ask yourself: how much were you paying the waitresses? Right? You weren't paying the serving staff much, I'd bet. Money talks."

Virgil was listening and watching, as were Shilo, Pish, and McGill, while the gearheads still piddled around with the old caddy. For once, the sheriff stayed silent. I could ask and say things he, as a police official, could not, and I was willing to take advantage of that. I thought for a moment, as Percy eyed me with suspicion, then said, "You paid off Juniper Jones, I'll bet. I'll let you in on a little secret; she was only trying to get rid of your daughter and would have let you in for free. Didn't you see Zoey? She was *here*, all right, at the party. Did you miss her? Again?"

"Damn it!" Percy exploded, shaking his fist in the air, his face getting red down to his thick neck. "How the (expletive) does she keep getting away from me?"

Virgil was restive, and I knew I had not taken the

investigative route he would have preferred. He was right, if that's what he was thinking. I had blown my chance just so I could take a cheap shot at the guy; I guess I'm not much of a Watson.

"Mr. Channer, we have some things to talk about, but not here," Virgil said. "If you would have your driver follow me to the police station—" He took the shorter man's elbow, ready to lead him back to his car, but Channer surprised him by yelping and cringing.

"Get away from me. Police brutality!" He whirled toward his chauffeur. "You dingbat, what am I paying you for?" As the chauffeur leaped to get between his employer and the sheriff, Percy sneered at Virgil, "I don't need your crap; I'm just looking for my daughter."

I was horrified by his swift and weird changes in personality. The chauffeur had now leaped over to the car and was opening the back door. I did not envy that guy his job, looking after someone like Percy Channer.

Virgil didn't rise to the bait, but did say, through gritted teeth, "If you truly want to know where your daughter is, you'll need to talk to *me*. She's in the hospital right now."

"Hospital? What happened to her?" He glared over at me, and his eyes traveled my body, pausing on my sweater. "Did *you* hurt her? If you did, I'll have you locked up so fast you'll spin like a top."

"I did *not* hurt her," I exclaimed, shocked at the suggestion. "Why would you even think . . . ?" I stopped as Shilo, eyes wide, glanced up and down at my bloodstained sweater and slacks. "Oh. That. This is her blood, actually, but I didn't—"

"What is going on?" Channer shouted, stamping his foot and balling his fists, punching them in the air. His face and thick neck were completely suffused with red. "Where is my daughter?" he screamed.

I backed away toward my friends, alarmed.

"She's in Ridley Ridge," Virgil said. "Mr. Channer, I can take—"

"Then I don't (expletive) need you at all, do I? You try to manhandle me again, cop," he said, jabbing his finger at Virgil, "and I will have a lawyer on the phone suing your ass so fast, you'll have to ask my permission to fart." He stalked away to his car, shouting at his chauffeur to find out where the hospital was and drive him to it. He got in and slammed the door as the chauffeur hopped in and gunned the motor, and they took off down my drive.

"What a *jerk*!" McGill said, and I think every person in earshot would have agreed with him.

Virgil was furious; I could tell by the way his jaw twitched. But his tone was even as he turned to me and said, "I'll bet I know now the identity of a short, stocky Dracula seen arguing with Hooper. One of your out-of-town guests witnessed it and told me, but we didn't have an ID on the man." He shook his head, a look of disgust on his face. He glanced over at me and said, "I shouldn't have said that; I'm just guessing."

"It's okay. I'll keep it under my wig."

He smiled. "I have to go." He cupped my shoulder and moved closer, staring down into my eyes. "Merry, please stay out of this. It's a vicious murder, and I don't want you mixed up in it."

My breath caught at his warm tone of voice. "I'll be careful."

"That's not what I told you to do," he murmured. "Stay *out* of it, Merry; I mean it. Let me do my job. I've got to go." He jumped in his car and zoomed off after Channer.

I took a moment to compose myself before turning back to my friends, who were watching, wide-eyed. Just then I heard the roar of an engine and a celebratory hoot from Gordy and Zeke. "What's going on?" I asked, heading that way.

Pish smiled slightly, creases bracketing his mobile mouth. "I think we could ask the same of you, but given that I'm assuming—thank heavens—that is *not* your blood smeared all over you, I will wait for my explanation until after our little surprise." Shilo skipped over to me as Pish took my arm and started me strolling toward the old car. "Darling, I know you've been looking around for a mechanic, but I found Mr. Hayes, the best one in a fifty-mile radius, and invited him out to fix the Caddy. He came, hauled it out of the garage, and took a look at the engine. It needed a bit of work, but look . . . he's got it going!"

"What *is* it?" I asked with trepidation, listening to the engine, which sounded pretty darn good, actually, given that it must not have been started for a long time. I circled it, which was a looong walk. "I mean, I know it's a Cadillac, but . . . what is it?"

The mechanic, a skinny older fellow with gappy teeth and grease-covered hands, said, "Ma'am, she's a beauty, that's what she is." He wiped his hands on a rag and caressed the smooth, dust-covered line of the cream-colored body. "A 1967 Cadillac Fleetwood Brougham, good body, low mileage, gorgeous ride. Like a well-built woman," he went on, looking me over with a grin and waggling straggly eyebrows.

I didn't mind being compared to the Cadillac, except that it looked like it could use a good scrub. Actually, that described me at that moment, too, after the dustup with Juniper and Zoey. Did I have a lot to tell my friends!

"Mr. Lincoln, I'm gonna take it back to the shop and give it a good once-over. Gordy here is gonna drive it for me, since, miracle of miracles, it seems to be running all right.

It'll do it good to get out on the highway and have a run. Work all the kinks out. Just like a woman," Hayes said, with a wink in my direction. "She gets a little rusty without good hands on her."

"This is the surprise you guys were working on!" I exclaimed. For a week they had been whispering together and laughing, and yet wouldn't tell me what it was about. I was relieved it was just this.

Pish turned to me and took my skinned and bloodied hands, the remnant of my scuffle with Juniper, in his own. "My gift, darling," he said. "It'll save us all from having to rent vehicles, or use Shilo's . . ." He paused and looked around, a puzzled frown twisting his lips.

My friend also perked up and looked around, then down the lane, as if she expected her heap to materialize out of the woods. "Where's my car, Merry?" Shilo asked. "Where's Jezebel?"

"That is a long story," I said. "Short version: the jalopy is broken down and still sitting in the town that decency forgot."

"What were you doing in Ridley Ridge?" Pish asked. "And does it have anything to do with the blood on your clothes?"

"Like I said, long story. Mr. Hayes, could you do me a huge favor?" I asked him to help us out with Shilo's car, and he agreed to go take a look. I handed him the keys.

"Anything for you," he said with a slow wink and a toothy smile. "I live out that way anyway. Can take a look as I'm taking the girl home." He patted the fender again.

"My poor baby!" Shilo mourned, and McGill pulled her to him and whispered that he'd take her to see her Jezebel the next day. She would probably take the car flowers and sing to it. *Kumbaya, my car, kumbaya.*

Zeke and Gordy got into the Caddy and pulled slowly down the lane, followed by Mr. Hayes in his tow truck. I had a car—or I would if the Caddy worked out; it was a strange feeling. I hadn't owned a car in years.

I was exhausted and still had a lot to tell my friends, but a hot shower and food would come first.

As it turned out, Pish was the only one left by the time I got out of the shower and into yoga pants and a long T-shirt. He and I settled by the fireplace in the kitchen with a pot of tea on the low table between us, and a selection of Chopin nocturnes lilting through the castle from the sound system. Becket snoozed on the hearth, two inches from having his whiskers singed. I was breaking my own rules about a cat in the kitchen, but we were nowhere near the work area. I pondered what I had learned and experienced that day.

"So . . . how did you come to be covered in blood?" he asked, pouring me a cup.

I told him everything, from my stops in Autumn Vale to my impulse drive into Ridley Ridge and the resulting fracas. "I feel like there are a hundred threads in this thing, and not a one of them is woven in with the others."

"Such as?"

I took a long drink of perfectly brewed tea, sighed, and sat back. "Such as . . . we have a whole lot of players here, all connected in some way: Zoey Channer, Percy Channer, Les Urquhart, Juniper Jones, Davey Hooper. And you." I watched him. "I've been assuming Davey Hooper was here because this is close to where his brother died, but do you think Davey Hooper was perhaps here to track you down?"

Pish shook his head. "There is no reason to think that it's anything more than a huge coincidence. How would he even know I was here? And why, if he was tracking me, did he not contact me?"

That was a good point, and it answered one of my other questions, which was if Hooper had contacted Pish. So, no. "And you didn't arrive at Wynter Castle until the very moment his mother was being arrested, so your whereabouts certainly could not get back to him that way." I thought about it, but I just couldn't figure a way that Pish's location could have gotten back to Davey Hooper. "So he was here at the castle for some other reason. Why?"

Pish stared into the fire. I watched his face and wondered: What kept him here? Why was he so determined to help me? Though I have never known his age, I have always known that he is old enough to be my father, if just barely. He treats me like an ideal father and worries over me. He and Miguel were so close, and . . . was that it?

"Pish, I have a completely unrelated question for you."

"Yes, my darling child?" He smiled over at me, the flickering flames lighting up his eyes and highlighting the faint creases around them.

"Your whole life is in New York City . . . your friends, your family, the opera, the symphony . . . your *life*! Why did you decide to stay here with me?" The enormity of his sacrifice weighed on me suddenly, like something sitting on my chest. "Does it have anything to do with Miguel?"

He pondered that for a while. We sat enjoying the lovely piano music and the crackle of the fire. "Miguel and I both loved the opera, as you know. That is what drew us together as friends rather than just investor and advisor."

I nodded. At first I had not understood their adoration of opera, or what Shilo calls "foreign folks in fancy dress screeching how much they hate each other in Italian." But I have come to enjoy some bits and pieces of classical opera. I get the feeling that comes through, although I don't understand the words.

"I knew him as well as anyone, and even more than his family, he once said. He called me his brother." Pish glanced over at me, then back to the fire. "I had seen him with other women, but once he met you, there was no one else and never would be. When he introduced you to me, I understood."

I was mystified, as I had long been. Miguel had been sophisticated and worldly, where I was not. Pish was deeply intelligent and just as sophisticated. What did these two men see in me? It was not false modesty that had me puzzled; I am a good person, and smart. I am attractive and compassionate. But I'm also deeply flawed, hasty, and impulsive at times; full of faults. They, both Miguel and Pish, had always seemed to be so much *more*.

"You still don't understand, do you?" Pish asked gently. I shook my head.

"You were his rock, someone with whom to build a life. Miguel didn't speak of it much, but his first wife cheated on him many times, and it wounded his soul. He was a passionate man, more sensitive than he let on. Besides the deep love he felt for you, he knew he could trust you, and so do I. Trust is a rare commodity." He paused, his feelings too heartfelt for easy expression. "We were both so grateful for you being you."

I reached out blindly and he took my hand, squeezing it. For a time I thought about Miguel and what we would have built if we'd had the time. He would have made me a better person, because he was so good himself. I had been jealous of what I perceived as his mother's hold over him—she disliked me, and I found her difficult—instead of being grateful that he was so good to her and what that revealed about him. I hope I would have overcome those feelings and justified his faith in me, given time.

But thinking of Miguel, as painful as it was, was thinking

about my past. There was no future with my beloved husband, and I was at peace with how our relationship had developed. I would have grown as a person, within our love, and become a better mate to him in time, if I had only been given that chance.

My heart hurt, though, for the relationship with which I was left. Though I would have trusted him with my life, there were still things Pish did not share with me. I was sure it was a habit born of his care for me and determination not to burden me, but still . . . He had subtly changed at the end of Virgil's questioning, and that led me to wonder: had Pish Lincoln ever paid Davey Hooper off, and had that crook followed my friend to Wynter Castle looking for more? It wasn't that I didn't trust Pish, but he kept trying to shield me from the harsh realities of life, even though I didn't need protection anymore. I was hurt that he had not told me about being sued in the first place. Was he protecting me again? Or still?

I could never ask him that because I didn't want to imply doubt and I didn't trust myself to be able to explain correctly how I felt. It didn't matter anyway. Even if Hooper had come looking for money from Pish, my dear friend would never kill a human. Unless he was protecting someone he loved, someone like me. But no . . . he would *never* slash someone's throat.

"Where were we?" I asked with false brightness, tired of the back-and-forth in my brain. "I think we can safely assume Percy Channer was here to try to get his daughter back."

"But why was Zoey here?" Pish asked. "And why was she watching the house from the woods?"

"That's what I can't figure out. She reminds me, though, of the kind of kid who belonged to that wannabe gang in LA who robbed people's houses for fun."

My friend nodded. "Maybe you're on to something. Could that involve Les Urquhart, too? And Davey Hooper and maybe even Juniper Jones?"

It was an attractive theory; a falling-out among thieves with one of them as the murderer. Alternately, Percy Channer made a great suspect as the angry father determined to take his daughter away to keep her out of trouble. Had Davey Hooper had a confrontation with Channer? It sounded like Virgil had concluded that, from his statement, he now knew the identity of the fat vampire who'd argued with the cowboy.

We sat in silence for a long while, and I looked over to find Pish drowsing off. "I'm going to tell Virgil all we've talked about," I said.

Pish opened his eyes and smiled over at me. "I think I nodded off. You do that, my dear, tomorrow. Right now I am getting these weary old bones to bed."

Chapter Fourteen

※ ※ ※

THE NEXT MORNING, I felt miles better. I'd had a good sleep and wonderful dreams, though I wasn't going to tell *anyone* that those dreams had involved Virgil Grace and his throaty voice and marvelous hands and swirl of chest hair. Not a single person. Especially not him.

I hadn't thought of Miguel all day the day before until Pish and I had spoken of him in the evening, and though a little guilt tugged at me, I had always known in my heart that my darling husband would *not* have wanted me to mourn as long as I had. Oddly enough, Wynter Castle and Autumn Vale were doing what New York had never been able to. If I was beginning to move ahead with life, beyond the pain of losing the most wonderful man I had ever known, Miguel would be happy for me.

After the gloom of the previous misty, rainy day, a bold and beautiful morning followed a foggy dawn. It was November 1, All Saints' Day. Over breakfast, Pish and I told

Shilo what had gone on the day before and what we had discussed. Shilo was going to see her darling wreck. McGill picked her up right after breakfast, and they headed out to confer with Mr. Hayes, the mechanic, who had towed Jezebel to his shop.

I called the sheriff's office but was told Virgil was out of town. I left a message for him to contact me when he got back, and was told he had left a message for me: the "scene," as the policewoman called it, had been released, and I could clean it up if I so desired.

Well, goody gumdrops for me.

How could Virgil leave town in the middle of a murder investigation? That only fueled my desperation to solve the murder of Davey Hooper and clear Pish of any involvement.

I had other things to do. Elwood Fitzhugh was coming out for lunch and to tell me what he knew about my mother, and before that, I was determined to make some headway in the turret bedroom. But first . . . oh, first I had to face my fear and go look at the scene of the crime, and I had to do it alone. For too long I had been leaning on Pish in every crisis. He was a good and loyal friend, but his reluctance to tell me anything sad or difficult revealed volumes about the amount of my life I had placed on his shoulders. I had come to Autumn Vale alone, knowing in my heart that I had to start facing my battles head-on; the crime scene was a battle I chose to *win* on my own.

Pish was ensconced in his suite working on his next book, the follow up to *Cons, Scams, and Flimflams*, this one specifically having to do with banking scams and the folks who create them using naïve insiders and employees. The situation at Autumn Vale Community Bank was tailor-made for the book, and he had the inside track. His first book had been a resounding success, and this one, with his trademark wit and drollery, would no doubt be the same. Somehow he could make a dull subject like banking fascinating.

And I was going to clean up a crime scene. I took a bucket of suds, a cloth, and a scouring brush, not knowing what to expect. I hadn't seen the area since the night of the party. I opened one of the big terrace doors and stepped out into the cold, clear air, taking a deep breath first and staring off at the far forest, a solid edge of green pines and brown trees. Then, quivering slightly, I stepped along the terrace to my hastily constructed smoking pit.

There was a short bit of crime-scene tape left, fluttering from the stone wall, but nothing else beyond the tables and chairs, the propane outdoor heater, and the lantern. I had already been told that the police were confident that the murder had indeed been committed out on the terrace, but it took me a while to make any sense of that. The casket was gone, and there was no sign of the mannequin. In fact, it was hard to tell that anything at all untoward had happened.

But then I began to see the evidence of the crime: rusty splatters on the pea gravel, a rut where the coffin had been dragged, and there, on my castle wall, a brownish stain in the shape of a hand. I set down the bucket and wandered over and put my hand up against it. It was almost the same size as mine, and the breath was sucked right out of my chest.

I remembered the night, and crouching by the body, so vividly . . . Had I put my hands on him? Yes, I had, and I thought there had been a wetness. Was the handprint my own? I stared at it, but though I vaguely remembered wiping my hands on my dress, I did *not* remember putting my hand on the stone. I examined the stain more closely, but to my untrained eye it was just the shadowy outline of a palm and some fingers. I put my hand over it. Now, with my brain more in gear, I thought the handprint indicated a hand slightly smaller than mine. A woman, then, had been at the scene of the crime, but which woman? Zoey Channer? Juniper Jones?

I lost heart and decided to leave the cleanup to Zeke and Gordy. Baby steps to independence, I thought . . . baby steps. A half hour later, I was painting trim, my dark hair wrapped up in a scarf so it wouldn't end up paint-flecked and my legs clad in an old pair of Miguel's cargo pants. He'd loved cargo pants for the numerous pockets that he'd used to stow stuff in, even when he'd had his assistant doing all the filter and lens changes. He was a big man, so the pants sagged on me, but they were comfortable and comforting.

It took two more hours to finish the trim in the turret bedroom, and I finally worked my way up to the curved section of ceiling that had been coated with wallpaper, of all things. It was hard to describe: the wall curved up to the ceiling, but the curvature was bracketed by raised filigree all the way around the room, similar to the design in the great hall. The castle was so big that I felt like my eyes were only capable of seeing so much at a time. As a result, I kept discovering new design features, nuances and details I hadn't the vision to see previously. Maybe it was just that I was putting new, stronger lighting in every room as we cleaned and painted.

I climbed the twelve-foot ladder feeling a little shaky and peeled back an edge of the wallpaper, seeing if it would come off intact. I was going to have to decide if this curved area should be painted like the wall, in the straw yellow, or the ceiling, a soft ivory.

I misted it with dishsoap and tepid water, let it soak in—I have stripped many an acre of wallpaper, and I have my methods—then peeled off a big hunk of the paper. I stared at the result, astounded. Maybe the frieze would not be painted at all. Under the wallpaper, I revealed a patch of peachy paint with some kind of design. I worked carefully and slowly, forgetting my fear of the ladder, and finally sat on the top, gazing up in awe at the treasure I had uncovered by pulling off a four-foot section of wallpaper. In one fell swoop I had changed my idea about the whole direction of the room's color and décor.

What I had uncovered was a lovely painted border of celestial blue and peach, with puffy clouds and putti—classical representations of chubby children with wings, peeking out mischievously from behind clouds. The frieze was gorgeous, and the wall below and the ceiling above would need to be painted in complementary colors to offset it appropriately. Peach for the walls, I thought, and blue for the ceiling. Whoever had covered it up with wallpaper had probably done it a favor, preserving it. If I could get all the wallpaper off without damaging it, I'd have a gem. So far, so good.

Somewhere in my family's past, someone—a wife, an owner, or a designer—had good taste and adequate resources, enough to hire a professional painter who had an awareness of classical painting. The frieze could not be original to the 1820s but had likely been done in the Victorian or the Edwardian era. Had my ancestors traveled and been inspired by the great houses of Europe? I was beginning to wish I could know them, understand them better.

I was sobered by my find, but time dictated that I stop. I cleaned up and prepared for my lunch with Elwood Fitzhugh in a thoughtful frame of mind. How could I bear to part with so much family history, undiscovered as of yet? My mother's family had very little in the way of information. A couple of generations of only daughters had left a shallow maternal pool, and neither my grandmother nor my mother had talked about family much. They'd died when I was still a callow twenty-one-year-old, self-absorbed and uninterested in such things as family history. But the Wynter family . . . well. There was a history here.

I did my hair up in a French twist, fastening it at the side with a clip Miguel had found in a French antique store, and dressed in an Anna Scholz belted-tunic-and-pants outfit, then descended to make lunch: salad, soup, and savory herb muffins. I had found a straggly patch of herbs growing in the once-great garden; there was oregano, thyme, savory, tarragon . . . lots of hardy perennials. I used to grow them in little pots on my New York windowsill, and here they were growing practically wild! I had snipped and dried a lot, but even in early November the weather was mild enough that I was still able to pick fresh for the muffins.

I thought my new friend would appreciate being fed in the breakfast parlor rather than the kitchen, so I cleared the round rosewood table, put on a hand-tatted vintage lace tablecloth that I had found at Janice's Crazy Lady Antiques and Collectibles, and laid it with my own china. I was such a romantic when I married Miguel; my china pattern was Royal Doulton's Juliet, a lovely ornate pink-and-blue pattern that suited the lace tablecloth. I did not have the matching soup tureen, but I had found a beautiful vintage one at Janice's. It was Blue Willow and had a small chip under the lip but looked magnificent in the center of the table filled with cauliflower and cheddar soup.

I stepped back to look it over, and tears filled my eyes. Miguel would have loved this place! Soaring gothic arched windows flooded the room with light on this bright, clear, chilly November day, and the big Eastlake sideboard, now filled with china and my beloved teapots—the very best of the best for this room—gave the place interest. There were a few old paintings on the gold-and-cream papered walls—landscapes, mostly—and comfortable chairs surrounding the table. I had never dressed it for a meal before, and the tears surprised me. I adored the castle.

Elwood was prompt, and Pish joined us. The two gentlemen kept the conversation light and varied. The former zoning commissioner shared the result of the meeting the day before, that he had been asked to come back to work for a time just to help Autumn Vale out. There was a mess left by Junior Bradley, who was now jobless and skulking about town in shame, and Elwood felt an obligation to assist. I thought the town would be in good hands, and I looked forward to working with him on the confusion over the zoning of my castle property.

After lunch we enjoyed a cup of coffee and piece of pie. Pish doesn't cook much, but he is a genius with pies. He had made Dutch apple for our guest, and it was delicious.

"So," Elwood said, sitting back and patting his small, rounded belly. "You want to know about your mother, eh?"

"I do."

"Well, I remember her very well, and this is why: she called Melvyn Wynter a fascist reactionary reprobate. Your mama did not mince words."

Chapter Fifteen

❊ ❊ ❊

I WAS STUNNED at first, then I laughed. That was my mother, all right. He had certainly met her—not that I'd had any doubt—and spent enough time with her to hear her political views, likes, and dislikes.

"Melvyn Wynter was my brother, you understand, of the Falconry," Elwood went on. "I'd been a member from early on. But she wasn't far off about a lot of things. Melvyn was a feisty cuss even then, and he only got worse."

"I've heard all about him," I said. I told him all I knew about my great uncle, from his hermit ways to his tendency to drive people off his land with a cocked rifle.

Elwood hadn't heard much of this because after he retired he spent most of his time in Florida and traveling. "Bored myself stupid," he said. "Had to come back home to get some excitement! I'm just not a Florida sort, I guess."

"What did you think of my mother?" I asked, returning the topic to my past.

A gleam of appreciation twinkled in his eyes. "She sure was a looker, almost as pretty as you," he said, winking one eye.

Pish smirked and snickered. I gave him a cross-eyed look. I had seen Elwood's behavior toward the ladies—he was an equal-opportunity flirt—and did not want to encourage him.

"I was a young buck myself, just on the sad side of forty and divorced. Wouldn't have minded taking her out for drinks and dancing, but I never did ask. She had you in tow and was headed back to New York City." He frowned. "Besides, she didn't seem to set much store by having fun."

If he only knew. My mother's idea of fun was rabble-rousing, and she loved a good picket line. While I appreciated her civic mindedness, it wouldn't have hurt her to lighten up a little. He then told me about his ride into Rochester with my mother and myself. It was like stepping back thirty-four years.

I was in the backseat, kneeling and looking out the car window; there were no seat belt laws back then to restrain me. It seems to me that the car radio was playing oldies, like Buddy Holly and Bill Haley. I vividly remember "Rock Around the Clock" because I was bopping along to it and humming. Mom told me to hush. She favored Joan Baez folk over old time rock 'n' roll.

"Charmaine asked me what I thought of Melvyn," Elwood said. "I said he was an okay sort if you didn't cross him, but stubborn as all get-out if you did. Melvyn and I dealt just fine because we didn't have much to talk about but Brotherhood issues. She said he was . . . well, she called him something I won't say in mixed company, and then she shot a look over her shoulder at you, but you were playing some kinda game of your own. You were a dreamy kid, lost in your own world."

That was true of me until we moved to Grandma's apartment. Looking back, I know that losing Daddy meant I'd lost the most fun fellow I have ever known and the love of my life until I met Miguel. I had a kind of epiphany in that moment, that losing two men I'd cared about had made me afraid to love someone too much. I'd think about that later. Maybe. "Did she say why it bugged her that Melvyn asked if she wanted to move here?"

"Well, that's the thing," Elwood said. "He didn't so much ask as demand, is my impression."

That would have angered my mother, all right. "I know my father spent time here as a kid, but do you know how much? Doc, Melvyn's old friend, has been kind of close-mouthed about anything to do with my dad and grandfather." As soon as I said it, I regretted it. It implied an aura of secrecy, and my guest picked up on that, his saggy bloodhound eyes squinting.

Elwood twisted up his mouth and nodded. "Lemme think on that," he said, his gray eyes misty with evasion.

What the heck was everyone keeping from me? I shifted my butt on the seat. "Please, Elwood, I just want to know more about my family! What's wrong with that?"

Pish reached out and covered my hand with his. I felt the warmth of his touch, and it soothed me.

Elwood nodded. "I know; nothin' wrong with it at all. Not many as remember the old days. I'm not trying to be a pain in the bee-hind, I just need to think on it. There was a falling out between Mel and Murg, and it had to do with your daddy, but I don't think I'm remembering all the details. Give an old fellow a little time."

"Surely you remember what the falling out was over and can tell me at least briefly," I said, clutching Pish's hand, feeling like I was close to understanding or finding out something about the father who was just a shadow figure and the grandfather I'd never known.

Elwood rose suddenly, stretching out his shoulders and flexing his hands. "Need to move, get the kinks out," he said. "Show me around? I'd sure like to see the old place again. Haven't been here since 1983, when we had a Brotherhood dinner and dance at the castle."

That was a new one. A dinner and dance at the castle in my great uncle's time? Okay, if Elwood wanted to walk and talk, then that's what we would do. Except that he was a master of small talk and even better at avoiding questions, so I learned nothing more of significance. We finished up in the turret room I was working on. Pish hadn't seen my find from that morning, and he was stunned.

"Oh, my *darling*, this is magnificent!" he said in a hushed voice.

Elwood stared up at the frieze. "It surely is," he said, his voice echoing in the high-ceilinged room.

"I can't imagine who would have covered it up," I said.

"Melvyn, I'd guess," Elwood said, his tone dry. "Old Mel was a master at covering things up."

"What do you mean?" I asked sharply. There was a subtext there that I did not yet understand.

The old man glanced down at his watch, and exclaimed, "Well, boy howdy, am I late! I'm s'posed to take a lady out to dinner, but her idea of dinner is the early bird buffet in Batavia, so I'd best get a move on."

He headed out of the room and to the stairs while Pish and I trailed him, me stupefied by the continuing string of half stories about my great uncle, grandfather, and father. Elwood clattered down the stairs to the great hall as we followed.

"Elwood, perhaps you can elaborate for Merry," Pish said, as the older man took his jacket from a hook on the oak Eastlake hall tree and shrugged it on. "She knows so little."

"Maybe. We'll talk some more. I *can* tell you: there is a bit about your family history in a book. If you can get ahold of it—"

"Yes, I think Hannah gave me a book on the Autumn Vale area and the Wynter family practically the day I got here," I said. "Is that the one you mean? I've been so busy, but I think I still have it somewhere."

"Read that, and then we'll get back together sometime and I'll tell you what I can. I don't know everything, you know. Just bits and pieces."

He was already heading out the door, and I had to be satisfied with that, even though he had left me with more questions than when I'd started. There seemed to be some kind of family mystery to do with Melvyn and my grandfather, Murgatroyd, and I just wanted to know what it was. Once he was gone, I went back up to the turret room with Pish and we lay on the floor, staring at the little section of frieze I had uncovered and the cavorting putti.

"It's so beautiful," I said.

"It's going to take time, though, certainly. But the more you do *this*," he said, waving his hand at the peeled-back wallpaper, "the more valuable the castle becomes."

I turned my head and watched him. He seemed lost in thought. "What have you got up your sleeve?"

He smiled. "Nothing at all; just trying to figure out a way to give you the time you need to fix this joint up. To change the subject: have you given any more thought to the puzzle in Becket's collar?"

I frowned up at the ceiling. "I know I should have been looking into it, but do you think it's anything more than a paranoid old guy's fantasy?"

"Who knows? You were wondering where all his money went."

"True. It's getting kind of cold for a walk in the woods, but I'll go if you'll go."

"Tomorrow morning, then, if the weather is decent. You and me and Becket, and maybe Shilo and McGill."

I lay there and thought for a long moment. "What do you think of that, Pish? McGill wants to marry her, you know."

"I know." He reached out and took my hand, squeezing it. "I've often worried what would happen if she didn't have you, my darling. And I've worried that you are too caught up in taking care of people, *especially* Shilo, to look after your own needs. Those needs being possibly met by the *delicious* Sheriff Virgil Grace."

"Pish, enough," I warned. "He has shown no interest at all in me."

"Well, now, I wouldn't exactly say that. And not *showing* it is different than not being interested. Anyone who knows you just for a short time knows how you still feel about Miguel. Virgil Grace does not strike me as the kind of man to compete with a dead saint."

I stood, and so did Pish. "That was hurtful, Pish. Please don't talk about Miguel that way."

He reached out and cradled my face in his warm hands. "Honey, you *know* how much I loved Miguel Paradiso. He was an extraordinary man, and my friend. I didn't mean anything, except that you have idealized the man over the last seven . . . no, *eight* . . . years since he was killed."

I took a deep breath and shook it off. "I don't know how we got from talking about Shilo's love life to mine, but that is it for me."

Pish was silent, but he pulled me to him and wrapped me

in his arms. "All right, I won't press. We'll concentrate on your late uncle and the mystery he concocted."

I laid my head on his shoulder and then pulled away and went to look for the book on Autumn Vale and the Wynter family history. After dinner I read long into the night, and what I learned was fascinating. And illuminating. It gave me a lot to mull over about the Wynter family.

The next morning was frosty and brilliant, with a sparkling rime on the grass that caught the rising sun. It was like faeries had scattered diamonds over everything. We dressed warmly, and Pish, Shilo, and I were just heading out, with the able accompaniment of Becket the wonder cat, when McGill pulled up and screeched to a halt. He leapt from his car—a more difficult feat than it sounds, given his height and the tininess of his car—and we all headed toward the woods with a written list of the trees and info found on the cat's collar.

We had developed a theory that the list of tree names was a path that would lead us to whatever treasure my uncle had hidden. I had no clue what to expect, but it would require time and patience, and I didn't have much hope of success. However, a treasure hunt was a nice respite from thinking about murder and worrying about the castle. I handed Shilo a book on upstate New York trees I had borrowed from Hannah's library and took the small shovel from Pish and handed it to McGill. I needed Pish's brain engaged, not his body. I had the list of trees, copied from Becket's tag; the cat was our mascot.

"Tallyho, my intrepid band. Our reward will be split equally, whatever treasure we find." As we approached the forest, I inhaled deeply. One of my favorite things about walking in the woods is the scents: the heady drift of wood and dampness, the aroma of leaves fallen underfoot as you crunch through them, and the meaty smell of nuts.

"What is the first tree on the list?" Pish asked, shifting aside the camera he had around his neck. He loves photography, and it was no surprise he had the camera with him. He was not as good a photographer as Lizzie, but he was certainly adequate.

"*Quercus macrocarpa*," I pronounced awkwardly, reading from the list.

"Sounds like a big fish," McGill joked.

I groaned as Shilo giggled. "I get it: macro carpa," I said. "Ha ha. What does it look like?"

Pish grabbed the book out of Shilo's hand, since she was too busy with other things to focus on the work at hand. He flipped through the pages. "Aha! Bur oak with one *r*, sometimes spelled *b-u-r-r oak*. If it was planted fifty years ago or so, it will be tall, even though it grows slowly, about a foot a year." He held out the book, and I saw a cluster of oak leaves with an acorn.

"I know this tree," I shouted with glee, poking the photo with one finger. I went directly to where it stood, alone and majestic, ten feet or more beyond the edge of the forest. It was gnarled and still held a lot of its leaves, though they were brown and crispy. Under it was a bed of acorn shells and whole acorns. "So this is our starting point . . . no big surprise," I said, since we were at the path entrance to the woods. "Next is the *Acer pseudoplatanus*. What the heck is that?"

"Uh . . . sycamore maple. Here's the photo."

It had maplelike leaves, which was no help at all now in November, but the bark was scaly, and I saw right away that the tree was one on the other side of the path into the woods. "Okay, so all it does is mark our way into the woods. Next is the *Juglans nigra*, the flowering black walnut," I said. I looked up from the list, trying not to notice Shilo and McGill, who were canoodling and kissing behind me.

"Here is a photo, my dear," Pish said, holding the book out. "It should have dropped green-husked walnuts on the ground, since that occurs in October. According to the book, we are in a little pocket in New York State where it will grow."

The tree apparently grew tall and stately when in a forest but would spread more if it was near the edge of the arboretum forest. I stepped along the path a short ways and came to some green husks, chewed through by some critter, as well as a few walnut shells. "Here!" I said, indicating the black walnut. It was a tall tree stretching up to the sun, the last leaves clinging to it a dull brown, withered and curled. "We're doing well!"

My merry—pardon the pun—little band followed the trail of trees deep into the woods, with Becket racing ahead as if he knew where we were going even before we got there. We had to venture off the beaten path, but it seemed to me that there was still a kind of path here, just not one that was used much. The discordant screech of a blue jay cut the quiet, and it chattered as we advanced, scolding us for our intrusion.

"You ought to invite some of the professors from Cornell out here, you know, to investigate your arboretum," Pish said, his voice hushed in the deep chilly shade of the woods. "I've been to their arboretum—went to a wedding there once—but this is a little wilder, less cultivated. Quite, quite amazing."

I felt a chill race down my back as I stopped to look around me. This place . . . it wasn't just an inheritance, it was a *responsibility*, and I hadn't thought of that until now. Melvyn had named me the inheritor rather than donating the estate to the town or whomever because he assumed someone with the name Wynter would care about it more than someone who might just see the commercial value of the castle and the trees. Which was basically how I was viewing it. There was so much I just didn't know about my paternal family history, and there was nowhere else I could find it out but at Wynter Castle and in Autumn Vale. The book entries I had read the previous night had just been a beginning.

Wynter Castle was my home more than any other place on earth besides New York City. For the first time I experienced a moment of certainty that I would exhaust every avenue to see if there was any way to keep this place rather than just give up on the notion. Though if Cranston ended up being my cousin, then I might have no choice but to sell to satisfy any claim he might have on the place. I would still go through with my plans to market the place for now, but I was having real doubts as to the wisdom of selling. Maybe I should be fighting tooth and nail to keep it.

But how? I just couldn't imagine.

"Where are Shilo and McGill?" I asked, then realized I was talking to myself. I looked around and spotted them nearby, at one of the faery structures Alcina had constructed by a mossy log. Shilo was sitting, and McGill was *kneeling*! It was *the* moment, the one he had told me would happen. Pish was taking photos as McGill drew out a ring box from his jacket pocket. I softly approached, coming up behind Pish as he shot photo after photo. Shilo sat trembling, staring raptly down into McGill's eyes.

"Shilo, Hannah says your name means 'peaceful,' but you say you're not peaceful at all. I disagree. You are more yourself than any person I've ever met, and that's a kind of peace." He was speaking quickly and gazing up at her with hopeful adoration. "Most folks struggle to be someone—someone else, someone important, someone who matters or makes a difference—but you . . . you just *are*. And I love you."

His voice was trembling, guttural with emotion. "It happened in a moment, that *first* moment when you asked me directions to Wynter Castle, and it gets deeper every day. If you will do me the honor of marrying me, I will make it my life's work to give you a home in my heart and in this community so you will never be lonely or afraid again."

I choked back tears. They must have talked about Shilo's desperate fear of being alone, with no one to love. McGill understood, and he had the heart to give her the love and security she needed for the rest of her life. Shilo cried, "Yes!" and threw herself into his arms. They tumbled to the forest floor, laughing and joyous, as Pish clicked away with his camera and I chuckled, viewing it all through a misty veil of tears.

McGill had to practically hold my dear friend down to push the ring on her finger, and she danced around the faery structure, a little stump hut with a tea party set of Pepto-Bismol-pink Barbie doll furniture outside of it. Pish finally stopped taking photos and stood with McGill as I dashed to my friend and pulled her into a dance. When I was out of breath, I said, "Shilo, will you just show me the ring, already?"

I had advised McGill to get a ring as unusual as Shilo, and he had done a magnificent job. It was white gold, a circle of flowers with amethyst and emerald stones alternating in the center of each posy.

"Gems have a language, you know," Shilo said. "Amethyst means 'peace,' like my name, and emerald . . ." She broke off and blushed, giving me that under-the-lashes look she was famous for. "It means 'love and rebirth' . . . new life, actually. And fertility."

McGill and Pish approached, and Jack put his arm over his new fiancée's shoulders. "Now we just have to set a date and plan the wedding!" he said.

"When do *you* want to get married?" Shilo looked up at him, her eyes shining.

"Soon as possible," McGill said fervently, tightening his grip. "You name the time and place and I'll be there with bells on."

"Christmas. At the castle!" she said, and then met my gaze. "If that's okay with you, Merry. Just our friends and that's all."

Could we do a wedding in just over a month and a half? We sure could try! I nodded, smiling at the joy it gave her.

"And now, on with the treasure hunt," McGill said, clapping his hands together and rubbing them. "I have a bottle of wine in the car for later, to celebrate whatever we find."

"Even if we don't find a thing, we'll have something to celebrate!" I said.

Chapter Sixteen

�֍ ✖ ✖

BECKET CAME CRASHING toward us through the woods and I jumped, then we heard bickering voices. "Who the heck could that be?" I asked, then hollered, *"Hello!"*

Lizzie and Alcina clambered through the bush . . . or rather, Lizzie clambered and Alcina hopped and skipped through the brush. Lizzie looked cross, her dark frizzy hair escaping from a ponytail and flying in wisps around her red face. That's a perpetual expression with Lizzie, so I wasn't concerned. Alcina seemed serene as always, her long, silky blonde hair falling in waves over her shoulders and a ratty camo jacket covering a chiffon dress that looked like a fifties vintage party dress. She wasn't wearing wings, for once. She bounced over to Shilo. Those two were kindred spirits, and it didn't surprise me when the child grabbed Shilo's hand to drag her off somewhere to see something. Shilo would tell us what it was when she got back. Alcina rarely spoke—to us, at least.

"What are you guys doing in the woods?" I asked.

"Alcina said we had to come out here early to see what the freakin' frost faeries left," she griped. "A half hour on a bicycle, freezing my butt off, just to see frost. I thought she meant something special!"

"I suppose to her it is special. I'll bet you got some great photos," I said.

"Well, of *course* I did," she said in that teenage tone that meant "duh." "What are *you* all doing here?" Lizzie's gaze took all of us in, lingering on the book and shovel. She eyed Pish's camera and nodded, looking down at her own. Hers was better, I surmised from her satisfied look. I had originally wondered where she'd gotten it, almost afraid to find out, but now knew it had been a gift from Tom Turner, her father, before he was murdered. He had told her to keep it a secret, and she said she'd thought he might have been a perv, but she'd taken the camera anyway.

Though we'll never know for sure, Binny figured Tom had wanted to give his daughter a gift, but because he hadn't yet worked things out with her mother, and hadn't acknowledged his paternity, he didn't want to tell her *why* he was giving her such a costly item. I think it became doubly valuable to Lizzie when she learned it was the only gift her father would ever be able to give her. It had given purpose and a goal in life to a kid who was going through a rough patch. How had he known to give her a camera? It made me wish I had known him apart from our very brief confrontation before his death, because his gift had been a stroke of genius.

I heard a squeal of delight off in the woods, and would have bet that Shilo had told Alcina about her engagement. "We're following my weird old uncle's treasure trail," I answered my young friend.

Lizzie's eyes lit up, gleaming with greed at the word

treasure. "What have you found? What did he leave? Was it gold? Jewels? Can I have some?"

"We haven't found anything yet, and we won't unless we get a move on. The weather looks dicey." I had been noticing the change in light for a half hour now, as a frosty brilliant morning turned gloomy above us. In the depths of the woods, you can't see much of the sky, but I was beginning to appreciate how the shifts in light revealed all you needed to know.

We moved on, with Alcina and Shilo bouncing around us like puppies at an off-leash park. The trees fascinated me as we followed my uncle's quirky path. Who knew there were so many species of oak and maple, sycamore, birch, ash, and beech? I'd always loved walking in Central Park in the different seasons, watching the changes taking place, but now I wondered about all those trees . . . what were they? Pish was right; I would need to contact someone to come and tell me more about my forest and how to take care of it.

And there I went again, thinking about the place as if I was going to be able to keep it.

We trudged on, and the forest began to thin somewhat as we crested a hill. It was as if Melvyn's tree trail had been designed to show all the beauties of Wynter Woods, as I thought of it. There were open marshy areas where wetland trees thrived, and occasional ponds around which wildlife proliferated. There were high hilly mounds and a windswept open vista or two that looked across a pine forest and down to the valley in which Autumn Vale was nestled.

I had not yet explored so much of the woods; it was a revelation and a lesson. The woods may not have been perfectly planned—and indeed there were quite a few dead or dying trees as well as some that were completely down—but still, it was glorious. My uncle had done well in planting the woods, and he had done magnificently in planning his little journey.

"This is the last tree in the list," I said. *"Nyssa sylvatica."*

Pish examined the book. "Ah, here it is. It is commonly known as the black tupelo, tupelo, or black gum. It likes a wetland area."

I looked down the hillock to a marshy area and saw a tree standing alone. I scaled down, slipping and sliding on wet leaves, and rooted around at the base—a lot of the trees had identifying markers at the base of the trunk—and uncovered a metal tag. " *'Nyssa sylvatica*: black tupelo'," I read. "Here it is."

We all looked at each other, and McGill said, "Well, no time like the present, right?" He looked up at the lowering sky, now visible because of the space in the canopy. "Gonna rain soon."

He dug, and we helped as much as we could by clearing sticks and leaves away, but mostly just watched him work. If Melvyn had buried something, it would likely be on the side where the tag was, so that's where McGill started. It wasn't long before he hit something with a hollow *thunk*. Alcina skipped and Lizzie let out a *woosh* of sound. Pish grabbed my hand and I held my breath.

McGill reached down and rooted around and yanked on something. He dug some more, then grabbed and pulled and fell backward in a great shower of dirt and leaves. We all crowded around. As Jack got back up, I wiped off the item; it was an old leather satchel. I was trembling with excitement and cold as a pelting rain started, the pitter-patter on the layer of dead leaves like tiny feet on patio stones.

I looked up. "Let's wait to open this until we get back to the castle," I said.

I was grateful that Lizzie, who knew the woods a lot

better than any of us, was there. She led us back to the actual
path, and we sped through the woods in the cold rain shower.
McGill took Shilo's newly repaired car to pick up the girls'
bikes out on the highway, making us swear to wait until he
got back before we opened the satchel.

It was the least I could do, since he had done all the actual
digging, but it was difficult looking at it sitting there, mys-
teriously full of something. So we got busy, hauling some
more comfortable chairs into the kitchen near the fireplace.
Pish laid a fire and lit it while I made some double-chocolate
muffins, coffee, tea, and cocoa.

Finally, we all gathered together with the filthy satchel
on newspapers on a low table in front of us. Lizzie had already photographed it from every possible angle: with the
fire as a backdrop, from above, and close up. With trembling
hands I worked at the latch, a shot of WD-40 squirted on it
helping immeasurably. I had discovered, in my crash course
in Care and Handling of an Old Castle, that WD-40 fixed
everything from squeaky hinges to locks that wouldn't work.

I opened the satchel and found a black plastic bag
securely wrapped in brittle duct tape. It was like unwrapping
a mummy. I carefully slit the plastic and pulled it open. Inside was a crumbling pile of documents.

"What are they? Gold certificates?" Lizzie asked.

How she would know such things exist, I could not tell
you. "I don't know what they are yet," I said, unfolding the
documents. I examined them, Pish reading over my shoulder.
When I had finished one, I looked up at him, and he shook
his head. He looked as sad as I felt. I sighed and slumped
down.

"What is it? What are they?" Shilo asked.

"They're stock certificates," I said.

"How much are they worth?" McGill asked.

"Nothing," Pish said, sadly. "Not even the paper they're printed on."

"What? Why?" Lizzie asked. She examined my face with a skeptical frown and narrowed eyes. "What do you mean they aren't *worth* anything?"

I flipped through the rest, and it confirmed Pish and my pessimism. "They're investment bonds from the early nineteen seventies for South African companies, most of them small steel manufacturing and mining," I said.

"Ah," McGill said. He understood immediately.

Pish, McGill, and I explained about apartheid, the horrible system of segregation in South Africa. I knew a lot about it because of my mother's involvement in the anti-apartheid movement in the 1980s. "Divestment—in other words, selling off investments in South African companies—was meant by other nations to pressure South Africa, to isolate it until the government repealed apartheid. As a result, some companies went belly-up," I concluded. "And we're pretty sure that these are investments in those companies."

"I recognize some of them," Pish said. "I gave seminars on ethical investment in the eighties and nineties. I used some of these companies as examples of where not to invest. Both from an ethical standpoint and from a risk standpoint, they were not good investments. Just at a glance, if they all have similar face value, I'd estimate that these were probably worth in the neighborhood of between two or three hundred thousand dollars when they were bought."

Jack whistled through his teeth. "That's some ritzy neighborhood."

Alcina giggled, but everyone else was somber.

"I think I'm beginning to understand why my mother and Melvyn did not get along," I said. "She would have been horrified if she had known about his investments. Rightly so. Conditions for black African workers under apartheid were appalling, which is one of the reasons university students across our country rallied to force their schools to divest from companies like these."

Pish got his laptop and did a little research, and confirmed our suspicions. There was not a single stock certificate in the bunch worth a dime.

I decided I couldn't mourn money I never had and never would. Despite our differences, I was still my mother's daughter, and the idea of the profit Melvyn intended to make on the broken backs of poverty-stricken African workers made me ill. I was glad they were worthless, happy those companies had gone bust.

"Who's hungry for lunch?" I asked, and got a show of hands. Everyone was, even Alcina.

I made lunch, and we ate in the breakfast room I had used just the day before for lunch with Elwood. As we finished, I decided I needed to draw Alcina out a little. She seemed silent and uncommunicative with any adult but Shilo. I rarely saw her face, since it was shielded by a curtain of silky hair. "So, Alcina, how are your lessons coming along? Do you study, or just . . . uh, read and . . . um, learn?"

She lifted her head and stared at me for a long moment, her beautiful blue eyes wide and her head cocked. I felt like she was deciding if she should talk to me or not. "I explore," she answered in her lilting voice. "My mother says if you keep your eyes and ears open, you can learn as much as from any book ever written."

I am a passionate advocate of books and didn't agree, but I needed to keep an open mind. Even from the little I had seen, it was clear that the child was already a gifted artist, and I believed the world needed to nurture artists. "What have you learned lately from keeping your ears and eyes open?"

She kept her gaze fixed on mine and said, "At your party, the dead cowboy was with the fat vampire, and the fat vampire said to him that he better get his chaps out to the terrace if he didn't want to get okay corralled. I didn't know what that meant so I asked my mom, and she told me about the Gunfight at the O.K. Corral. I read a book about it, but I don't think it happened the way they said. My mother says all written history is . . ."

She paused, searching for the right word, then said, "Suspect. She said suspect. I don't know what she meant by that. She says, 'History is a bunch of stories written by the winners.'" She paused, tilted her head to one side, and swiped her silky hair behind one ear in a Shiloesque movement. "Later I heard the cowboy died. So was he shot? Is that what the vampire meant by 'okay corralled'?"

I was bewildered by Alcina's sudden stream of verbiage, and I noticed that Lizzie looked just as surprised. "Wait . . . fat vampire?" I said, finally catching the one important part. This was independent corroboration of what Virgil had told me about a stocky Dracula and his argument with Hooper. "Did any of the rest of you notice a fat vampire?" I asked my friends. Not one of them had. "Are you sure of what you saw and heard, Alcina?" I asked. She was such a dreamy child, and I wondered if she had made the story up.

She nodded but wouldn't elaborate, saying that was it. I met Pish's gaze, and he nodded, then bustled off. I thought he was probably going to phone Virgil to give him the corroborating information and relate what Alcina had indicated about Channer telling Hooper he wanted to talk to him out on the terrace, because that fit with what we suspected about Percy Channer. How *had* he avoided me so successfully? "No, he wasn't shot," I said. "What time would this have been?"

She shrugged.

"Was it late in the evening or early? Was there anyone else around? Did anyone say anything to the fat vampire?" I watched her face. What had been bothering me for some time was that whoever killed Hooper should have had blood on him. How had that escaped notice? "Did you see him again later?"

Alcina shrugged again, and I could feel her withdrawing.

"Shilo?" I pleaded, and nodded toward the girl.

"Aly," Shilo said, and the girl looked up at her. "Why did you notice the vampire and the cowboy?"

It was not the question I would have asked, but I held my tongue.

Alcina shrugged again. "It was funny, this little fat, sweaty vampire and the tall, skinny cowboy. It was like . . . a cartoon."

"Did you notice anything else about the vampire?" I asked.

She shrugged and shook her head.

Lizzie watched me, then her gaze flicked over to Alcina. "Why didn't you tell me that stuff, Aly?" she asked, her feelings hurt.

"Let her answer me," I said to Lizzie.

But Alcina was done. She jumped up, smiled at us all briefly—a look like sunshine—then said, "I'll race you home, Lizzie."

It had stopped raining and, though it was cold, the sun was shining. I followed them outside hoping to get more info, but after offering me an apologetic shrug, Lizzie took off after Alcina. I stood on the terrace, watching them cycle down the sloping drive and disappear around the curve. Maybe Virgil could get something more from Alcina. It left me wondering about the timing. Who among my friends and acquaintances had seen Channer and Hooper arguing and told Virgil about it? Was that inside or out on the terrace? If it was late, then Channer just might be the murderer.

I reentered the castle. Pish said he was going back to work on his book, but after our morning expedition, I was at a loss for what to do.

"Why don't we go up to the attic? You have to see it, Merry," Shilo said, looping her arm through mine.

I thought about it for a second as McGill joined us in the great hall. There were a thousand things I ought to have been doing. I should have been following up on the sighting of the vampire who I thought might have been Channer. I should have gotten back to work peeling wallpaper off the frieze in the turret room. But I didn't want to do anything. My heart and mind felt overburdened with worry for Pish, about Cranston, and over the fate of Wynter Castle.

Virgil had warned me that some of the townsfolk were worried about what was going to happen to the castle and property when I sold. I was beginning to worry about that, too. Who would appreciate Wynter Castle more than I would? That was probably not the right frame of mind to go up and look through a century of Wynter family memorabilia. Even after two months it was still a shock to me that I had such a deep and storied family history.

But I needed something to distract me, and I was suddenly curious. "Okay. Let's do it!"

The stairway to the attic was behind a narrow door tucked away in a corner of the gallery hallway. I followed Shilo and McGill up there, and we turned on the lights that hung from the rafters. It was a revelation, not at all like other attics I had known. It was huge and spacious, with high ceilings and windows that let light in even through dust. "Wow," I breathed, coughing a little from the dust. "This is amazing,

like an entire third floor! McGill, there's even room up here
for more guest suites, if a buyer was interested."

He simply nodded, but he looked troubled.

I paced the length, then explored the groupings of furniture shoved to the side. There were at least two entire sets
of Eastlake bedroom furniture, the design along the top of
one headboard reminding me of eyelet lace, as well as a
couple more complete sets of Victorian furnishings. The
dressers were heavy as heck, as I found when I tried to move
one. McGill came to my aid, and we turned one around so
I could have a look at it.

"Magnificent!" I breathed, staring at a chest of drawers
with an ornate mirror topping it. It made the set I was using
seem modest in contrast.

We actually moved some of the furniture downstairs to
an empty room so I could use it for the turret bedroom once
I was done redecorating. It was fortunate that I was a strong
woman and that McGill looked stringy but was strong, too.
We then moved a bunch of stuff to the edge of the attic stairs,
ready to take downstairs as well. I could already picture the
turret bedrooms finished. One would be the Eastlake room,
complete with a washstand topped by a pitcher-and-bowl
set, with a wardrobe that was too big to move without help
but was earmarked for one of the few walls without windows.
The other turret bedroom would be done up in traditional
Victorian style. I was having far too much fun with the
planning, and it was worrisome, given that I was doing all
of the work for someone else.

I dug through a stack of boxes, many of which had china
and serving pieces I couldn't wait to investigate further.
Then I came across a box of photo albums and started trembling. Was my dad in there, in that box? Would I recognize

him if he was in a photo? I moved it from place to place, then finally shoved the box aside. I was on the edge of my nerves shattering. I told Shilo I'd had enough and needed to go back downstairs.

It's hard to explain to people who have had family their whole lives, but I've been independent a long time, and my "family" has always been my circle of friends. It was hard to get a grasp on this whole other part of my past, a Wynter family that had existed for hundreds of years and of which I was the living relic. I had to get away, out of the stuffy attic, where I sensed the ghosts of Wynters. Shilo understood and let me go.

It was time for me to make dinner, anyway, and cooking soothes me like nothing else. I put on a pot roast, surrounding it in the Dutch oven with lots of potatoes, carrots, garlic, onions, and wild herbs. The aroma was divine, wafting in puffs of steam from the pot. While it was cooking, I tried to go back to planning for the sale of the castle, but my mind was just not in it. I was in no-man's-land, wandering between worrying about a second death at the castle and who was guilty to Pish's situation as a suspect to Cranston's claim on the estate to what the heck I was going to do with it all. Despite how frantic the uncertainties were in my mind, at least it was a change from a few months before, when my worries had been about my career, how I was going to make a living, and who would hire me.

We ate in the kitchen, Shilo, Pish, McGill, and I. The tension began to unknot from my shoulders as I listened to Pish's plans for his book. He was using the Autumn Vale Community Bank as an overarching story line, with chapters in between discussing various aspects of bank frauds. He was going to have to travel some for it, but he was wealthy and had the time and means. I wondered when he was going to get bored with the isolation of Wynter Castle and want to go back to the city. What would I do without him?

I turned to ask Shilo something and caught her smiling over at McGill; his expression, goofy with love, made me smile. I was just so grateful for friends at a time like this that I forgot about my worries for the moment. "Let's retire to the parlor," I said of the newly furnished room just beyond the dining room. "We can start a fire and plan a wedding!"

The parlor was a smallish nook, in comparison to the size of the other rooms, and was furnished now with antiques, some that belonged to the castle collection and some I had found at Janice's shop. I loved the room, from the rich wine-colored Victorian draperies to the Persian rug, and including the antique settee and low rosewood table, upon which I had centered my silver tea set, a wedding gift from my mother-in-law.

While Pish worked on building a fire in the parlor, McGill, Shilo, and I paced out the great hall, and I expanded on the ideas I'd had for a winter wedding the very first time McGill had shown me the place. It amazed me how the last two months had progressed: he hadn't known the wedding we'd be planning would be his own! I had them stand, hands joined, in front of the fireplace, and my vision blurred. Suddenly I had become a crybaby, but I was so happy for Shilo, who looked up at McGill with trust and love in her eyes, her head back and long dark hair flowing down in waves. I had styled her many times, and this time I could see her in front of a roaring fire, a vision in white, a circlet of flowers on her hair. McGill I would put in a jacket but no tie, and certainly no tuxedo. He didn't suit anything too formal. It was going to be beautiful.

We gathered in the parlor around the fire with Shilo and McGill on a low settee, and Pish and I, like a mother and father, sitting in wing chairs opposite them with the low round table between us. I made tea for myself and Shilo, while Pish cradled a brandy and McGill sipped his ever-present Dr Pepper. We chatted about the wedding, but then the conversation inevitably turned to the murder.

It was a ball of confusion to me, I admitted.

Pish said, "You've assumed that Juniper attacked this Zoey girl because she was dumped by Les in Zoey's favor, right?"

I nodded. "There wasn't anything specific that gave me that idea, except . . . well, I assumed Les fired Juniper because their relationship ended, and it sure seems like Zoey is with Les now."

"But you just told us that there was a long-haired guy hanging around Les, right? Maybe you didn't notice, but Davey Hooper had long hair. And couldn't he equally as likely be the guy Zoey met through a cellmate? Hooper was in jail, too."

"Yeah, I had thought about that. And actually, I did tell Virgil about the guy hanging around Les's store, and that maybe he was Davey Hooper, but I guess everything that happened just knocked the waitress's skinny, long-haired 'vampire' out of my mind. So you think that maybe *Hooper* is the guy Zoey was hooked up with, not Les? If so, she sure doesn't seem cut up that he's dead."

"But Juniper does, right?"

I thought about Pish's conjectures, but McGill was ahead of me in some ways.

"So maybe Davey Hooper was hanging out in Ridley Ridge to be near Autumn Vale so he could get close to where his brother died?" he asked.

We had gone over the possible reasons behind Davey

Hooper's sojourn in Ridley Ridge many times, and I had privately considered that he was setting up to blackmail Pish some more. But how had he figured out Pish was at Wynter Castle? It wasn't something I could talk to anyone about, so I was left to my own conjectures.

Shilo said to me, "Maybe he was out to hurt you because you were his mom's downfall, you know?" She paused and shook her head. "No, I guess that doesn't work. He wouldn't wait for the party to attack you, would he? That would be a bad time. He'd just . . . I don't know, run you off the highway or something."

"That's not a bad point, though, Shilo, that he may have been stalking me using Zoey. After all, I'm the reason his mom's in prison. But the fact remains: I am not the one who ended up dead—Davey is." I pondered that for a long moment. "I feel like there's this big part of the story we're not seeing, something that would make it all gel. Something that would connect it all together."

"Let's go back to Juniper," Pish said, sitting back and swirling his brandy. "She was distraught after the party, as you learned from Binny, or if not right after the party, once word got to her about who was *killed* at the party."

I thought about that for a moment, because if Juniper hadn't been upset until she'd found out who had been killed, that let her off the hook as the killer. "So you're saying maybe Juniper Jones had been hooking up with Davey Hooper, and that's why she was distraught when she found out the identity of the victim." I stared into the fire briefly, then said, "I know the timing of her meltdown seems to indicate otherwise, but I still say we can't rule Juniper out as killer, if she was the spurned lover. I can attest to that girl being handy with a knife." I stared into the fire. "And the handprint!" I explained my finding of the bloody handprint on the wall by the smoking terrace.

Shilo shivered. "It's like some gothic book . . . *Curse of the Bloody Handprint*!"

"Maybe she became distraught because she *was* the one who murdered Hooper and the police questioning scared her," I mused. "I keep coming back to one question: why did she disappear from the party? Well, she would have had to if she were covered in blood. No one knows how she got home, or even if she went right home." Unless she had told the police all of that.

Shilo shuddered and clung to McGill. "Do we have to talk about this right after planning my pretty wedding?" she complained.

"Yes, we do, honey," I said, sitting cross-legged in the wing chair. "I won't rest until this is cleared up."

"I know," she murmured. "Sorry, go on!" McGill patted her hand on his arm and kissed the top of her head.

Pish said, "Let's go back first, before talking about Juniper as the possible killer. Say something happened between Hooper and Juniper, and maybe he dumped her for Zoey Channer."

I readily adjusted my thinking to having Hooper and Juniper and Zoey in a love triangle instead of Les Urquhart as the male lead.

"Zoey is rich, or at least her daddy is," Pish went on. "We know the Hooper family is all about the money. That's Zoey's attraction . . . money."

"But if Alcina's fat vampire is Percy Channer, I still think *he's* our most likely killer," I said. I like simplicity, and it just seemed so obvious now that I knew someone fitting Channer's general description was at the party, had fought with Hooper, and had clearly avoided me. "He was seen arguing with Hooper, and now we know he told him to get out on the terrace. Wouldn't be the first dad to kill a guy like that if he was buzzing around his wealthy daughter just to score some money."

McGill said, "You know . . . that guy, Percy Channer, he may be stocky, but he's short. I never noticed, but maybe he has small hands and the handprint is his! You have longer fingers than a lot of men, Merry."

"That's true. Okay, you may have a point: the handprint could even be Percy Channer's."

Pish looked unsettled. "But how do we know—"

As sometimes happens in real life, two things happened at once: Pish's cell phone rang, and there was a loud gong that meant someone was at the door.

Chapter Seventeen

❈ ❈ ❈

I TROTTED OUT of the room and toward the front door as Pish answered the phone. Who on earth would be coming to my door late at night in the middle of nowhere? I got nervous for a moment, but McGill had followed me, perhaps with the same thought. We advanced, and I cautiously opened the heavy door, surprised to find that it was pouring rain. In the castle with the drapes drawn, it could be World War III outside and you wouldn't notice.

Standing on my doorstep was a very wet, bedraggled Juniper Jones. I started back, and McGill stepped in front of me.

Wearily, she held up one hand, and said, "Give it up, already. Do I look freakin' dangerous?"

I exchanged a look with McGill as Shilo drifted into the great hall after us. She saw Juniper and bolted forward. "You poor kid!" she cried, her voice echoing. "You're soaked. C'mon in and get dry." She gave us both a look that told me she wasn't impressed by our defensive attitudes and pulled the young woman through the door.

Fine for her, I thought. She had not witnessed the Tasmanian-devil side of young Juniper. I could not forget the way she'd slashed out at Zoey, and I kind of wished I had a metal detector over the castle door, like in your average high school.

I followed McGill back into the parlor, where Shilo had Juniper ensconced in my chair and was helping her dry her matted hair with a kitchen dish towel. Pish, still on the phone, met my gaze, his eyebrows up around his sparse hairline. Neither of us had seen this side of Shilo. She was a great girl, but humans were generally not her thing. Nurturing was saved for her bunny, Magic. Perhaps she was practicing becoming a mother.

Becket, who had been sitting on the hearth purring contentedly, paws tucked under his big orangey body, now sat upright and glared at the intruder. Pish had turned away and was murmuring into his phone, so there would be no guidance on this particular social situation from him. What to do with a fugitive from justice, someone I considered a murder suspect?

She didn't appear to be dangerous for the moment, though, so I would do what I do best: feed folks. I scooted to the kitchen and made the girl a plate of warmed, buttered muffins and a hot cocoa. She scarfed it all down as Shilo combed out her wet hair.

"You know the Ridley Ridge Police are looking for you after that little performance at the Party Stop the other day?" I finally said, hovering nearby and watching her.

"What else could I do?" Juniper said, tears rolling down her cheeks. She swallowed her last bit of muffin and took a long drink of cocoa. "That little rich bitch stole my Davey away and then killed him, like a dog she was tired of."

"Zoey Channer *killed* Davey Hooper?" I blurted out, only part of my brain dealing with wondering what kind of people Juniper knew who would kill a dog of which they had tired. "How do you know? Did you see it?"

"No, but isn't it obvious?"

"Not to most people." I crouched down beside her and looked up into her troubled face. "Juniper, you have got to have some evidence if you expect us to believe that. Right now *you* are a contender for the position of suspect number one."

"Me?" she cried, sitting up straight in the chair. "Why would I kill Davey? I *loved* him!"

"People have killed out of jealousy before; you just told us Zoey stole him from you." Which was news to us, but I'd ask her about that in a moment. "You were angry about it. And you sure are handy with a knife." I was wondering what I should do about her showing up out of the blue like this. Turning her in to Virgil would be the obvious choice, but somehow, sitting on my chair full of muffins and cocoa looking young and scared, she just didn't seem like a killer. A grief-stricken young woman yes, but not a killer.

Pish hung up and approached us, eyeing Juniper warily. "Why don't you tell us what happened the night of the party, then, if you want us to believe you didn't kill him?"

She sighed, heavily put-upon by our determination to view her with suspicion. My shoulder still ached from trying to pull her away as she slashed at Zoey, so Juniper could just take her martyr attitude and stuff it.

"I have a better idea," I said, pulling over a footstool and setting my butt down. "Why don't you start at the beginning, when you hopped off a bus in Ridley Ridge and got a job at the Party Stop. Or before that, when you first met Davey Hooper." If I got a feel for whether I thought she was telling the truth, it might help in my decision about what to do with her.

Had she killed Davey Hooper, as we had speculated? Now I seriously doubted it, and if the police got her in custody, it could possibly end any search for the real killer. I hadn't ruled out turning her in, but I wasn't going to leap up and do it that moment. She lowered her gaze and stared into the fire.

"Juniper, how did you meet Davey Hooper?" Shilo asked, her tone soft.

Somehow the question sounded better coming from her. Pish took his chair back, and McGill perched beside Shilo. Juniper looked up at Shilo, tears in her eyes. "I met him at a party. I was living in Buffalo working for this dude, this guy who organizes parties and books entertainment. I was just supposed to clear tables and stuff, but he kept harassing me, making me do sh . . . crap jobs. There was this table of guys; I went over to ask if they wanted anything, and when my boss started hassling me, Davey—I didn't know his name then— said why didn't the guy go f-f . . . uh, forget himself."

It was interesting to me that Juniper was censoring her language in our presence. Why was she bothering?

"So Davey Hooper stuck up for you," Shilo said.

"Yeah," she said with a broken, tearful smile. Her gaze became dreamy, her complexion in the firelight taking on a rosy hue. I was reminded of how young she was, only about twenty or so. "He asked me if I had a place to crash. I did, kind of, a friend's couch, but he told me he could put me up."

I was silent. Such offers usually came with strings of the booty-call type from what I had heard and observed.

"So we started going together," Juniper continued, "and it was so cool. He was such a chill dude and looked after me, you know?"

"I heard he had been in jail before," I said.

She gave me a withering look. "Who hasn't been?"

Everyone else in the room, I was about to say caustically, but I restrained myself. While she gushed, I wondered what she was leading up to. I wasn't *completely* certain of her innocence just yet and questioned why she had shown up at the castle door. Could she have attacked Hooper in a fit of jealousy over his new relationship with Zoey? Pushed beyond endurance, had seeing them together at the party, Zoey in her expensive clothes while Juniper served her hors d'oeuvres, driven her to murder?

I tried to do the mental gymnastics, to stretch my belief system to picture her killing the guy she adored, but on reflection, I didn't think so. If she was going to kill anyone, it would have been Zoey. I still strongly favored Percy Channer as the culprit since finding out he had been at the party. I tuned back in to her story as she admitted to following Davey to Ridley Ridge. "Why on earth did he come to Ridley Ridge in the first place?" I asked.

Juniper looked uneasy. "He, uh . . . he was mad about his twin brother dying and his mom being put in jail."

As we suspected. My skin crawled when I thought of someone plotting revenge or trying to come up with a way to make me sorry. I didn't know if that was his intent, but just knowing he had been out there and angry about Dinty's death . . . Had he sent Zoey to spy on me? Is that why she had been watching the castle?

"How did you know where he was going? How did you know to follow him to Ridley Ridge?"

"He had started hanging out with Zo-bitch in Buffalo, you know, but he was still with me, too. He kind of went crazy when he heard about his brother. His mom and he were on the phone ranting and raving about it, so I heard a lot about Autumn Vale, and then she sent him a message through someone else to get the people responsible and make them pay."

"Dinty Hooper died in Merry's woods, but no one here killed him, for heaven's sake," McGill said, his tone unusually acerbic, voicing what we were all thinking. "Merry didn't even live here when he died, and neither did these other two. As far as we know, Hooper never made a move against the guy who actually killed his brother in self-defense. Why the heck did he come to the castle?"

Juniper shrugged. "Look, don't ask me about any of this, 'cause that's about when he cut me out of his life. I decided to go to Ridley Ridge after he dumped me for that flossy-haired floozy because I knew he was heading there himself. I just wanted him to tell me why, you know?"

Ah yes, the continual girl cry: Why? Why don't you love me? Why did you choose another girl over me? What is wrong with me? She needed to read *He's Just Not That Into You* or *Guys Who Make Girls Crazy and the Crazy Girls Who Love Them*, but she didn't seem like the book-learning type. And Davey was dead anyway. If not an answer, it was at least an ultimate end to the "why" query. But there were still so many questions about her story. She curled up in her chair, looking so tired and sad that I began to feel for her. "So Davey was heading to Ridley Ridge," I prompted. "And so were you. Why Ridley Ridge?"

"He was going to stay with Les, who was a buddy of his brother's. That was about the same time he took up permanently with that bleached freak and dumped my ass." She choked back a sob and sat up, doubling over.

I shared a look with Pish. Why had Rusty, who had actually killed Dinty, gotten a free pass? And why had Davey been lingering about in Ridley Ridge without taking his revenge? We knew they had all been there for the better part of a month. I asked her those questions.

With a helpless shrug, she said, "Look, like I said, Davey cut me out of his life. He started up with Sleazoid Barbie, and after that I was, like, no one to him. It hurt so bad. Les and Dinty were buddies from jail—"

Aha! That was true . . . Dinty Hooper was a jailbird, too. Birds of a feather . . . "So you headed to Ridley Ridge to be near Davey, even though you two were no longer an item."

Juniper sniffled back a sob and wiped her nose on her sleeve. "I didn't know what else to do. I just wanted to be close to Davey so that when he figured out I was better for him than her, I'd be close by. When I got off the bus, I told Les that Davey and I were engaged, but Davey and Zo-whore showed up and told him the truth a coupla days later. I asked Les to let me stay anyway, and he said okay." She frowned and started chewing on a ragged fingernail. "I don't know why."

None of this made a bit of sense to me yet. I kept expecting something she said to add up, but in her storytelling style, one plus one equaled fritters. It seemed like they had all just collected in Ridley Ridge and done. . . nothing. "Did Davey Hooper ever talk about me?" I asked.

She gave her fingernail a break, looking up at me as she shook her head. "Never heard of you until I started working for Binny. Not by name, anyway. I think I heard about some bitch who sent his mom to jail."

Still didn't make sense. Why did Hooper come to the party at the castle if not to accost or attack me for having some tangential part in his family drama? "Why did you come to Autumn Vale to get a job?"

"After Les tossed me out, I had to go somewhere, and I saw Binny's ad for help. It kept me close to Davey. I kept hoping . . ." She sighed hugely and flopped back in the wing chair. "It seems so freakin' dumb now, but I kept hoping Davey would ditch that Channer witch and come back to me. Or that she would ditch him and he would need me, you know?"

It was hard to believe Davey Hooper, lowlife scum, jail rat, and son of a grifter, could have had two girls in love with him. Though, for a girlfriend, Zoey did not seem particularly broken up about his death. I surmised that for her it was thrill seeking, some way to fill a hollow life. I had seen her type all too often in the fashion world, the celebutants who turned to men, booze, or drugs—or all three—for excitement. I was anxious to get to Juniper's version of the night of the party. "So the night of the party you found out he was still with Zoey Channer, right? And you were jealous. You accosted him, or he talked to you, right?"

Pish made a face at me and jerked his head. He had something to tell me.

"Hold that thought," I said, and followed him out to the hallway.

"I just wanted you to be cognizant of everything before we speak more with young Miss Jones," he murmured. "Earlier I made a few calls of inquiry about the people involved; that phone call just before she arrived was an answer. I'm starting to lean toward our theory that Channer might be the guilty one. I know of the man's financial dealings, of course—some of them are questionable, and many downright illegal—but what I didn't know is the latest Percy Channer news. . . . He is a suspect in a case involving the disappearance and probable death of a business rival."

"Wow," I said. "It doesn't surprise me, somehow, having met the charmer."

"We're pretty sure now that that Juniper let Percy Channer into the party, and she would have been watching Hooper more intently than anyone else. Maybe she can tell us something about Channer's movements that night. And I have more. I got another call at the same time; my federal friend tells me that he heard from an unnamed source that someone was trying to blackmail Channer with shameful photos or video of his daughter. Zoey Channer is a wild little thing and, as we know, has a liking for bad boys. It's possible Davey Hooper was the blackmailer."

"If that's true, Channer had an even stronger motive than just splitting them up," I mused. "I know I said he was just the kind of guy to kill someone who got in his way, and I wouldn't want to cross the man, but still . . . would he kill Davey Hooper to prevent photos or video of his daughter coming out? Wouldn't he be motivated to keep him alive at least until he got the photos or video?"

"The killing may not have been a planned ending. He could have met Hooper to pay him off and ended up arguing with him."

"True. Okay, let's get back. I'm anxious to hear if she saw anything that night. I just don't know whether to call Virgil or not." Agitated, I stepped back and forth from foot to foot. "What do you think I should do, Pish?"

He thought for a moment, then said, "Let's hear her out first."

It was what I wanted to do, too, so I agreed. We returned.

"Why did you come here, Juniper, to Autumn Vale?" I asked, to ease her back into her story. "Why not just go back to Buffalo once you figured out Davey really was hooked up with Zoey? You couldn't have thought he'd dump her. She was rich."

She swallowed hard and stared at me. "There was stuff going on, stuff with Davey and his crew, that I didn't understand. That I *wanted* to understand."

"What kind of stuff?" Pish asked.

Juniper was silent, just looking miserable and shaking her head.

I exchanged a look with Pish as Shilo and McGill looked on, a little puzzled, perhaps, but silent. "Okay, so you let Percy Channer, Zoey's father, into the party that night. Is that true?"

She nodded.

"Did you know who he was? Did you tell him Davey was there? How did that go down?"

She shifted around and looked off toward the fire. "He met me at the bakery and asked questions. I found out who he was and told him I knew Zoey. Then he told me he just wanted to get his daughter and shove her in rehab to get her out of her parole-violation rap."

It made sense that Percy would approach her that way, though I wasn't sure the plan he shared with her was the complete truth. It would have appealed to Juniper as a way of getting rid of her rival and maybe getting Davey back. I thought for a second and asked, "Did he seem to know your name?"

She nodded. Channer had done his homework. "He offered me a hundred bucks to get him into the party without anyone knowing about it. It was so easy! The ladies in the kitchen didn't know who was supposed to come or go."

"So you figured turning her over to her father would get her out of your way, leave the field clear for you to get Davey back." I said it just to keep her talking while I thought.

She nodded.

"Did you see him talking to Davey? What went down?"

"I don't know; I lost sight of the guy. Those damn football goofs kept talking to me, and they tried to hoist me up on their shoulders until I jabbed one in the arm with a canopy pick."

"Canapé," I corrected.

"Whatever."

"Who all was here? We know Davey and Zoey were, but who else?" Pish asked.

I held my breath, waiting.

"Zoey, yeah, and Davey, and Les."

"Les Urquhart was there, too?" I glanced over at Pish. "He told me he wasn't . . . or, well, not really. He just avoided the question, I guess. He must have slipped away, maybe with Zoey? But why did he leave? Did he know Davey was dead?" I mused aloud. "Did he maybe kill him for some reason?"

"I told you, it was that bitch Zoey who killed him!" Juniper said, her face reddening and twisting into a grimace.

"That is entirely possible," I mused, pondering again the small handprint, "because she left, too, and why would she if she wasn't guilty? I mean, Davey Hooper was her boyfriend. Surely she came with him and would expect to go with him." Juniper had taken off, too, but I would get to that later. No point in treating her as a hostile witness. Yet. My mind tangled a bit, as I wondered when Zoey and Les became as chummy as they seemed to be now. Before or after Hooper's death?

"Why were they all at Merry's party anyway?" Pish asked.

"I asked Les," Juniper said. "He told me that Davey was there to meet up with someone, some business associate."

"Davey Hooper meeting a *business* associate at my party?" I asked, skeptical.

She nodded.

I exchanged a look with Pish; was that business associate Zoey's father? Had Davey taken Zoey there, giving her some kind of story, so he could meet with Percy, get a payoff, and hand the girl over to her father? It hung together, pretty much, except then I wondered: why had Percy needed Juniper to get into the party? I could explain why Les and Zoey had disappeared from the party; if things went bad between the two men and Percy killed Hooper, they wouldn't have wanted to be involved. "Did you actually talk to Davey at any point?" I asked, remembering seeing her with the cowboy who'd turned out to have been Davey, aka the murder victim.

She hung her head. "Yeah, for a minute. He told me he was sorry for how Les canned me."

"Juniper, you're so insistent on one point, and I want to know . . . *why* do you think Zoey would kill Davey?"

"She had taken up with Les, the little sleaze."

So . . . before Hooper's death. "Zoey Channer was having a fling with Les, too?"

Juniper nodded, tears welling. She fisted the tears from her eyes like a little kid, any attempt at grown-up world-weariness gone. "She had Davey, and she treated him like crap. I just don't understand. How *could* she?" In a second her expression changed to loathing. "I hate her. I want her dead."

Wow, the girl had mood swings! Not that I hadn't dealt with my share of mood swings; with Leatrice it had been much the same, from weepiness to giddy laughter and back again in minutes. "But why would she *kill* Davey?"

She shrugged and sobbed.

If Davey Hooper had come to my party to meet up with someone, who was that someone? Was it Percy, as I now suspected? It wasn't Juniper, certainly. And why had he had Zoey and Les with him? I frowned. The only thing that made sense was that Hooper planned to meet Channer at my party so he could receive a payoff, and he needed Zoey there to hand her over. But had Zoey been in on it or not? It could have been her plan all along to blackmail her father.

"I am sorry for all the pain you've been through," I said in all sincerity. "It hurts to lose someone you love." No matter if he was a big jerk.

She covered her face and wept, clearly brokenhearted.

"Did you see him talking to anyone that night?" I pressed, feeling like she might still be holding information back.

"We do want to figure out who did it," Pish said. "And we *can't* assume Zoey is guilty."

I know women, and there was no way Juniper did not follow Davey Hooper as much as she could that night. I remember what being a lovesick twentysomething is like, and it is exactly like being a lovesick teenager but with more freedom. She wasn't responding to questions, but I had to keep trying. "Who did Davey talk to? Did he argue with anyone? When did you last see him?"

She took a deep, heaving breath and looked up. There was no denying the depth of her loss, and I actually felt sympathy for her. I didn't know what in her life had led to a piece of crap like Davey Hooper being worth crying over, but her pain was real.

"Juniper, I know you think Zoey killed your Davey," Shilo said, the first she had spoken in a while. "Maybe it *was* Zoey, but if it wasn't, you still want whoever did it to be caught, right? And pay?"

Shilo's voice seemed to work some kind of soothing magic on Juniper, who said, "Yeah, I do. I'll tell you what I can. I only saw Davey now and again, because I had to take food around. He had Zoey tagging after him when she wasn't taunting me. I swear, I should have taken her out then, and maybe Davey would be alive."

She was getting distracted again by her Zoey-as-murderess

theory. "Who else? You said Les was there, but I didn't see him. What costume was he wearing?"

"I don't know who he was supposed to be. He had some weird wig on and a white lab coat."

My eyes widened, and Pish and I shared a look. Les Urquhart was the Demon Barber? And had he indeed been carrying the straight razor that we suspected was the weapon? I had to tell Virgil this! I kept a hold on my excitement and said, "How did Davey and Les get along?"

She scrunched up her face. "Good. Why?"

"No conflicts?"

"No, of course not. Look, Les can be a douche, but he's no killer, if that's what you're thinking."

And just because he brought the weapon, didn't mean he'd used it, I realized. He could have put it down or given it to someone else. "So, who else did Davey talk to?" I asked.

Juniper bolted up out of her chair, pointed toward the door, and hollered, "You!"

Chapter Eighteen

❋ ❋ ❋

I REALIZED RIGHT away she did not mean me, and I whirled in my seat. There, at the door of the parlor, was Cranston Higgins. "What are you doing here, Cranston?" And how the hell did he keep getting into the castle? I turned back to our guest, who was still standing and staring. "How do you know Cranston?" I asked Juniper.

"I saw him at the Party Stop a couple times," Juniper said. Her voice was steady, but she looked spooked. Her gaze moved around the room to each of us. I was frankly puzzled.

"Hey, Merry, Pish, Shilo, McGill," Cranston said, nodding to each of us in turn. He pulled off his black wool bomber-style jacket and slung it over a table, then unwound the scarf from his neck. "Well of *course* I've been at the Party Stop! I've been staying at a boarding house because you didn't want me staying *here*," he said to me, pointedly. "Even though you've got lots of extra rooms. So I went to the Party Stop to pick up cheap paper plates and plastic utensils. It's a rough life for a bachelor, am I right, Pish? McGill?"

"Actually, I won't be a bachelor much longer," McGill said, and held out Shilo's engagement finger with the pretty ring encircling it.

Cranston hooted and said, "Congratulations, you two! Couldn't be a nicer couple." He charged across the room and grabbed Shilo up in a bear hug, then pumped McGill's outstretched hand with enthusiasm.

"I don't feel well," Juniper said, hand on her stomach. "Those chocolate muffins . . . they're sitting like . . . like freakin' rocks. What do you put in those things? Where's the bathroom?" She put one hand over her mouth.

Damn. Maybe they were too rich on an empty stomach? Allergies? I hoped to heck she didn't have a nut allergy. I had many questions for her, because I still didn't know where the girl had gone after the party nor where she had been staying, but it would all have to wait until she felt better.

I showed her to the ground-floor bathroom, a little powder room tucked away behind the butler's pantry near the back doorway, and went to the kitchen to get a glass of cold water and a damp cloth in case she vomited. I could hardly wait to ask her about seeing Cranston: why had she been so surprised to see him at the castle? I also wanted to ask her why she'd come to the castle this night. I stood staring out the kitchen window into the darkness and lost a few minutes pondering that. How much could I trust Juniper?

After a few minutes I went to the hallway outside of the powder room. "Juniper, are you okay?" I asked. I tapped, then put my ear to the wood door and listened for the sound of retching. Nothing. "Juniper?" No sound at all. I pushed open the door to an empty room. Sometimes I wonder . . .

Am I really as bright as people tell me I am? I should have figured on this.

She was gone, and she had a good ten minutes on me. I didn't even know how she had gotten out to the castle, but she must have driven. For all I knew she had stolen a car, and with the time I had allowed her in the bathroom, she could be past Ridley Ridge by now. I called the police station, giving the dispatcher a detailed message for Virgil about Juniper's arrival and abrupt departure. Maybe I should have called them right away, but there was no use beating myself up over that now. I hung up and girded my loins to tackle my "cousin." There was something fishy going on, and there was more to it than just his spurious claim to my castle.

Why had his arrival scared off Juniper?

I paused briefly before going back to my friends and did a little happy dance as I experienced a tingling of relief; Cranston, or whoever he was, was not my cousin. I didn't need a DNA test to tell me that now, not with the fishiness of Juniper's fear of him. All along I had not really believed him, but something inside of me wanted family. However . . . Wynter Castle was mine, all mine, and Cranston was a con artist. There were still a whole lot of questions Cranston was going to have to answer, particularly about his acquaintance with Les Urquhart, but I definitely had a skip and a hop to my step as I returned to the parlor. Silence reigned. Everyone looked a little uncomfortable. Cranston was sitting where Juniper had been.

I met Pish's gaze and raised my brows. He nodded. We had partnered at euchre before, and he knew what that meant; I was going to try a little bit o' the old bluff. "Juniper is so upset, Cranston . . . or *whomever* you are. *She* says you were good buddies with Les Urquhart. She's weeping so hard right now that I can't figure out all that she's saying."

Cranston stood and faced me, dainty, ring-laden hand on his chest. "I am wounded to the heart. Let me just talk to the girl to explain to her why I was talking to those fellows. We were no more than acquaintances, I assure you."

Those fellows . . . not just Urquhart, then, but Davey, too. My stomach clenched. "You can tell *me*," I said, as Pish, McGill, and Shilo all stood. "I'll tell her. Who exactly are you, and what are you doing here?"

He bridled. "If you don't believe me, that I am Melvyn Wynter's grandson, then you are impugning my grandmother's deathbed confession! Any court in the land would—"

"I think we'll let the DNA talk," Pish said, watching Cranston, who was puffing up like a toad, his face turning red.

"Cranston, there are so many holes in your story, it could be used as a sieve, but I'm willing to let the DNA test do the talking," I said calmly. "The test is in a few days, so let's agree to disagree until then."

"You've humiliated me," he said, and I swear that one big, fat tear rolled down his cheek. In a practiced, dramatic voice, he declaimed, "I'm leaving, and I will see you in court! You'll be sorry, Merry Wynter!"

He whirled and stormed out of the parlor. I followed, but he didn't have anything more to say except, as he paused, trembling, at the door, "You have wounded me. I thought I had found family, but all I found was . . . heartbreak!"

"And . . . scene," I said, once he had exited.

We all trooped back into the parlor, and I told everyone about Juniper's skipping out on me and my surmises. "I can't get over the fact that she was fine with us until she saw Cranston."

"Yeah. What the heck was that all about?" McGill said.

"She looked like she'd seen a ghost," Shilo said.

"Pish, what's your take on it?"

"On what, Cranston? That fellow, whatever his name is, is a classic con man," he said, sitting back in the wing chair and wrinkling his brow. "I've met a lot of them, and he has all the earmarks. I thought so from the beginning, but you never call a bluff until you have all the facts."

"Violent? Not violent?" I asked.

Pish considered for a moment, then said, "I don't see him doing more than disappearing into the mist; the bluster of suing was classic 'con man caught in the act and bluffing until he can escape the situation.'" He paused and grimaced. "What I can't figure out is his connection to Davey Hooper and Les Urquhart."

"You didn't buy his claim of coincidence any more than I did," I said. "But we don't have a lot to go on, except Juniper saying she had seen him at the Party Stop. I guess we just don't know enough."

"Let me ask around," McGill said. "I know folks in Ridley Ridge, and maybe they've seen Cranston there. Too bad you don't have any photos."

"His real name can't be Cranston Higgins," I said. "Maybe Virgil will have his real name by now, since they were looking into the background of everyone who was at the party."

"Why don't you call Virgil tomorrow and meet him somewhere?" Shilo said, her open gaze all innocence. "You two can talk."

"I'll do that," I said, refusing to "get" her subtext.

After the long, busy day, I slept like a log or a baby or a dead man, whichever phrase you prefer to mean deep and dreamless sleep. I awoke early, made muffins, both savory and sweet, brownies, and lemon squares, and headed into town. The mechanic had promised to get my new/old car to me within the next few days, and I looked forward to having wheels of my own. In my situation, it had become a necessity. Jezebel was fixed up for the moment, but Hayes had said to treat her nicely, so I spoke sweetly to her and hoped I made it into town and back home without too much trouble.

I had called the police once again, told them I had information for Virgil, and gave them my schedule. Muffins and squares to the Vale Variety and Lunch, then on to Golden Acres. I went to the back door and had a chat with the cook, who was now my good friend. I then wound my way past Gogi's office—she wasn't there—and to the front desk, where Mrs. Dotty Levitz was kicking up a fuss, as she sometimes did. The crafty lady, who suffers dementia but is nobody's fool, was tossing her array of small stuffed animals willy-nilly out of her walker basket and heading for the door. She had done this before as a distraction to try to get away, certain she had to meet her mother somewhere. This time the receptionist was smiling because she'd had the foresight to lock the door already when she saw Dotty heading in her direction.

Hannah, I could hear from the buzz of voices and conversation in the lounge, was there for one of her bi-weekly visits. She brought books and her sunny personality to Golden Acres. Her eyes lit up when I entered, and she gestured me over.

"Merry, I have *such* news! I did research, using the maiden name of your great uncle's girlfriend. Remember you told me Doc said she still had family in the area? Well, guess who our Yolanda-also-known-as-Violet is related to?" Her big gray eyes sparkled.

"You've got me there."

"She had a sister, remember? The sister's name was Dorothea, or Dorothy, but she is now known as . . . Dotty!"

Dotty? I gasped. "Is her married name Dotty Levitz?"

"Exactly!"

Interesting, but disappointing in a way. Dotty couldn't remember what she'd had for lunch, much less anything else. Gogi came looking for me. She had helped Hannah with the investigation, and she confirmed the finding.

"That won't help, then," I said. It probably didn't matter at this point, given that I now thought Cranston was a con man, but I still wanted to have proof to throw in his face.

"On the contrary," Gogi said. "I think Dotty has something to tell you that you'll be interested to hear. She remembers very well the events of that summer, better than what happened yesterday, if you read between the lines." She led the elderly lady into the lounge and sat her down, and with some prompting, got the story out of her.

It took a little time, so I will give a synopsis: Violet, who'd hated her name, Yolanda, as much as Dotty had disliked Dorothea, had gone out with Melvyn Wynter through high school, but when he enlisted, they had a big argument. He went off to boot camp, and she felt she was free to do what she wanted. So Violet got herself a boyfriend who was older, classifed 4-F, and had a good job. She married him in secret, then had a big going away party just so Melvyn would read about it.

Dotty looked from side to side, and then at Doc, who sat over in the corner listening in as he played a game of chess with Hubert Dread. "She was a jealous, horrible sister, though, and I'll tell you why: poor Violet couldn't have a baby, no matter how she tried." Dotty laughed out loud, her eyes twinkling with seventy-year-old mischief. "I had three, and she didn't have a one! Poor old Violet."

I looked over to Gogi. "Are you sure this is true?"

Gogi nodded, petting Dotty's spotted arthritic hand

gently. "Oh yes, I'm sure she's right. In fact, I looked into it and found out that Violet is still alive and well and living at Camelot Corners Nursing Home in a small hamlet just outside of Batavia, so for any number of reasons she *can't* be Cranston's late grandmother. She never did have children, and she is still alive and relatively well."

I nodded and sighed. If I hadn't already been sure, this would have driven a stake in Cranston's claims, but this was the confirmation I needed. A slow burn of anger was sparked in my gut. How dare he put me through this . . . and for what?

Gogi touched Dotty's wispy hair, and the woman put her head down on the nursing home owner's shoulder. "I guess the sisters lost track of each other," Gogi gently said. "Dotty's son is so pleased that he's going to take his mother there so they can visit. He told me he remembers his aunt Vi from the old days, but she dropped out of sight in the seventies. I guess the two sisters didn't get along very well and stopped talking to each other. He is *so* grateful, you have no idea. And to think, if it hadn't been for a con man, the two sisters might never have gotten back together."

Hannah spoke up. "He planned it well, I must say. Cranston must have used public records, old newspapers, and whatever else he could find."

"Why did he target me in the first place?" I asked.

Hannah scrunched up her little face. "I don't know. I wonder if, when Andrew Silvio posted for heirs when he was doing the Wynter estate stuff, that Cranston caught wind of it and planned his con?"

"But that was ages ago. Why wait so long?"

She shrugged. "Maybe it took that long to figure everything out? I don't know how con artists work. I think he must have used photos of himself with his real grandma, and maybe even an old photo of his grandmother for the locket. He would have bought the locket at an antique store and had it engraved with the name and sentiment he wanted."

It still didn't solve who Cranston was, but he and I were going to have a talk, and then I was going to turn him over to Virgil. I looked over at Doc, who nodded and dropped a wink at me as he took Hubert's bishop.

I was getting ready to leave when who should arrive but Virgil Grace himself, looking handsome and spiffy in his uniform. He kissed his mother on the cheek and then turned his gaze to me. My heart skipped a beat. I wondered: would Miguel like this man who was so completely different than he? I had been going to go to the sheriff's office anyway, and in anticipation of meeting up with Virgil I had dressed with care. Not that I don't always, but today I wore a challis skirt and soft smocked tunic in autumn colors with cowboy boots and a scarf. I had a heavy sweater coat on.

"Hey, Merry," he said, rubbing the back of his neck as he looked me up and down. "I got your message last night about Juniper Jones and passed on the information to Baxter in Ridley Ridge. We think she's driving Binny's car, which was parked behind the bakery. Binny said she'd loaned her the car while the girl worked for her. She hasn't shown up again, has she?"

"No, but I have a lot more to tell you. I may want to press charges against the guy posing as Cranston Higgins, and I was wondering if you'd come up with any information about him. Could we talk privately?"

"We can talk here," he said.

I was flummoxed, I don't mind saying it, because I was convinced in that moment that he did not want to spend time alone with me. What the heck was wrong with him? I glanced over at Gogi, but though she was smiling, her eyes were wrinkled with concern. Hannah smiled up at me, oblivious to the undercurrents. "I have a lot to talk about, and I don't want to do it here," I insisted.

"Okay, all right. Let's go somewhere and talk."

I wanted to tell him just to get lost. I wanted to sling back: *I don't want to twist your arm, dumbass*, but I held my temper and said, "Let's walk, Sheriff."

After saying affectionate good-byes to Gogi and Hannah, I strode ahead of him out of Golden Acres to the street. I hadn't had a chance to explore the town too much at this point, but from the highway above I had noticed a little park, and I wanted to see it. Let him follow me.

I walked, not letting myself be concerned that he was seeing me from an unflattering angle, and made my way down to the corner, turned left, then down to another short street, another left, and into a small pocket park of the type that had delighted me in New York. I entered through a wrought iron gate over which were the words *Come and Partake of Nature*.

I stopped and took in a deep breath, and the rhythm of my walk slowed. I love parks, and this one was a gem, enclosed by lovely old wrought iron fencing and with a meandering gravel path through it. I wondered if my grandfather had courted my grandmother here, those many years ago. I knew so little; I didn't even know if my grandmother was a local girl or if Murgatroyd, my grandfather, had met her somewhere else. As I followed the path past big trees—some of which I now recognized, thanks to my uncle's arboretum—I pondered all the mysteries of my life. If my father hadn't died when I was so young, would everything have been different? Would I ever have moved to New York City? Would I have even gone down the same career path, or ever met Miguel?

Virgil caught up with me. He took my arm, saying, "Why don't we sit for a moment?"

We found a park bench, and I told him about Cranston, why we thought he was a fraud, and what Juniper had told us about seeing him at the Party Stop, as well as her admission that Les Urquhart was one of the unknowns at the costume party, and that it sounded like he was the Sweeney Todd. I worried at Cranston's link to the whole affair; could he possibly be connected to Les Urquhart and Davey Hooper? Was that the key to the whole mess and the timing of the con? How was that possible?

"What I can't understand is: what did he expect to get from it?" I mused, staring up at a big old bur oak. "He stopped asking for a payout after the first few days and seemed content to wait to do the DNA test I needed before sharing the estate with him. But he wasn't related to me. What, then, is the con?"

"Wait a sec," Virgil said, and took out his phone. He walked a ways away and spoke to someone for a few minutes. He made a second call, then came back. "I have a few ideas on that, so I've put in a call to an acquaintance on another police force. I'll know more shortly. Can I ask you: have you spoken to everyone you invited to your party since that night?"

"No, not at all. I've tried to get ahold of some of them, but I'm not getting answers and haven't had time to follow up properly. I've been kind of distracted about things." I glanced at him; he had a hawklike profile, with dark brows that sloped down over his brown eyes when he was deep in thought, as he was now. He sat back on the bench and put his arm over the back behind me. I was a little cold and wanted to cuddle up to him, but I figured that would send him running for the hills. I longed to ask him about his ex-wife, the daughter of the Ridley Ridge sheriff, but now was not the time.

"I have to think he's connected to Hooper," he said. "We now know that Hooper received a message from his mother through someone who visited someone else in jail. It's possible that this was how he met Zoey Channer, since she was at the same jail for a very brief period while being transferred."

"You mean maybe Dinah sent a message to Davey via Zoey when she got out?" He nodded. So the rumored jail-cell friendship was between Dinah and Zoey, and that's how Zoey had met Davey. "What did Zoey do that had her in the same jail as Dinah?"

"Drug offense. She's wanted right now on a parole violation, so she'll be returned to custody as soon as she gets out of the hospital."

"She's still in the hospital? Was she *that* badly hurt?"

He rolled his eyes. "That's Baxter for you. As you know, Percy Channer headed to Ridley Ridge General—he's been there raising a stink nonstop about his precious daughter and how badly she was hurt because a homicide suspect from Autumn Vale was on the loose. Baxter is eating it up, blaming it all on me, and letting her stay at the hospital so she can consult a plastic surgeon that Channer flew in. Something about the gash in her leg needing special care."

Again, there was a subtext about the tension between him and the Ridley Ridge sheriff because of Baxter's daughter and the divorce. As I had already decided, though, this was not the time to follow up on my questions about Virgil's ex-wife, so I turned my mind back to the conundrum of how Cranston, Hooper, Les, Juniper, and Zoey were all connected, and who had done Hooper in. "So, is it feasible that it wasn't Cranston at all who came up with the con? That Hooper used information from his mother plus a little research to construct it?"

"Good thinking," Virgil said. "Given the skill sets of the folks we're talking about, that's logical. Dinah probably figured there was more money there than anyone was acknowledging."

"Even though there's not. She was after my great uncle's rumored millions. If only she knew that the secret hidden money my uncle constructed a grand puzzle and search for turned out to be a satchel of worthless stock certificates from long-gone South African mining companies. But . . . okay, I'm trying to figure this out. Dinah set her son up to try to con me into giving them money—through Cranston, who-ever he is—thinking I would pay up to get him to just go away?"

"Makes sense. Davey looked so much like Dinty that we would have recognized him right away—like I did recognize his body—so they needed someone else to play the part of the Wynter heir. I have a report of Hooper spotted at the library in Ridley Ridge and an Internet café in Batavia, and we think he accessed the same information Hannah has discovered about the woman Melvyn was connected to in his youth."

We had already figured that out, but it was news that Virgil had been investigating the same avenue. Of course, what did I *think* he'd been doing? "Virgil, where were you when you were out of town?"

He shifted. "I was in Cayuga, getting information on the lawsuit Davey Hooper tried to file against Pish from jail. No one there believed Hooper at the time, and they still don't."

"Did you really believe Pish could have killed Hooper?"

"That's not how law enforcement works, Merry," he said, meeting my gaze. "I can't figure I like someone, so there's no way he could be a murderer, and I won't go into any in-vestigation with a preset idea of the outcome."

"But you can't totally shut off your feelings!" I exclaimed. "That's inhuman."

"Merry, I won't let my 'feelings,' as you call them, influence the direction of an investigation. That is crappy technique, though I'm not saying there aren't cops out there who do it. I call it lazy. I don't mind a hunch now and then, but I need to find facts to back it up, and I *won't* close off other avenues of investigation while I look into it."

At least I knew he was passionate about something . . . his job. "I *know* that." I paused, letting the heat between us subside. "Virgil, when I went out to the terrace, I noticed a bloody handprint on the wall. Whose was that?"

"We don't know yet. There are no ridge details."

"Ridge details?"

"Sorry—fingerprints. It appears the perp wore gloves. Problem is, a lot of people wore gloves as part of their costumes. If we find a set with Hooper's blood, we could look for the killer's DNA on the inside."

"Have you tested our costumes for blood?"

"Yes, and before you ask, there was blood on both yours and Pish's, but that doesn't mean much, since by your own admission you both touched the body."

I shuddered. "You've talked to a lot of people who were at the party. Did anyone see anything?" I knew the Grovers, Gogi, Doc, and all the other locals had given the police their statements, and I had heard through Zeke and Gordy that the police had tracked down and talked to the football boys and the Frobisher twins.

"No one has admitted to seeing anything yet. I haven't been able to question Percy Channer, in case you're wondering, because his damned lawyer has him clammed up." Virgil rubbed his eyes. "That concerns me but isn't particularly damning. That's what guys like him do, lawyer up even when they aren't hiding anything. Nobody's admitting anything, but that's pretty much the usual in a murder case. We've searched every Dumpster in town and beyond for clues, and we've interviewed everyone we can think of and followed up every lead."

"So . . . are you at a roadblock?"

He glanced over at me, then looked straight ahead. "I have a few ideas, but I can't discuss them with you. I'm sorry. It wouldn't be right. I'll find whoever did it, Merry; I promise you that. I'm beginning to get a sense of something, but I can't talk to you about it."

"Okay, I get it. I do." I understood his point and decided to go back to the con. "What doesn't make sense to me is: why did Cranston stop making demands? He started out pressuring me to buy him out, but lately he's seemed completely willing to wait until the DNA test was proved. Why?"

Virgil's phone chimed just then, and he answered, just making noises like *mhmm* and *okay*. There was a gleam in his dark eyes as he turned to face me on the bench. "You know your friend Melanie Pritchard?"

"Yes. She's a real estate investor and agent in New York. Why?"

"That was my source, a guy pretty high up in the New York City PD. Apparently, a few days ago Ms. Pritchard reported to the New York cops a phone call she got from a man who identified himself as Cranston Higgins, a fellow she met at your party. He told her that you and he, joint heirs of the Wynter estate, were going in together to develop the property as a high-end spa, but you needed investors."

I let it sink in for a moment, then exploded. "That *jerk*! I should have whacked him when I had the chance. Oooh! Last night I had the urge, but I held back, and I don't hold back often." I jumped up and paced back and forth in front of

Virgil. "Oh my lord! How many other of my friends did he try to hit up?" I said, hands over my eyes. I dropped them and looked down at the sheriff. "How many friends am I going to lose over *this* one? I've already lost a ton of friends from that crap with Leatrice, and . . . I'm so mad I could spit!"

Virgil grabbed my hand and tugged me down to sit on the bench. I turned to face him. He still held my hand, and it was enveloped in his.

"Merry, *relax*. Ms. Pritchard did the right thing. She strung him along, then called the cops and gave them his cell phone number. She told the police she didn't want to come down on you because she knew you were *not* involved."

I slumped down, and he stroked my back, sending a chill down to my cowboy boots. I felt like weeping and laughing all at once as things finally started to make sense. "I wish she had told me, though."

He let go of my hand and stopped stroking my back. I wished he'd kept it up, because it had felt lovely. "She thought he really was your cousin and coheir," Virgil said, "but that he was maybe doing a little con. She didn't want to alarm you until she checked it out."

"This explains a lot, and it tells me why folks aren't getting back to me. They've probably all been contacted." My face burned at what my friends must be thinking, that I'd invited them to Wynter Castle hoping to pry money from them. "Now I know what he was doing on the days he wasn't plaguing me about the castle. But it doesn't tell me if he was involved in Davey Hooper's death. However . . ."

I had a thought and stared off into space for a long moment. "So, what we surmise is: Davey Hooper set up the con and brought Cranston in as the Wynter heir. But Cranston went rogue, parting from Davey Hooper's plan to get money out of me. Would that be why Les, Davey, and Zoey came to my party, because they knew he'd be there and they could blend in unnoticed? If that's so, if they confronted him, Cranston *could* have killed Davey Hooper." Could I picture Cranston killing anyone? No, but that was Virgil's point, that you couldn't just decide what you thought you knew about someone and proceed from that.

"As soon as we figure out who Cranston is, we may have a better handle on him." Virgil paused, then went on: "I can tell you this much: I checked out his ID, and there actually is a Cranston Higgins about his correct age and with a bit of the right backstory, but then, there would be if he's any kind of a con man. I have questions in to other law enforcement agencies about him, and I'm waiting for word back. One of my officers is doing background checks using every bit of info Cranston gave us about his life. This is all the collection of information that will eventually let me nail him to the wall on the con, and maybe even make a murder charge stick, if he did it."

I nodded. Investigation for the police was a matter of following leads, coming up with theories, and checking the known facts against them. It was being picky and careful and painstaking that would get Virgil to the answer. I had to learn to be patient.

"Right now we're missing Cranston and Juniper, who I would also like to ask a few questions. Baxter has first dibs on Juniper, though, because of the attack on Zoey Channer. If you had called us the minute Juniper showed up at your door, we'd be further ahead."

"I'm sorry, Virgil. You're right, of course." And he was.

He looked a little taken aback at my ready admission of fault. "Good. Next time, call me. Let me handle things like that. Now, I just put in a call to Baxter in Ridley Ridge to pick up Les Urquhart for questioning."

I was relieved at that. I did have one more question, though. "Virgil, tell me the truth about this, because it's very important to me. You've told me all you did to check out Pish's involvement with Hooper. Honestly . . . *did* you suspect him of killing the guy?"

"Merry, what can I say? It was a possibility," he admitted. "I had to investigate it, especially when I traced a deposit Pish Lincoln made into one of Hooper's bank accounts. He gave that guy ten thousand dollars. I know he didn't exactly tell me he *didn't* pay him off; he fudged in a very expert way. It *had* to be hush money, Merry. I'm sorry. I like Pish, and no, I *don't* think he killed Davey Hooper, but it would have made it a hell of a lot easier if he had told me the truth. I wish he had trusted me."

Me, too, I thought. I sure wish Pish had trusted me enough to tell me about paying off Davey Hooper so I didn't have to hear it from Virgil.

Chapter Nineteen

✻ ✻ ✻

I DIDN'T SAY that to Virgil, though. He had been remarkably helpful and forthcoming. I opened my mouth to casually ask about his ex-wife, but he got a call just then and said he had to go. He almost ran out of the park, and I watched him leave with regret. Maybe Gogi could tell me more about his ex, but I did not want to question his mother on something so sensitive if I could avoid it. I wanted it to come from him.

There was something between us, I could have sworn it. I liked him more than I had any man since my husband died, liked him in that "way" every girl knows once she reaches puberty: the stomach turning over, the sense of attraction, the tingling, the wish to know more and be closer. But he was avoiding me, and it either meant he liked me, too—I remember a boy from childhood who pulled my hair and made faces at me because he liked me, and some fellows never get over that method of wooing—or he wanted nothing to do with me. There was no middle ground, I was afraid. My instincts were rusty from not paying much attention to them in the last ten years since I'd gotten married. But if those instincts *were* to be trusted, I suspected that he was attracted to me.

I pushed my hands deep into my sweater coat pockets and strolled back through the park as a cool wind whipped up, gathering dead leaves and sending them into tiny tornadoes. I vividly remembered a time walking in the Volksgarten, a beautiful park in Vienna, in the autumn. Miguel had hummed snatches of Haydn and Mozart, but otherwise we were silent. It was enough just to have his arm around me, keeping me warm. I would give anything to have him back, I thought.

But that memory took me by surprise. Why, I wondered, did I think of Miguel *every* time I had been with Virgil? Did my attraction toward Virgil feel like cheating, eight *long* years after my husband's death? I would have to think about that . . . another day.

Shaking off my mild depression, I strode purposefully through the wrought iron arch—I had partaken of enough nature for one day—and back along the town streets toward Jezebel. I needed to go home and talk to Pish about why he didn't feel that he could confide in me about paying Davey Hooper off. We were better friends than that, I had thought. I wanted to weep; how could he not trust me with the truth?

Thank goodness our miracle mechanic had old Jezebel working much better, and she started up without so much as a whimper of protest. Once again the clouds had come in to close off the celestial blue of the sky over Autumn Vale, and as I began the climb out of town, thick rain sheeted across the windshield. I tapped my thumbs on the steering wheel in time to the *slap-slap-slap* of the wipers and hummed "Me and Bobby McGee," singing out the line about windshield wipers slapping time. My mother had played the guitar and sung that song, along with Joni Mitchell and Joan Baez songs.

As far as the murder went, Virgil would take care of things. Whoever had killed Davey Hooper, it had to be among those three men: the spurious Cranston Higgins, angry hotelier Percy Channer, or drug dealer/Party Stop owner Les Urquhart. I supposed Juniper was a distant possibility, and Zoey even more distant, but both were possible. Or it could have been a combination of two or more of them.

I climbed and climbed as the weather got nastier. What was winter going to be like at the castle? How was I going to afford to stay? What was I going to do about Pish? How should I handle Virgil? Questions and troubles raced around in my brain, zinging from one to another until I settled myself down, needing to focus on the road in the worsening weather. Little bits of the gravel road had washed away down the slope. I sure didn't want to wreck Jezebel.

A couple of miles before the castle I saw a car half off the road in the ditch. That was exactly what I had feared happening! I screeched to a halt on the wet gravel and flung myself from the car, racing to where a girl huddled on the gravel shoulder of the road, blood on her leg. She was soaked, makeup-smeared, and shivering. "Zoey!" I cried, as I approached her.

She turned, her face wet with tears and rain. "Thank God someone's here. I was coming out to talk to you, but my car went off the road!" Blood soaked the bandage on her leg, visible under a short skirt.

"Come on, let me help you up, and I'll get you to the castle."

She sobbed and shivered, holding out her hand for me to

help her up. But she couldn't put her full weight on her injured leg. "Can you take me back to the hospital? I have stitches, but I think I've ripped them open, and it hurts like hell!" Moaning, she bent over, touching the bandage. Her hand came away red with blood, and she began to wail.

I thought for just one second, pulling my sweater jacket off and wrapping it around the shivering girl, but my course was obvious. I led her to Jezebel, supporting her as she limped/hopped down the road, and said, "You're right. The hospital is the best place for you." I worried about hypothermia and the risk of infection, and in the awful shape she was in I would rather have a doctor take care of her than us. Once she was settled into the passenger seat, I revved the motor and turned on the heater. I wasn't sure it would work, but it was worth a try. Mr. Hayes must have performed some voodoo spell, because the heater kicked in with a stream of warmish air, probably the first time that had happened since 1989.

I turned the car around and sped off. I knew where Ridley Ridge General Hospital was, as I had seen it in passing while looking for the Party Stop. Glancing over, I saw that Zoey had stopped shivering and looked almost asleep. I hoped that wasn't shock. *Don't die on me*, I prayed fervently. "Zoey, wake up! How did you run your car off the road? Why were you coming to see me?" I asked. "Zoey, open your eyes! Are you okay?"

"I'm okay, I think," she said, looking over at me blearily. "It just . . . hurts."

"I'll get you to the hospital. Why did you even leave in the first place? I understood that you were staying at the hospital until you worked things out legally, and until you saw a plastic surgeon." No answer. "Zoey, honey, keep your eyes open. Why did you leave the hospital? I didn't think you'd be allowed. You're on parole, right?"

I looked over at her, but she had her eyes closed again. "Zoey, the police want to talk to you about what happened the night of the party. Did you see anything? Is that what you were coming out to the castle to tell me? I hate to say it, but you're not hanging out with the best crowd, especially not for someone on parole. Either Les or the guy posing as Cranston Higgins had to have been the one who killed Davey Hooper." I didn't want to mention her father as a suspect.

She was silent, but at least she was sitting up now and looked more alert. She rummaged in her little shoulder bag, took out a pack of cigarettes, and shook one out of the pack, her slim fingers dexterous.

I plucked it from her fingers and tossed it in the backseat. "Sorry, not in the car." I turned onto the highway into town.

We were silent for a long moment, and she had closed her eyes again. The bandage on her leg was a weird red, practically a fluorescent color, and there was a *lot* of blood, drying into a strange drippy pattern. That could not be good. But it made me think of the bloody handprint on the wall and what Virgil had said about there being no ridge detail. Whoever made the handprint had been wearing gloves. Who had been wearing gloves with their costume? Gogi was as La Dame Aux Camélias. Juniper had gloves on to serve with. My eyes widened. That was true! I wondered if she had gotten rid of the gloves or if she had still been wearing them at the end of the evening.

"I'm sorry, Zoey. It must have been a shock, Davey Hooper dying like that." I thought over all I had heard. There were so many things that just didn't add up, but one thing that stuck was the fact that Zoey Channer didn't seem to care about Hooper's death. That was true from what I had observed at the back of the Party Stop.

Lots of stuff did not add up. I invited Les and had him on the guest list, but he hadn't checked in at the door like he should have. Why not? He had come in costume, because it was clear to me at that point that he *was* the Sweeney Todd with the straight razor. "How much did you know about Davey's con, the plot to make money off me?" I suddenly asked.

She sounded drowsy as she said, "He hired some jerk, some guy who makes a living swindling old folks, to play your cousin. Usually the guy works the grandson scam, you know? Finds a mark, then makes the phone call: *Grandma, I'm in trouble. Can you send me money to get out of jail?* What kind of loser scams little old ladies?" She giggled, ending on a snort and a snuffle. "But the guy went off script on his own, and Davey was mad as hell."

That much I had already figured out. So Davey Hooper was coming to my party to have it out with Cranston. For the first time, I wondered when Cranston had left that evening, why he had left before other locals, and if he still had his lab coat from his Doctor Frankenstein costume on? Why had I not wondered about that before? "You were Davey's girlfriend, right? You met through his mother, who you met in jail; she sent you to him with a message about me and the castle."

She glanced over at me, her makeup-streaked face marked by a surprised expression. I looked back, needing to keep my focus on the road. We were almost to Ridley Ridge, and I was relieved that she seemed better than she had at first, when I'd thought she was going into shock.

"How involved were you in the plot?" I asked, slowing to go around a branch that had fallen in the road. I wove around it, waiting for her answer. Involved enough that she'd come in costume to the party . . . the Mardi Gras mask and gaudy costume, complete with gloves. She had been involved enough that she could be going back to jail, I suspected, for more than just the parole violation.

Wait . . . gloves? "How involved were you, Zoey?" I said, my blood running cold. "Involved enough that you were at the scene of the crime?"

"Enough. Shut up now!"

I felt something poke into my side and looked down at the barrel of a gun. I jumped and the car swerved.

"Geez, will you watch what you're doing?" she screeched, grabbing the door handle. "Just drive and stay steady, 'cause my finger's on the trigger."

My hands were shaking and the weather was getting worse, and I didn't know what else to do but keep driving and hope I could figure something out. Zoey with a gun, holding it on me. What the heck was going on? Maybe as I slowed to go through town I could catch someone's attention. At the edge of Ridley Ridge, as I began to brake, Zoey moved across the seat, put the gun to my head, and stomped on the gas. I had no choice but to stay straight, weaving around the very few cars that were on the road in the storm, and we zoomed past the hospital and out the other side of the town like a greased pig slipping through a narrow doorway. I was terrified, and I struggled to keep control both of myself and the car. I shouted at her to get her foot off the gas, and as the gun wavered away from me, I kicked at her, completely forgetting about her wounds.

It was all I could do to control the car for a long two or three minutes that felt like an eon as I slowed it to a moderate speed. She still held that gun on me, cursing me out the whole time and telling me to smarten up. Then she suddenly grabbed the wheel and wrenched it hard to the right, sending us and the car careening into a parking lot by an abandoned-looking gas station about a quarter mile past Ridley Ridge.

I shrieked, but she just laughed hysterically; we bounced and jolted down a rise and slid to a stop in a shower of gravel as I slammed on the brakes. I was shaking badly, my heart pounding and bile rising in my throat, the seatbelt having taken my breath away. I undid it, rubbing my breastbone, which ached from the sudden stop. Before I could collect myself, Les Urquhart dashed out of the gas station, jerked open my door, and yanked me out by the hair. I scrabbled for footing on wet gravel and whacked at his hands, only succeeding in smacking myself in the head.

"Shut up and get the hell into the station," he growled, as unlike the lackadaisical man I had met on two occasions as could be imagined.

"What's going on?" I gabbled, clucking like a chicken about to lay an egg. Frigid rain poured down, soaking me in moments as he pushed me, stumbling and staggering, toward the door. "What are you doing this for?"

"Between you and effing Juniper and Davey, you've ruined a beautiful, elegant, *simple* plan." He wrenched my arm behind me and frog-walked me through a rickety screen door into a dark and musty interior. "Move the car, Zoey," he yelled over his shoulder.

He pushed me down on a wheeled office chair that skidded across the cement floor, screeching all the way. As I was about to spring up to bolt, he grabbed me again, shoving me back down on the chair. He was a lot stronger than I ever thought he could be, and he used the weight of his body to hold me down in the heavy vintage office chair, which was more steel than padding, as he efficiently zip-tied my hand to one armrest. "Stop struggling or I'll kill you, I swear to God."

"He'll do it, Merry," came a voice out of the darkness.

I squinted my eyes and peered through the dimness as Les zip-tied my other arm down. My eyes adjusted, and I could make out Cranston.

"He will," my faux-cousin repeated. "He's dangerous!"

Les turned on a small office-style gooseneck lamp on a desk. That's when I noticed that Cranston, too, was tied securely to an office chair. "What's going on, Cran . . . What the heck *is* your real name?"

He looked scared. His blunt, pudgy face was streaked and dirty, with tear trails running through the dust. He was always so neat and tidy, but now he looked disheveled, like he had slept in his clothes the previous night. "Bob. Just . . . Bob." His voice cracked and quavered.

"So, Just Bob, what gives?" I said, trying to keep my own voice from shaking, since he was doing enough quivering for both of us. Les Urquhart had disappeared, but he came back carrying a gun.

Bob glanced fearfully at Les, who waved the gun casually, and said, "Go ahead, tell her. Tell her all about it while I figure out what to do."

I didn't like the hint of desperation in his voice, but I thought I'd just ignore that for the moment and try to keep everything calm. "I don't know anything at this point, you know," I said to Les. "Not a thing!"

"Right," he said, glaring at me through squinty eyes. "Nice try. You spend half an hour in the park with the damned sheriff of Autumn Vale, he suddenly up and calls the Ridley Ridge PD to pick me up for questioning, and I'm supposed to believe you don't know anything?" Sarcasm and disbelief threaded through his tone.

"How do you know all that?"

"You have some enemies in Autumn Vale, or didn't you know that?"

I thought of the woman who had screeched at me that I was ruining things. "Who is that woman and why does she hate me?"

He chuckled. "What, you don't like my mom? Well, she doesn't like you, either. She thinks you are a snippety know-it-all from New York, and my aunt Minnie thinks so, too. My brother hears all about you from those losers, Zeke and Gordy, and he thinks you're some kind of nutcase, fixing up that dump and thinking anyone is going to buy it. My brother's wife works at the police department in Ridley Ridge. I have a lot of family!"

"So . . . your aunt is Minnie, the local postal worker and the town gossip." It gave me the creeps to think about how he had been monitoring my every move. I didn't have anything else to say to Les, so I turned to Cranston—or Bob. He was terrified, and I wondered why Les was holding him. Would he kill the con man? Sure, he had departed from the script, but that was not a killing offense. Or was it? The story was beginning to make sense in my head. Davey Hooper had, after doing the requisite research, recruited this fellow to play the unacknowledged grandson of Melvyn Wynter. "So, Bob, what happened? Why did you change up the script Hooper had given you?"

"I just thought . . ." He trailed off on a sob. "P-poor Davey . . . he was an old friend."

"Old friend? Nice company you keep."

He scuffed the dusty floor with one foot. "I won't speak ill of dead," he said, a little huffy. "I think the company *he* kept—him and his sleazy brother, Dinty—was much worse!" He shot a look of fearful hatred toward Les. "*Anyway,*" he continued, taking in a deep shuddering breath, "Davey was smart, but this time I just thought he was being shortsighted. You've got a lot of friends, Merry, a lot of *rich* friends!" he

said, earnestly, like it was news to me. "It was an opportunity. I figured, why not do both? You know, score off you
and mine your rich friends, a kind of side business. Davey
didn't see it that way, so I just kept him happy, told him what
he needed to hear, and stayed out of his way while I conducted a little . . . a little personal business."

Les snorted.

"Personal business as in trying to rip off my friends," I
said.

Zoey slipped in through the screeching screen door and
kicked it shut as the wind wailed outside; she perched on the
edge of the steel desk, pushing aside the old gooseneck lamp,
and fired up a cigarette. She had my purse—an older Balen-
ciaga bag that Leatrice had given me when she was in a good
mood—and casually overturned it, going through the con-
tents on the desk. I gritted my teeth. I do *not* like people
pawing through my things. She held up a Lancôme coral
lipstick and nodded. "Not bad!" She lipsticked her mouth,
so that was one lipstick I would be tossing out. I noticed she
exhibited no trace of the pain she had claimed to be experi-
encing. She could have had a career on the screen if she had
stayed out of trouble, that's how convincing her pain and fear
had been to me. I stifled my natural reaction, which was to
tell her to leave my stuff alone, and turned away.

How was I going to get out of this? It didn't seem like
Les had any plan, and that was almost more scary than if
he had. It left his responses wide-open, and he could flail
widely between ransoming us and killing us. Or me. I
doubted anyone would pay to get poor Bob back. How could
I turn this situation to my benefit?

I decided to let my mind work on that in the background
while I kept the info stream flowing. "So Les, the night of
my party, you and Davey and Zoey came to the castle to

corner poor old Bobby here, and let me guess . . . Hooper kicked up a fuss? Was *that* his downfall?"

Zoey shifted on the desk, and said, "Poor Davey . . . he really thought I was into him, you know? Thought I was a solid-gold good luck charm, me and my daddy's money. He played the badass, but he wasn't truly a tough guy, just a kinda pretend tough guy."

"What happened in your life that you prefer the kind of guy who is only after you for your money, as opposed to someone who might give a damn about you?" I asked brightly.

I didn't see it coming. Les struck me, hard; I yelped and felt a burst of pain across my jaw. I skidded backward on my wheeled chair and hit Bob, who cried out in fear.

Zoey chuckled, and the chuckle turned into gales of laughter as she saw my no doubt dazed expression. "Now see, that's worth it all right there!"

"I told you," Bob whimpered and pushed his wheeled office chair away from me as if I had some kind of communicable disease. "Don't make him mad."

I stretched my jaw, wishing I could touch it. Okay, so it hurt, but no teeth had been damaged. However, I'm no idiot and I don't like pain. I would never make it as the kick-ass heroine of an action drama. My tone was milder when I said to Les, "So you came to my party to corner Bob, and things got out of hand?"

Les, hoisting himself up to sit cross-legged on the desk next to Zoey, looked at me with an expression holding some respect. Maybe the fact that I wasn't whimpering like Bob made me look a little more stoic. If he only knew that inside my guts were quivering like jelly. He took the cigarette from his girlfriend and lit a joint, inhaling and holding the smoke in his lungs as he handed the butt back to Zoey.

"Just bad timing. It was all cool, but then Davey

overheard something I said to Zoey," he said, exhaling a great cloud of smoke, the grassy herbal smell drifting toward me. "For a while I had been the only one talking to Davey and the only one talking to Bob, so I was the go-between, but I was playing both ends. You know how it is. He figured it out and then started kicking up a fuss with Bobby, here. Said he didn't appreciate the crap little old Bobby was pulling behind his back. I would have made our whiney friend here pay, but Davey was cut from different cloth and decided to ice him."

"Imagine that . . . a con man who didn't like being conned." I wasn't sure I bought Les's explanation completely. Davey Hooper was planning to kill Bob? I didn't think so, but I would bet that's what Les had told Bob to keep him quiet about the whole affair. Les, defender of the helpless . . . *right*. "Why do I think that maybe it was you who suggested killing Bob, and Davey who kicked up a fuss?"

Bob moaned in fear, but Les, mellower now, ignored my interjection. "Anyway, Davey heard me tell Zoey that we needed to cut Davey out of the con somehow. Course, I didn't know that then, did I, that Davey overheard? Or things would have gone a whole lot different. When Davey asked him about it, Bobby here used it to get himself off the hook and got Davey all worked up about me intending to cut him out of the payoff."

"So you killed Hooper, just like that?"

Bob whimpered and scuttled even farther back until he was in the shadows. Apparently being a good con man did not make him physically gutsy.

"Course not," Les said, taking another drag and relaxing even more. "Things were getting complicated, though. Davey told Zoey's papa that she was there at the party, after Channer confronted him. When Davey told me what he'd done, I wanted to deck him. Zoey had to stay out of sight after that, because the moron was wandering around looking for her while ducking out of sight of you." He chuckled and stared at me, his eyes half closed in stoned mellowness. "Channer told Davey he didn't want to listen to your freakin' sales pitch again! Said you made him want to tell you your castle was a piece of crap in the middle of nowhere."

"Ticked me off, having to stay out of sight of Daddy. I'd been having so much fun playing tag with those dumb local bimbos!" Zoey said, with an exaggerated pout. "Les, can I get my cell phone back now? I want to check in with a couple of friends."

"No. You're not using it until we get some money and get out of this hellhole."

She slumped down and pawed through my stuff some more, surreptitiously taking my cell phone and thumbing through it. I desperately wished she'd accidentally dial 911 or something. Where did he plan on getting money? I wondered.

"Anyway, I got Hooper settled down . . . told him it was just a misunderstanding," Les said. "But he was bringing me down, saying he just wanted to get the con done and be gone. If Bob and I went along with his original plan, he'd forgive and forget. *Forgive and forget!* He didn't even freakin' care about getting the old dude who killed his bro. Can't stand lack of loyalty. Brothers should stick together, you know? If someone was in any way responsible for my brother dying, I'd gut him like a pig."

"So Davey, Les, and I were out in the smoking pit arguing," Zoey said, tucking my cell phone in her skirt waistband.

He shot her a look and she shrugged and went back to smoking and pawing through my stuff.

"No one else?"

"Too damn freezing, I guess, and not many of your hoity-toity crowd smokes," Les said, watching me. His eyes were cold, and I thought I could see him calculating what to do.

"You were there, Zoey, while the whole thing went down?"

She nodded but didn't look up. She picked up my silver compact, a gift from Miguel, and opened it, checking herself out in the mirror. I bit my lip to keep from telling her to put it down. She took a tissue, licked it, and began blotting the dark streaks of makeup off her cheeks.

Les continued his story. "Davey got on my case about Zo. I looked over and saw the coffin sitting there, where a bunch of your goofball guests had dragged it and the mannequin." He paused and smirked. "Seemed like a good idea—serendipitous, you might say—so I took care of it." He drew his thumb across his throat in a cutting gesture and made a graphic slitting and gurgling noise.

Bob started crying, and Zoey glanced over at Les uncertainly. She was trying to be Miss Tough Girl, but she wasn't selling me on it. She flashed a look at me, and she looked so old, so detached, and yet . . . so scared. She looked frightened and hopeless. I wondered, had Les chosen the Sweeney Todd costume for that reason, knowing what he planned to do?

"So, the handprint on the wall . . . it was yours, wasn't it, Zoey?"

"She did her bit, didn't you, good girl?" Les said, patting Zoey on the shoulder. "She helped me get Davey into the coffin." He broke out in laughter. "My God, that was funny! Poor old Davey bleeding like a stuck pig and both of us trying to stuff him into the casket, arms flopping around! We dragged away the dummy, acting like it was a drunk guy we were helping out. Your dumbass doormen, Zeke and

Gordy, were too busy looking after two girls, and no one else thought anything of it when we left."

"You left alone? What about Juniper?"

Les shrugged. "She wasn't with us."

"She was helping me," Bob said in a tiny voice. "I wasn't feeling well, and she helped me. She's not a bad girl, you know."

Aha! Had Juniper begun to wonder after she heard about Davey being killed if Bob had been distracting her to keep her away from the scene? Or had she even put two and two together and begun to think he was involved in the murder itself? That would account for her freak-out when she saw him at the castle.

"Not a bad girl? Are you *kidding* me?" Zoey shrieked. "She's psycho! She tried to kill me with a knife, and if that isn't psycho, I don't . . ." She stopped before she finished and glanced over, eyes wide, at Les, who glared at her with narrowed eyes.

"So, now, what do we do with *you*?" Les asked, glancing at me and then taking out a knife and cutting his fingernail, paring it like an apple. His gun lay on his lap like a favorite puppy.

I was attached to an office chair in a dim back room with a killer, his clueless girlfriend, and a useless con man who was quietly snuffling away in the corner. What was I going to do? I needed to keep alert for any way out of this, because I had a feeling Les would come to the conclusion that his best bet was to snuff both Bob and I.

Stay alert; that was good advice to myself, and I took it. As well as excellent vision, I have pretty good hearing, certainly better than a stoner. I heard, through the wail of the wind outside, what sounded like the thrum of a heavy motor, but that suddenly stopped.

Was it possible? Was rescue close at hand?

And then, above the wind, I heard a megaphone-amplified voice, gruff and sexy, say, "Les Urquhart, we know you're in there, and we know you have a hostage. If you come out with your hands up before anyone else gets hurt, we might be able to cut you a deal."

It was Virgil!

But . . . *really*? Did they honestly think that Les was going to play nice with so much at stake? Bob, still whimpering, dragged his chair across the floor toward the door, and Les jumped down from the desk to stop him, but he tripped and fell flat out on the floor as his gun skittered across the cement. I stood as best as I could and with one mighty swing I lifted the office chair and flung it down on him, forgetting that, because I was attached to it, that swinging motion would take me flying, too. The weight of that old steel office chair carried me with it, and I flew on top of Les, just as Virgil, my hero, burst into the deserted gas station office, gun drawn.

"Am I interrupting anything?" he asked.

Chapter Twenty

❊ ❊ ❊

I T WAS A bit of a tangle for a while. In the confusion that followed, no one was sure who the good guys were or the bad guys. Bob, aka Cranston Higgins, got away but was caught staggering and stumbling down the highway in the storm, still attached to his chair, which was, I must say, lighter in weight than mine. Thank goodness I had the heavier one, because it had knocked Les out.

The arrest was anticlimactic, since the villain was out cold. When Virgil saw the bruise on my jaw, *his* jaw clenched, a rock-hard stubble-covered line; it seemed to me that he "helped" the paramedics by flinging Les onto the gurney with just a little more force than was needed.

Zoey's father and Sheriff Baxter showed up about then, the whole parking lot area filled with cruisers, blue and red lights blinking, reflecting in the rain puddles on the pavement.

"Daddy!" Zoey cried, and flung herself at her dad. "Les

Urquhart . . . he kept *me* captive, too, and threatened that if I didn't go along with him, he'd hurt *you*! Oh, Daddy, I was so scared! What was I going to do?" She blubbered like a little girl.

Girl missed her calling; she should have been a soap star.

"That is a load of bull feathers," I said to the Ridley Ridge sheriff. "She's the one who faked an injury—you can check out the supposedly 'off the road' car on the Wynter Line—then held a gun to me and made me drive here. Then she let Les tie me down to the chair while she pawed through my purse and stole my silver compact, which I want back, by the way! *And* my cell phone!"

We all trundled off to the Ridley Ridge PD. It took another couple of hours to sort everything out, and I did get my compact and cell phone back. Sheriff Baxter got an earful from me about Zoey Channer, Les Urquhart, and my faux cousin, poor Chicken Bob. I told them honestly that Zoey Channer did seem scared of Les—and who wouldn't after seeing him kill Davey Hooper? The mannequin from my party, with Hooper's blood on it, was found at the Party Stop, I later heard, indelibly tying Les Urquhart to the murder at the castle.

"How did you find me?" I asked Virgil in a lull in the action at the Ridley Ridge PD.

"There is a waitress named Susan in a café in Ridley Ridge, and she called the cops to tell them about a car zooming through town with you at the wheel and someone holding a gun to your head."

I would have to thank that girl. She probably saved my life, just because she decided to do something rather than ignore it. "I would have expected that would cause the police to be there sooner!" I exclaimed.

He shot a glance across the room at Baxter, who was

sitting in a squeaky office chair watching one of his officers flirt with Zoey. "It took a while before anyone believed her. I heard the call on the scanner, and that's why I got here first, even though I was fifteen miles away."

I hugged him and kissed his cheek, and he turned a becoming shade of red.

In the days that followed, Zoey's daddy wasn't much use to her, since he was indicted on charges of conspiracy to commit murder in that other little trouble he had. I thought that Zoey might be spending the rest of her actual jail term in jail once her parole was revoked. I hoped she got along real well with Dinah, once that woman found out Zoey had been peripherally involved in her only other son's death. The Hoopers had many friends in the prison system.

After a couple of days, things calmed down. I waited until Shilo and McGill were gone out to dinner one evening so I could talk to Pish. We were sitting together on the settee in the parlor, hand in hand, while Debussy's *Prelude to the Afternoon of a Faun* played. "Why didn't you tell me you had paid Davey Hooper off? Why did you do it, Pish—pay him off, I mean? When you *knew* you hadn't done what he accused you of."

"Two different issues, my love. So I'll tackle the easier one first: why I gave him money." He sighed and let go of my hand, staring into the fire, the glow of the flames on his lean, handsome face as the lovely orchestral music flowed around us. "I had already turned him in to the jail officials at that point, on the threat he leveled at me, that I had harassed him. I don't suppose Virgil actually followed the time line and figured that out. But then Hooper contacted me again once he got out of jail. Crafty fellow, Davey Hooper was. He could have done so much in his life if his bent wasn't toward the criminal. But he had gotten ahold of a piece of information that was damaging, not to me, but to someone I cared about very much."

"Who? What information?"

He shook his head. "It doesn't matter anymore, my darling. That person is gone from my life. But I wouldn't let Hooper destroy someone who deserved to be let alone. I gave him money, he abided by his deal, and that is the end of that story. He was, as I remember him, a different person from his mother in that way, not nearly as vindictive, nor as dangerous."

"So . . . did you truly not remember him when you first heard his name?"

"He was going by a different name then, remember: David Isaac Smith. No, I did not remember him until Virgil told me the details. The part of his face I saw, below the Lone Ranger mask, looked vaguely familiar, but that was all."

I told Pish what Les had said, about Hooper's unwillingness to go after his brother's killer, poor old Rusty Turner.

"Yes, that coincides with what I thought he was about. I have, by the way, since told Virgil all of this, and he has checked out my story. Everything is, as they say, copacetic."

"I understand that you can't tell me who this involves, but why not tell me the truth that you've shared with me now? It must have been a difficult and upsetting time."

"My dearest darling, my problem is that you have me so high on a pedestal, and I am merely human. I am so afraid of disappointing you."

I put my arm over his shoulders and hugged him tight. "You never need to worry about that, because you've got *me* on that pedestal beside you. How about we both climb down so we can be honest with each other from now on?"

We agreed on that, and I felt at peace.

The next day, as Shilo and McGill were off ordering wedding invitations and Pish was in Autumn Vale using my lovely new/old Caddy, I put on a CD, a collection of romantic music with a Spanish guitar thrumming through it, one of Miguel's favorites. It was loud. The weather outside was cold and sleety, but beef bourguignon was bubbling in the Dutch oven down in the kitchen, and I was oddly content. I was almost broke and saddled with a gorgeous, impractical castle, true, but at least it was mine, all mine. For the time being.

I donned my painting clothes, Miguel's oversized cargo pants and a man's shirt, tied my hair back up in a scarf with a floppy bow in front, and climbed that twelve-foot ladder again. I was almost all the way around in the turret room, just another ten feet or so to go, uncovering the masterpiece that some long-ago painter had perfected. Working gave me a lot of satisfaction. I had looked through some of the other unused rooms and found that there were more treasures to be found under layers of wallpaper. There was furniture galore still in the attic, beautiful old bureaus and wardrobes and bedsteads, enough to furnish every bedroom, and then some.

My heart was full to bursting as I worked around, finally pulling off the last foot of wallpaper and sat, staring up at the ceiling. It was beautiful, my gorgeous turret bedroom.

"*Merry!* What the hell are you *doing* up there?"

I cried out and lost my balance at the loud voice and felt myself falling, falling . . . into Virgil's arms. But instead of him catching me in a perfect romantic clinch, I knocked him down and ended up lying across his chest, my butt in the air in a most undignified position.

I felt him heaving and grunting, and I struggled to get off, crossly muttering, "Stay still. . . . Let me get off! What the heck did you think you were doing, startling me like that?"

When I rolled over and off him, I saw that Virgil was

actually laughing, great gusty whoops of laughter that sputtered into a cough. I collapsed in laughter, too, and he turned me over onto my back, hovering above me for longer than was necessary, his handsome face and cinnamon-scented breath bathing me. I thought he was going to kiss me, I really did, and the world stopped for a moment as we stared at each other.

And then the phone rang, and the spell broke. He lumbered up off me and offered me his hand, pulling me to my feet. I ran to answer it, shouting out to Virgil that I'd make him a coffee if he'd meet me in the kitchen. I turned off the music and answered the phone in the little office off the upstairs gallery hall. The call was from a friend in LA. He had been sent photos of my castle by some mysterious person—Shilo or Pish? I wondered—and asked if he could come the next week to check it out. He was a location scout for movies and thought my castle might be a good external stand-in for a scene in a medieval drama. How much would it pay if the castle were selected? I asked. He told me. I was astounded, and as I set the phone back in the cradle, I counted up how many electric bills and how much of the property taxes even just a few days would pay.

Down in the kitchen Virgil was sitting by the fireplace. He looked awful, which I hadn't noticed before. His nose was red and his eyes bleary. "You've got a cold!" I cried.

He looked up at me with a quirky half grin. "You look so beautiful," he said.

"That is the cold meds talking, no doubt," I said, pulling the scarf off and shaking my hair out.

"You're always so damned perfect—perfect hair, perfect clothes, perfect makeup . . . everything perfect—and right now you're . . ." He shook his head as if to clear it.

"Yup, cold meds. And you *drove* like this?" I made some

soup and sandwiches and gave him coffee. We ate right there at the fireplace, and soon I saw him become more like himself: cautious, careful, alert.

He cleared his throat as I came back from putting the dishes in the dishwasher. "I'm sorry, Merry, for startling you like that. I rang the bell, but no one answered and the door was unlocked, so I came in."

"I had the music pretty loud. It helps me think." And remember my husband. "What were you coming out for?"

"I've got news about the case. Les Urquhart denied everything at first, but something interesting happened: he was attacked in prison, and when he was in the infirmary, he asked to talk to a detective and made a full, signed confession. Then he asked for protective custody."

"Davey Hooper had friends inside?"

He nodded. "Not that I condone what they did in beating him up, but his confession sure saves a lot of time and money."

"So what happens to Juniper Jones?"

"Zoey tells us that she's not pressing charges on the assault, so Juniper is free to do whatever she wants."

"That's good to know. And Bob? My never-was cousin?"

"He's wanted on so many outstanding complaints and warrants he's going to do time for a while. By the way, did you know he had a key made to the castle?"

"So *that's* how he kept sneaking in! I wondered."

"That guy is not going to do well in jail. He's pretty scared right now."

"Poor guy," I mused, then laughed. "I actually feel bad for him. How weird is that?"

"Don't waste your time," Virgil said.

"I never do," I retorted, and eyed him. "I *never* waste my time on impossible projects."

Chapter Twenty-one

�֍ ✖ ✖

FIVE WEEKS LATER, after a hectic, mind-blowing schedule—Thanksgiving at Golden Acres with Gogi, Virgil, Hannah, her parents, and a whole slew of the residents, and weeks of labor to get the castle in better repair—I stood in Wynter Castle's great hall beside Shilo and watched her and McGill marry in a tender, happy, laughing ceremony presided over by the local Methodist pastor. It was full-on winter in upstate New York. We had about six inches of snow that would, according to local wisdom, melt away, only to be followed by lots more.

The hall was filled with flowers and candles, the chandelier dimmed by swaths of draped white tulle donated by a designer friend of mine. The ballroom was set up for the reception and a professional photographer was snapping everything in sight, shadowed earnestly by Lizzie, who had volunteered to be his assistant. From the gallery above drifted the sound of a harp soloist from the Cornell

University Department of Music. Gogi smiled over at me; she had been responsible for that. She had always imagined harp music from the gallery above the great hall, she'd told me the first time she visited me at the castle.

I cried buckets as they said the words, sniffing and snuffling like a fool. McGill's honest, homely face shone with love and Shilo . . . She took my breath away. Alcina, that magical child, had made her a crown of flowers for her hair, and it sat on a blond lace veil, anchoring it. Shilo wore a vintage wedding gown given to her by McGill's mother, who sat in the front row, smiling with tears in her eyes. She loved Shilo so much, it was a sight to behold. My dear friend deserved the happiness she had found when she had followed me to my castle.

But I sure would miss her.

Oh, she wouldn't be leaving Autumn Vale, but she'd be living with McGill, of course, in his prudently bought-and-paid-for Autumn Vale house. And first they were going on a two-week tour of France, a gift from his mother, before coming back just in time for Christmas at the castle.

The reception went off without a hitch, and for one day I wasn't worrying about anything. I stood with my arm through Pish's as the dance floor was filled by Autumn Valeers. A local group provided peppy music, alternating with a classical string ensemble. It was weirdly wonderful. Hannah, in her motorized wheelchair, twirled with Zeke, her steadfast friend. Elwood Fitzhugh whirled Janice Grover, resplendent in a lovely winter white muumuu, around the dance floor. Simon Grover chewed contently on cake, happy now that it appeared that Autumn Vale Community Bank was on the track to recovery. Pish had kept me apprised of the progress made in the bank shemozzle, and it seemed that the bank manager was making a real effort to learn everything he needed to know. He just might keep his job after all. Gogi and Doc were slowly dancing, a kind of senior's version of a waltz.

"It has all worked out," I sighed, resting against Pish. "And thanks to the location contract," I went on, referring to the signed contract to use the castle for one month in the spring, "I'm good for about six to eight months, which gives me time for more work on the castle."

"My dear," he said, patting my hand, "I have a proposal for you."

"I *do*, my dear Pish. I'd marry you in a heartbeat." I squeezed his arm.

He chuckled easily. "An old dog like me? No, you deserve someone young and strong, like our friend Virgil."

I glanced across the ballroom floor to find Virgil's gaze on me with unsettling ferocity.

"Anyway, what was your proposal?" I asked, turning to Pish with a flutter in my stomach.

"I think it is going to take a while to get this place up to snuff. Meanwhile, there are dozens of folks who would love to stay in a castle, and many who would even like to rent a suite of rooms for a time. Not just a few days here and there, but a kind of residential inn."

"Like who?" I said, with a healthy dose of skepticism.

He had clearly thought about this a lot and was ready with an answer. "Like my darling, dotty Auntie Lush. She has been pining over Wynter Castle ever since I sent those photos to my mother. She has buckets of money, but she can't fly to Europe anymore. Her heart and her constitution won't stand airline travel. She owns a condo in New York in the same building as mine, but she and my mother don't like each other much and hate having to socialize. She would *dearly* love to get out of the city for a little while, as would a couple of her friends, especially to live in elegant splendor in a real honest-to-goodness castle."

I was silent for a moment. I knew his mother, and she hated me with a cold passion; I don't know why. Perhaps it was that we disagreed on almost every aspect of life. "What is your aunt like?"

"Darling, my mother's sister could not be more different than her. I know you and Mother don't agree, but Auntie Lush is a different matter."

I thought about it for a minute. "If she brought her friends, each one would need her own room and bathroom. Could they handle the stairs?"

"Oh yes. They're not invalids, just elderly."

"How much do you think I could charge?"

He named a sum, and I did some addition. It would give me almost a year to fix the place up. "I would need to hire help if I had guests," I mused. "But I know that Emerald would love to leave her job, and I've been trying to help her find something else that would let her stay in Autumn Vale. Binny needs to be able to hire someone who would be better at customer service than Juniper, but she won't ditch the girl. However . . . Juniper is a fiend about cleaning, and as long as she didn't have to interact with the guests, she could be a kind of chambermaid, if she wanted to." Juniper Jones had stayed on in Autumn Vale, telling Binny that it was the best home she had ever had. I had even come to appreciate her quick wits, which had been hidden by a taciturn disposition that now occasionally cracked to reveal a sweeter young woman than I would have expected.

I thought some more, then asked Pish, "When do you think I should have the ladies move in, if we go ahead with this?"

"Given that we'll need at least three suites done up, I'd make it February or March."

I nodded, as I noticed Virgil Grace, wearing a tuxedo—he had been McGill's best man—making his way around the edge of the ballroom, a determined gleam in his eyes. I felt that damned flutter again. He was headed toward me, and he was going to ask me to dance. I hoped.

"Okay," I said, a little breathless, turning to Pish. "How do I look?" I had found an off-the-shoulder gold lace brocade gown to wear as Shilo's maid of honor, while Pish had donned a crimson jacket with velvet lapels to give Shilo away as a stand-in father of the bride.

He looked me over, a smile on his face. "My darling child, daughter of my heart, you look glorious . . . lovely, breathtaking, positively angelic."

I made a snap decision that I hoped to heck I wouldn't regret, but the chance to make the castle better and give myself almost a year there . . . I couldn't refuse. And I have never suffered by taking Pish's advice, only by ignoring it. "I'll do it," I said on a sigh, as Virgil approached. "Tell your auntie Lush yes."

"Will you dance with me, Merry?" Virgil asked.

I nodded, speechless. He took me in his arms and swept me onto the floor, surprising me by being a pretty good dancer. I glanced back, and Pish was smiling with a self-satisfied look. As long as I could count on no more murders, I would be a happy camper, I thought dreamily. I was happy, since I wouldn't have to deal with Pish's mother, only his lovely aunt and her friends. What could possibly go wrong with three elderly ladies?

Virgil pulled me closer, his strong arms holding me with meaning and care, and as the music slowed into an old piece, "As Time Goes By," we danced.

Recipes

Savory Herb Muffins

Yield: 12

2 cups whole wheat pastry flour, or unbleached white flour

1 tablespoon baking powder

1 teaspoon baking soda

½ teaspoon salt

1 tablespoon fresh oregano, chopped (or 2 teaspoons dried oregano)

1 tablespoon fresh thyme leaves (or 2 teaspoons dried thyme)

1 tablespoon fresh basil, chopped (or 2 teaspoons dried basil)

2 eggs

1 egg white

1 cup nonfat buttermilk

2 tablespoons mildly flavored vegetable oil or canola oil

2 teaspoons sugar, less if you like

¼ cup grated Parmesan cheese

Additional oil for muffin pan(s), or cooking spray

Preheat oven to 400 degrees. Lightly oil or spray a 12-hole muffin tin.

Combine flour, baking powder, baking soda, salt, oregano, thyme, and basil in a large mixing bowl.

In another bowl, combine eggs, egg white, buttermilk, the 2 tablespoons oil, sugar, and Parmesan.

Add the liquid mixture to the flour mixture, stirring briefly, then spoon into prepared muffin cups, filling two-thirds full.

Bake for approximately 25 minutes, but check at 20. Let cool slightly, then remove from tins.

Fit for the King Muffins (Banana–Peanut Butter–Chocolate Chip Muffins)

Yield: 12

1 cup all-purpose flour

1/2 cup whole wheat flour

1 teaspoon baking soda

1 teaspoon baking powder

1/2 teaspoon salt

1/4 cup white sugar

1/4 cup brown sugar

1/4 cup unsalted butter, softened

2 ripe bananas, mashed

1/2 cup creamy peanut butter

1 teaspoon vanilla extract

1 egg

1 cup milk chocolate chips
1 Tablespoon turbinado sugar

Preheat oven to 375 degrees. Coat a muffin tin with cooking spray.

Mix together the flours, baking soda, baking powder, and salt together in a small bowl. In a second bowl beat sugars and softened butter. Add the mashed bananas, peanut butter, vanilla, and egg.

Stir the flour mixture into the banana mixture until just combined; add 3/4 cup of chocolate chips to the batter and mix. Spoon batter evenly into the prepared muffin cups. Sprinkle the tops of each muffin evenly with the remaining chocolate chips and turbinado sugar.

Bake in preheated oven for 13-15 minutes until a tester inserted into the center of a muffin comes out clean.

Remove from the oven and let cool for a few minutes before removing from the tray and placing on a wire rack to finish cooling. Enjoy.

Cauliflower & Cheddar Soup

Yield: 6–8 servings

1 medium head cauliflower, broken in florets
1 medium onion, chopped
2 cups chicken broth, homemade or commercial
2 tablespoons butter
2 tablespoons all-purpose flour
3 cups milk

2 cups (8 ounces) shredded cheddar cheese
1 tablespoon dried parsley flakes
1 teaspoon salt
1/4 teaspoon ground nutmeg
1/8 teaspoon pepper

In a large saucepan, combine the cauliflower, onion, and chicken broth. Cover and cook over medium heat until the vegetables are tender.

Meanwhile, in a medium saucepan, melt butter; stir in flour until smooth. Gradually add milk. Cook and stir until bubbly. Cook and stir for 2 to 3 minutes longer or until thickened.

Reduce heat; add cheese and seasonings.

Pour into cauliflower mixture.

Simmer slowly for 30 minutes: do not boil!

Serve with Savory Herb Muffins.